THE
DRY WHITE
TEAR

THE
DRY WHITE TEAR

A T.S.W. Sheridan Mystery

STEPHEN F. WILCOX

ST. MARTIN'S PRESS
NEW YORK

Library of Congress Cataloging-in-Publication Data

Wilcox, Stephen F.
    The dry white tear / Stephen F. Wilcox.
        p.   cm.
    ISBN 0-312-02909-8
    I. Title.
  PS3573.I419D79 1989
  813'.54—dc19   89-30120
                                        CIP

First Edition

10 9 8 7 6 5 4 3 2 1

FOR PAULINE,
who always knew.

CHAPTER 1

"SCREE-YEEEE."

A heron swooped into the swamp grass on the far shore, its manic cry sounding equal parts mugging victim and Lotto winner. I knew the feeling. Thursday morning up-state.

Back in New York, the Yankees were about to open a weekend home stand against Boston and Paul Simon was booked into Carnegie Hall with Phoebe Snow as the open-ing act. Not to mention the new Szechuan joint in Chinatown that Lev raved about.

Maybe that's why rural folk seem to live longer than the rest of us; no tough choices.

The lake's surface was polished turquoise and dead calm. From my seat in the little rowboat, bobbing se-renely at mid-lake, I could see both shorelines clearly. There were no cars on the meandering two-lane road that rimmed the lake and no other boats on the water. It was as if someone had canceled the twentieth century. Any minute now, Huck Finn would float by on a log raft.

I exhaled slowly and tried to shift into a more agreeable position on the uncompromising aluminum bench seat. "Okay, Uncle Charlie, this is it. Last wishwise, as they say in the NFL."

Reaching under the seat in front of me, I pulled out the ceramic urn and an old copy of *Playboy*. Carefully placing the urn on the seat, I opened the magazine to the center-fold and took a moment to admire the redheaded goddess and all her airbrushed charms. Then I ripped out the page and wadded the centerfold into a tight ball. Opening the urn, I sprinkled its contents into the coffee can at my feet, tossed in the centerfold, then reached behind me and grabbed the bottle of Johnny Walker Black. Finally, I raised the bottle to my lips and took a long pull of the dusky scotch.

"To Charlie Dugan," I recited my lines. "May his soul have reached heaven an hour before the Devil knew he died."

Toast completed, I set the bottle down and scavenged through my pockets for the Zippo lighter I'd had since Ft. Dix. The flint sparked true on the first strike. Reaching into the coffee can, I touched the flame to the edge of the crumpled pinup. There was only a whisper of smoke as the glossy paper burned down, curled, blackened, and, finally, settled in with Uncle Charlie's ashes. A moment of silence seemed redundant, so, instead, I made a half-hearted sign of the cross and dumped the ashes into the slow current.

Not exactly a high mass, but then, Uncle Charlie wasn't much of a Catholic and I was no Bishop Sheen myself.

I took another swallow of the Johnny Walker and, re-luctantly, poured the rest into the lake and tucked the empty bottle away under the seat. Ceremony completed, I reached back for the lanyard on the small outboard.

The instructions Uncle Charlie had left in his will were exact and particular, a reflection of the man. "Don't throw the empty J. W. bottle overboard, Tim, and defile my lake." Even in death, he had to have things done his way. Hold the mid-lake ceremony between 7 and 8 A.M. on a weekday, the better to avoid water-skiers and the odd curiosity seeker. Use a fifth of Johnny Walker—Old Bushmills is too dear to fritter away on sentiment. And the rationale behind mingling the centerfold with his remains: "Just my way of getting my ashes hauled one last time."

All in all, it was a suitable farewell for a man I remembered mostly as a pariah, the family black sheep. As a boy, I had seen little of Uncle Charlie outside of an occasional reunion picnic or somebody's First Communion brunch; times when my father was able to convince my mother that an invitation was obligatory. "Let's give him the benefit of the doubt" was my father's pat phrase. She'd stew about it, and then the two of them would go off somewhere and argue it out quietly, away from the children, as if Uncle Charlie were an unruly cat that made a habit of soiling the dining room carpet. Mom always voted to put the ornery beast to sleep, while Dad was ready to try housebreaking it one more time.

But then, it was easier for my father, who had no blood ties at stake. It was my mother's sister, Aunt Maureen, who had invested sixteen raucous years of marriage in Uncle Charlie. And when they finally called it quits— Aunt Maureen packing the two kids off to Arizona, Uncle Charlie hopscotching it with a series of barmaids and desperate divorcées—my mother was the first to send up a prayer of thanks for her sister's deliverance, and to call down an Irish curse on the head of Charlie Dugan.

As a result, I didn't get to know Uncle Charlie for years, until after the army let me go. I had returned to Rochester to finish college and, afterward, took my first reporting job with one of the local dailies. Uncle Charlie and I would run across each other at ball games or taverns and reminisce along parallel themes; his Iwo Jima and silk stockings, my Da Nang and panty hose; his two failed marriages, which put him one up on me.

"We're birds of a feather, you and me," he told me once, deep in his cups at a downtown bar. "Livin' for the

3

here and now, 'stead of the hereafter. Unconventional, I've been called, like it was a cardinal sin. Hell, I say conventions are for Masons and Jehovah's Witnesses."

Birds of a feather. I didn't agree, but I didn't argue, either. Guilt kept me quiet, I suppose. Because no matter how much I had come to like this mysterious man of my childhood, I knew I didn't want people ever to look at me and see Charlie Dugan. He had been a self-centered man, a man of extravagance and excess, capable almost simultaneously of great generosity and casual, offhanded cruelty.

And if his life was an enigma, his death was a conundrum. Who'd want to murder the life of the party? Why did Charlie Dugan die the way he did, alone in his cottage, a fishing knife's six-inch blade jammed between his ribs, puncturing the heart my mother claimed he didn't have?

I maneuvered the little boat to the left—port, I reminded myself—and putted toward the west shore of the lake and the cottage. That was the other thing, besides the letter, that my uncle had left me in his will and the principal reason I found myself here on Seneca Lake.

No doubt I could have handled most of it from the Greenwich Village loft I'd been sharing with Lev Ascher, a good friend who longed to write plays but was making too much money as a copywriter on Madison Avenue. I could have had Lev's brother, the lawyer, call Uncle Charlie's lawyer in Geneva. We sign a few papers, closing costs and fees are paid, and the cottage and its surrounding fifteen acres gets sold off as a summer diversion for some anonymous family from Rochester or Syracuse. I end up with a handsome windfall and life goes on, somewhat more comfortably, in the big city.

But in the few days that had passed since I received word of Uncle Charlie's murder and his bequest to me, I had decided it would be better if I packed my bags and moved here to the cottage, at least on a trial basis. I had to drive up anyway to carry out the lake ceremony as Uncle Charlie had requested. And there was another consideration; that proprietary urge I'd rarely felt before.

I had never really owned anything, at least nothing substantial. I had my books, my typewriter, clothes, a record collection, and an aging Plymouth Horizon to haul them away in. But that was it. Every place I'd ever called home had been either a dormitory, a barracks, a hotel room or an apartment that was mine only until a faceless landlord boosted the rent beyond my means. That had been the nature of my adult life, first as a cops reporter moving from one paper to the next, and then as a freelancer chasing down the crime stories in which I had come to specialize.

But now I had a piece of the American dream. I owned living room furniture and a gravel driveway and a little dock and, luxury of luxuries, three giant closets I couldn't even begin to fill. These things belonged to me now. In time, maybe I'd come to feel that I belonged in this place.

Those are the reasons I gave to friends and family for deciding to leave the metropolis for the small town of Mohaca Springs. I didn't tell them about the other motivators; my ambiguous feelings for Uncle Charlie, the tiny guilts I felt, the need to know the why of it all. Someone had brutally murdered my uncle and walked away. I couldn't just walk away, too. Not until I had the whole story.

The rowboat bumped rudely against a piling and began to drift backward. I jumped onto the dock, made a quick stab at the painter dangling from the bow, and looped it around a metal cleat fastened to the dock's weathered deck. The boat secured, I gathered up the miscellanea from the morning's observance and started up the walk to the cottage.

It was a modified A-frame with a natural-cedar exterior protected from the fickle upstate New York elements by a coat of clear stain. The locals called it a cottage but, like most of the vacation houses that rimmed the lake, it was fully winterized, with everything you could need for year-round living: an electric furnace, a full bath, a modern kitchen, a large master bedroom in the rear and a guest room in the loft. It had an expansive redwood deck overlooking the lake, a fieldstone fireplace, a cable television hookup, and a stereo system.

The place had bachelor written all over it. In the great room that took up the front half of the house, a stuffed rainbow trout, waxy and with gaping jaws, was mounted over the fireplace above a rustic mantel fashioned from an old railroad tie. The walls and vaulted ceiling were painted offwhite, highlighted by natural pine trim and heavy wooden crossbeams. The floor, partially hidden beneath an oval hook rug, was built of tongue-in-groove Georgia yellow pine. Double-pane insulating glass spanned the east end of the room and included a sliding glass door that opened onto the deck.

Two overstuffed chairs and an old leather couch were grouped around the fireplace while, across the room, four captain's chairs surrounded a round pedestal table. Along the wall behind the table sat a heavy oak hutch, its drawers crammed full of the things that make a cliché of an aging hedonist's life—decks of playing cards bound with rubber bands, a lazy Susan of poker chips, a solid silver corkscrew, a chess set of Mexican onyx, odd bits of fishing tackle, several frayed skin magazines. The shelves of the hutch housed an eclectic grouping of collectibles: a small plastic doll dressed in a Boston Red Sox uniform, a few precious pieces of Steuben glass, two Hummels—a little boy and his dog and a teutonic maiden carrying a bucket and stool—and a cheap ceramic statuette of a smiling angler, its base inscribed "World's Greatest Fisherman."

Not much of a monument to mark sixty years of hard living, I thought as I closed the cottage door and set the

6

empty urn on the table. But fitting, somehow, for anyone who knew Charlie Dugan. Two marriages and two divorces. Two kids by his first wife, my cousins, Mary Rose and Chuck, both of whom had long ago written off their father.

Of course, while they rejected the man, neither of them rejected the stocks and bonds he left to them. And it was a tidy sum. For all that he was, Uncle Charlie was one hell of a businessman. A failed insurance business at age thirty had proved to be merely an inconvenience that he soon followed up with a highly successful television and appliance rental chain. It grew to ten stores in upstate New York before, at age forty-two, he sold it and retired to the cottage, to lick the wounds from his second divorce while living comfortably on the numerous investments he'd made.

He spent the last eighteen years living strictly on his own terms, dividing his time between the cottage and a small apartment he maintained in Rochester. Playing the market and carousing with old friends. Fishing, playing cards, listening to his collection of jazz and big band recordings, indulging his tastes for women and whiskey.

I surveyed the great room's memories a moment longer, then turned toward the kitchen and a cold Molson's. It was hot for early June and already the humidity was on the air like a shroud. I ran the sweating bottle of ale across my brow and remembered James Dean in *Rebel Without a Cause*. Chuckling, I walked to the back bedroom and stripped off my sport coat and tie, tossing both on the bed. I didn't own a dark-blue suit and it wouldn't have mattered to Charlie.

Stepping out of my tan slacks, I was thinking about taking a cold shower when I spotted the woman through the bedroom window. She was standing on the porch of an old farmhouse across the cove separating the farm and the cottage. Standing rigid with her hands at her sides; a stern middle-aged woman, as far as I could tell from the three hundred-odd yards that divided us. She seemed to be staring at the cottage and, though I knew the glare on the bedroom window would prevent it, directly at me.

I stared back for half a minute until, finally, she wheeled around and went into the farmhouse. As I started again for the bathroom, another movie image flashed across my mind. Tony Perkins in *Psycho*. But I decided to take that shower anyway.

CHAPTER 2

SIMON and Garfunkel sang softly in the background while Janet and I sat facing each other in a dark place I'd never seen before. We didn't speak; the room was silent but for the music and a persistent tapping sound coming from out of the surrounding gloom. Janet smiled wistfully at the look of puzzlement on my face and leaned forward to hand me a book of poetry by Robert Frost. I reached out, but my hand was weak and the heavy book fell to the floor without a noise. The image of the dark room and my soon-to-be ex-wife began to fade just then, but the tapping continued. My eyes blinked open and slowly came to focus through the glaze of sleep.

I sat up in the chair, flexed a cramp out of my shoulders and took in the familiar surroundings of the cottage, just as the last verse of "The Dangling Conversation" played out on the radio. My watch said five past noon, but the drowsiness in my head and the three empty beer bottles on the end table said it should be much later. I switched off the stereo's tuner and answered the knocking at my door.

"T. S. W. Sheridan?" The caller recited my by-line as if

9

he was reading it from the newspaper. "I'm J. D. Staub, undersheriff of Quincy County. Mind if I come in?"

"Oh, yeah, certainly." I waved him into the living room and took a swipe at the film over my eyes. "I guess I dozed off."

"Well, I'm sorry to disturb you, Mr. Sheridan, but I figured I should come by, pass along my condolences on your loss."

"That's good of you. Please, have a seat."

He went directly to the morris chair by the fireplace, flicking an ash from his panatela into the grate as he sat down.

John Dankley Staub, right-hand man to Amos T. Skelly, the septuagenarian county sheriff. We had never met, Staub and I, but I knew something about the man from a conversation I'd had with his garrulous chief of detectives, Tony Areno. Areno had briefed me on Uncle Charlie's case—and J. D. Staub—the day before, when I stopped in at the Quincy County Sheriff's Department in Geneva on my way down to the cottage. A Gary Cooper type, Areno had said, and he certainly had the physique right. Staub was about six three, a half a foot taller than I, with the sinewy body of a long-distance runner and the contrasting pallor of an Attica lifer. He looked to be in his mid-forties but, according to Areno, he was closing in on fifty-five.

"Man doesn't take shit from anybody, 'cept maybe Amos himself, and that outta respect," Areno had told me between bites on a foul-smelling hero sandwich. "He's the one really runs the show around here, leaving the politicking to Amos. And you can believe me," the portly detective growled, spewing bits of Bermuda onion over the papers on his desk as he spoke, "he's ready to kick ass for a lead on this Dugan killing. They were buddies, y'know."

I took the platform rocker, the chair I'd been dreaming in moments before. "It's nice of you to stop by. Actually, I was hoping we'd get a chance to talk."

10

Staub nodded and inspected the ash on his El Producto. "Charlie used to tell us about his nephew, the writer. We played poker together up in Geneva every Monday night, at the Anglers Club. He'd get a few too many down him and start in on his family. You seem to be the only one he had a kind word for." He glanced at the empty beer bottles on the end table. "Said you were both cut from the same cloth."

"Funny, I always thought of Uncle Charlie as a tartan plaid," I said, a touch defensive. "I'm more a wool tweed."

Staub nodded again, patiently. "T. S. W. Sheridan. The *T* is for Timothy, right? Charlie called you Tim, anyway."

This time I nodded. "Timothy Seamus Wolfe Sheridan. Named after my father, my maternal grandfather, and an Irish Republican rebel named Wolfe Tone, in that order. Everybody in the family calls my father Big Tim and me Little Tim, or even Timmy. Which is why I don't like the name."

"Fair enough. So what do I call you? T.S.W.?"

"That's just for my by-line. Most folks just call me Sheridan. How about you? Is it Undersheriff Staub or what?"

"The troops call me Mr. Staub, to my face. Friends call me J.D. It'd suit me if you called me J.D." He leaned forward and flicked another ash into the fire grate, then studied the butt end some more. He was deliberate, careful in his movements and his speech, the way cops are when they're on the witness stand giving testimony for the prosecution. "I'm real sorry about Charlie, Sheridan. I guess Tony Areno briefed you on the particulars of the case."

"He gave me a look at the police report," I said. "You're the one that found the body."

He sighed. "Charlie didn't show up for Monday night's poker game and he didn't answer the phone when Tommy Melnick—Tommy's one of the regulars—called the cottage. So I came by here the next morning to see if

11

he was okay, thinking maybe he was just sleeping one off. Or got lucky."

"He didn't get lucky."

"No," Staub agreed solemnly. "Anyway, the door was unlocked, which isn't unusual around here. I let myself in and found him on the bedroom floor with a filleting knife stuck in his chest. Coroner says he probably died around ten-thirty or eleven Monday night. He would've gone quick, if that's any comfort."

"What time did your poker buddy call here?"

That drew a small smile. "Very good question. What I'd expect from a reporter. Tommy called about nine o'clock, then tried again around nine-thirty. The game usually starts at eight, but Charlie was late a lot. Sometimes he didn't show up at all, which is why nobody panicked."

"So Uncle Charlie was still alive when Tommy called, but he didn't answer the phone. Could he have been here, you think, maybe sleeping one off?"

"Could be. Or he may have come in later, around ten or so, and gone straight to bed with a big head. Autopsy showed quite a bit of alcohol in his blood. Of course, quite a bit for the average guy was more like normal for Charlie Dugan."

Staub paused and again looked at the empty bottles. I was half-preparing myself for a temperance lecture, when I realized that Staub wasn't the type. "You wouldn't like a cold ale, by any chance, would you, J.D.?" I asked.

He grinned. "Thought you'd never ask."

I swear I heard the sound of ice breaking.

We spent the next couple of hours sharing ale and corn chips and small talk, getting acquainted, testing each other like two people on a blind date.

I reminisced about the time years before when my parents rented a place on Seneca Lake and I had learned to swim and catch sunfish off the dock; then about college and Vietnam, the newspaper business and freelancing in the big city.

12

For his part, Staub stayed mostly with his relationship with Uncle Charlie. How they had met and become friends at a local euchre tournament fifteen years before, how their common tastes in politics and cards had helped to cement the friendship, and how, in spite of Staub's aversion to fishing, the two had spent many a summer afternoon out in Charlie's boat drinking, drowning worms, and "telling lies."

"Dugan was good at it, fishing, I mean. Me, I never caught much and damn glad of it. Hate fishing. I hate the worms, hate the smell of the goddamn fish, I even hate fish fries," Staub confessed as he stripped the cellophane from a fresh cigar. "Nope, I was out there strictly to relax with a guy who never asked more than that you go halfs with him on the booze and never call wild cards when you've got the deal. Charlie was something, all right."

"Yeah, he certainly was," I said as I drank down the last of a bottle of Molson's Golden. I was getting a little tight and I wanted some answers before I was too far gone to remember the questions. "So tell me about the investigation, J.D. Where's it stand?"

"Yeah, I guess that's really why I'm here, isn't it?" He took a deep draft on the cigar and exhaled a plume of smoke. "Let's start with the obvious scenario, the one Areno likes because it's neat and easy. A burglar, maybe some local kid on a dope high, maybe a transient passing through, whatever. He finds out Charlie plays cards Monday nights and so he decides to rip off the cottage."

I interrupted. "That would imply it was someone who knew Uncle Charlie pretty well, wouldn't it?"

"Not really. Charlie was a social animal, Sheridan. Drank in every bar from Geneva to Watkins Glen and back. Wouldn't take much for some sleazeball to buddy up to him over a couple of drinks and find out just about anything he wanted to know about Charlie Dugan."

"So the murder was just bad timing?" I asked. "Uncle Charlie decides not to go to the poker game that night— maybe because he'd been drinking and fell asleep, which

13

might explain why he didn't answer Tommy Melnick's call."

"And why he was wearing his pajamas when he was killed," Staub added. "Burglar comes into the bedroom, runs into Charlie and panics. He sticks him with that fishing knife and takes off." He shrugged his shoulders. "That's the way Areno sees it, but I don't know."

"It's got some holes, all right. Like, what about Uncle Charlie's car? If he was here, then his car must have been here, too, right? So why would the burglar come in?"

"I thought of that, too, but the fact is, Charlie often caught a ride to the game with one of the other regulars. I picked him up a few times myself, figuring I'd have to take him home later anyway, what with the way he drank. The perp could've found that out, like he found out everything else."

"But you still have your doubts."

Staub uncoiled his lanky body from the chair in segments, like a Slinky coming down a stairway, and walked over to the sliding glass door. Staring out at the placid lake, he scratched at the tip of his nose with a knuckle and sniffed hard. "Let's say I get paid to be skeptical, sort of like you journalists." Turning to face me, he said, "First, it doesn't have the physical characteristics of a foiled burglary. The place wasn't ransacked, beyond the usual mess Charlie had lying around. Far as we could tell, nothing was taken, not even the two-hundred-dollar poker stash Charlie always kept in his dresser drawer."

I decided to play devil's advocate. "The thief might have been going for that money when he bumped into Uncle Charlie. After the knifing, he just ran scared."

"Maybe. But then there's the method used by the killer. One clean thrust of the blade, between the ribs and smack into the heart. No mad slashing, no attempt to retrieve the knife. Just one poke and good night, Irene."

Staub's description of the death blow took me back to Vietnam and some of the things I'd seen and heard about there. "Maybe the burglar was a vet, J.D. Special Forces or commando. They're taught to kill that way, instinctively."

"Yeah, I knew a few of those guys in Korea. Only thing is, that type is also trained not to panic, right? I mean, if the guy was a trained killer, cool enough to dispassionately murder Charlie, why would he then get shook up and run out of the cottage without stealing anything? Without finishing the job?" Staub shook his head. "It doesn't add up, not to burglary, anyway. If the killer was a pro—and I say *if*—he wouldn't have left without getting what he came for. But maybe he did get what he came for."

"Premeditated," I mumbled, thinking out loud.

"That's what it feels like to me. I think the guy was after Charlie, not his money or his possessions," Staub said. "Damn, if only the bastard had left some decent evidence. Son of a bitch must've been wearing gloves. He didn't even leave a hint of a fingerprint on the knife."

"What about motive?" I smiled wryly, just to let him know my next comment was facetious. "I mean, other than my Aunt Maureen and my mother, I can't think of anyone who disliked Charlie enough to kill him."

Staub smiled back at me. "Yeah, well don't think we haven't looked into them, Sheridan, along with the rest of your family tree. They checked out okay."

"I'm relieved. So where do you go from here?"

He sighed. "Well, I don't know, really. I've got a half-baked notion . . . probably add up to nothing. Let me ask you, have you ever heard of a guy named Michel Humbert?" He pronounced it in the French style, Mee-shell Oom-bare, but it made no difference to me.

"Not that I can remember." I shook my head.

"How about Florio, Gabriel Florio?"

"Nope."

"I didn't think so," Staub said before adding, "Well, have you met your new neighbor yet? The plain-looking woman who lives over in that old farmhouse?"

15

CHAPTER 3

THE traffic along West Lake Road had picked up a bit by five o'clock that afternoon. A pickup truck, a station wagon, and two subcompacts that could have been Chevys or Toyotas passed me on their way north toward Geneva.

I was driving to the village of Mohaca Springs, located along the lake four miles south of the cottage and roughly in the center of the town of the same name. The difference between living in the town and living in the village, I'd been told, could be discerned by checking your property assessment. Villagers had sewers and paid a special tax for the privilege, while "townies" like me got by with septic tanks and no tax.

The ride along the recently repaved two-lane highway was pleasant; the blue lake to the left was beautiful despite the nearly unbroken phalanx of cottages and motels that hugged the shoreline. To the right, row upon row of grape vines, interrupted infrequently by farmhouses and barns, marched away over steep hillsides. Then just as the winding highway straightened and began a long graded descent, neat homes with high gables and balustraded porches and eaves trimmed like party cakes lined the road and a large royal-blue sign welcomed you to the village on behalf of sundry churches and civic groups. Main Street, U.S.A., and somewhere Norman Rockwell smiled.

Quaint is a word that might have been coined for Mohaca Springs and a score of similar communities scattered among the Finger Lakes, each with its liberal dollop of graceful Victorian homes and wide village greens; each a touch smug in its Chamber of Commerce image as a holdout for nineteenth-century architecture and values. Comfortably predictable places where summers mean cash flow from fishing and tourism, autumn signals the grape harvest, and winter renews high school basketball rivalries and snowmobile races on back country lanes.

As I drove toward the center of town, I remembered bits and pieces of the place from vacations spent in the area years ago. But those images seemed old and faded now, like the brown-hued tintypes of long-dead ancestors you come across while browsing through the family photo album.

"Dead relatives seem to be the dominant theme," I said to no one in particular as I wheeled the Horizon around a double-parked tour bus. I turned up the volume on the cassette player mounted in the dash and sang along to a favorite Buffalo Springfield tune, "For What It's Worth." The vocalist was Stephen Stills, but, minus the gritty guitar solo, it might as easily have been J. D. Staub. Something was indeed happening here, even if it wasn't exactly clear—to either of us.

We had used up most of the afternoon—and all of my Molson's—kicking around Staub's theory that my uncle's death had some connection to a three-sided land deal he was involved in with the two men Staub had mentioned, Michel Humbert and Gabriel Florio, and Maevis Kendall, the neighbor I had seen from my window.

"Charlie was usually pretty closemouthed when it came to his business affairs, but he did tell me a little about these two buy-out offers he got; one from this land developer Florio and the other from Humbert Winery," Staub had said.

"It seems both men wanted to buy Charlie's place, including the four acres the cottage sits on and the eleven acres of hilly scrubland he owned across the road, away from the lakeshore. I take it Michel Humbert hoped to use the land to cultivate more grapes—some kind of hybrid that thrives in that sort of location. Florio supposedly has a hair up his ass about building a fancy resort community along in there. As Charlie explained it, both guys wanted to buy his fifteen acres and the adjoining thirty or so acres owned by Maevis Kendall. Otherwise, neither project would've been 'cost effective.'" Staub snorted. "The thing was, Maevis Kendall wasn't hot to sell out to either one. Which left the whole deal in limbo."

According to Staub, Uncle Charlie—who didn't need the money but was always ready to listen to a good business deal—had been making a private game of the negotiations. He was playing Florio and Humbert off against each other to see how high the price would go, while simultaneously trying to charm Mrs. Kendall into teaming up with him and selling both parcels as a package deal.

"I think Charlie might've been close to getting his price from one of them—I don't know which—but he was having a hell of a time with Maevis."

"I thought Uncle Charlie was supposed to be able to talk a woman into anything." I'd smiled.

"Hmmph. Not a woman like Maevis. She's one of these born-again types. Always has been a strange bird, but she's been even worse the last couple of years since she lost her husband and her son."

"What happened to them?"

"Well, Ed, that's the husband, he deserted the family about two years ago. Just walked away one day and didn't come back, which didn't surprise too many people, owing to how Ed liked his whiskey and how Maevis harped about it. Then the boy, Edward Junior, went and hung himself from a rafter in that old hay barn of theirs. That happened just a few months back. We didn't really turn up a satisfactory reason for his doing it, but who can figure out teenagers?"

"He didn't leave a note or anything?"

"Yeah, he left a note. Four words. 'I'm better off dead.' That was it."

"Enough to drive any mother a little loony," I had said. "At any rate, you think these negotiations for the land may have something to do with Uncle Charlie's murder."

"It's remotely possible," Staub had said carefully, before throwing his hands up and continuing. "Look, to be honest, Sheridan, it's a pretty weak theory, but it's the only one I've been able to come up with. If Dugan's murder wasn't a botched burglary—and that's a big if— then the key to finding the killer becomes finding a motive. According to Dugan, both Florio and Humbert wanted the land so much they were salivating, and Maevis was just as determined to resist. Maybe one of them was desperate enough to commit murder."

"Yeah, but to what end?" I'd asked.

"Well, it could produce two results. First, it might stall the negotiations long enough for everyone to lose interest. That would be Maevis Kendall's motive. Second, it would pass the Dugan property to his heirs, who might be willing to sell, and at a better price, to settle the estate. That's where either Florio or Humbert stood to gain."

"And that also puts me right in the middle," I had said.

"Bingo," Staub had said. "The problem is, I've already had my people do all the sniffin' around we can legally do without Humbert or Florio or Kendall getting pissed off. I just don't have anything right now that I can use to justify an official investigation of the three. Humbert, for one, has a lot of political clout in this county, and don't think Amos Skelly doesn't realize it."

"The sheriff has pressured you to lay off?"

"Let's just say he prefers Areno's killer thief theory. It comes with fewer complications." He had tossed the cigar butt into the fireplace. "Look, I just wanted you to know the score. Like you said, if my theory holds water, you're in the middle of this thing. The negotiations have to come to you. I need more information, something solid to take to Amos. And you're an experienced reporter; you ask questions for a living. You catch my drift?"

For a man who hated fishing, Staub certainly knew how to bait a hook. Not that I needed much persuading. I wanted to find the killer, too. I owed Charlie Dugan that much.

Ralph and Kay's Diner and Outdoor Store sat on the northern edge of the village's modest downtown business section, sandwiched between a Rexall Drugs and a municipal parking lot. I pulled into the lot and parked the Horizon at the base of a large sign that said FREE PARKING COURTESY OF THE VILLAGE OF MOHACA SPRINGS—NO PARKING 1 A.M. TO 6 A.M. So much for the nightlife in rural America, but then again, try to find a free parking space in Manhattan.

The entrance to Ralph and Kay's led into a spacious foyer with a long metal coatrack along one wall and, straight ahead, a stubby glass display case with an old NCR cash register on top and a display of gum, candy, and cigars inside. An archway in the left wall opened into a room packed with the kind of outdoor gear on which L. L. Bean has grown rich. To the right of the foyer was the diner. A lunch counter ran across the back and perhaps two dozen tables and booths were stationed rank and file throughout the rest of the room, most of them occupied— old couples who spoke little and ate slowly, young marrieds with fidgeting kids, isolated groups of sunburned men sharing dinner and fish stories with a gusto one rarely sees outside of a beer commercial.

I took a counter stool three places removed from an old

man whose face looked like West Texas in August. He glanced up as I sat down, quickly lost interest, and went back to reading his paper and slurping his soup. I read the daily specials written on the blackboard behind the counter, then pulled a menu from a clip on the napkin dispenser and tried to find something that didn't come deep fried.

Half a minute later, the café door behind the counter swiveled open and the best-looking woman I'd seen all day was standing in front of me with pad and pencil. She was wearing a short powder-blue uniform. Her hair, shoulder length and a deep reddish-brown, contrasted favorably with her radiant green eyes. She was probably thirty-six or -seven, a couple of years ahead of me. Her body was firm and fleshy, the kind that promised a great deal. And she had the smile of a woman who never broke a promise.

"Hi," she said.

"Hi. Are you Kay?" Not exactly a memorable opening line, but I was out of practice. I cautioned myself not to ask her sign.

"No, I'm Sorrie."

"About what?"

She laughed easily. "No, that's my name. Sorrie. Short for Sorrel."

"That's a very pretty name." Maybe I should have gone with astrology after all. "I'm Sheridan."

"Well, that's a nice name, too. Can I take your order?" The smile downshifted from warm to professional. I thought about trying to reheat it with a witty remark, something that wouldn't make me look like a Vegas lounge lizard, but I drew a blank. When push comes to shove, Uncle Charlie used to say, most guys fall down.

I picked my ego up off the floor and ordered chicken and dumplings. She wrote it down, set a glass of ice water on the counter, and sashayed back through the café doors.

Like I said, I was out of practice. It had been six months

21

since Janet had given me the word and headed west with a guy named Tony, an itinerant electrical engineer she met at an "environmental art" exhibit in a SoHo gallery that specialized in bamboozling the upwardly mobile. Last I heard, they were billing and cooing in a Houston condo, waiting breathlessly for the divorce papers to come through. Which was okay by me. They belonged together, like a matched set of designer luggage. The thing I hated most about the impending divorce was that it seemed so damned trendy.

But we had been married seven years, long enough for me to have lost the knack of being single. Up to now, I'd been practicing on "safe" women, old friends and friends of friends. But now I was in a strange town with no convenient social connections to fall back on and it wasn't as easy as it looked in the movies.

"Here you go. Enjoy." Before you could say Chicken McNuggets, Sorrel had swooped back out of the kitchen and deposited before me a generous portion of chicken and dumplings with a side of peas. I thanked her, but she was already moving down the counter to clear away the old man's dishes and scoop up the miserly tip. C'est la vie. I reached over and grabbed the newspaper the old guy had left behind, then started in on my dinner.

Ralph and Kay's was the sort of place that boasted home cooking like mother used to make. They weren't too far off the mark. The chicken and dumplings were hot, flavorful, and filling. I took my time with the food and browsed through the old man's copy of the *Finger Lakes Daily News*. When I was finished, I left a hefty gratuity, figuring maybe cold cash would impress where watery blue eyes and muddy blond hair hadn't.

At the cashier's counter, I handed over the check and a five-dollar bill to the elderly man minding the till. I was almost out the door when I noticed, through the archway leading into the Outdoor Store, a display of knives. Including a bone-handled filleting knife with a six-inch blade, an identical match for the one Tony Areno had shown me.

"Good knife, fairly cheap," the stocky chief of detectives had said. "But common as fleas on a dog 'round here. Must be two dozen stores just along Seneca Lake that sell 'em. No way to trace where this one came from."

I walked over to the case and stared at the twin of the knife that had killed Uncle Charlie, mesmerized by the gleaming menace of the blade.

"Can I help you with anything?" The old cashier stepped out from behind the register and limped over beside me. He had to be past seventy, and when he smiled his permanently tanned face puckered like a baseball glove that's been left out in the rain.

"I was just curious about that knife." I pointed.

"Yeah, that's a good one. Lists for nineteen ninety-five," he said, taking it down from the display case. "But I can let it go for fifteen ninety-five, including the genuine cowhide sheath."

"Okay." Don't ask me why, but I dug into my pants pocket for the money and then followed the old fellow back over to the cash register. "Are you Ralph?" I asked.

"Yessir. Ralph Cramer, owner, along with my wife Kay, who's in the kitchen burnin' a few dinners."

"Sheridan." We shook hands. "Do you sell many of these knives, Mr. Cramer?"

"Call me Ralph." He rubbed his chin. "Y'know, I had a couple county detectives in here the other day, asked me the same question. Told 'em I sell maybe a dozen a month, in season. You aren't with the county, though, are you?"

"Charlie Dugan was my uncle," I said. "He left his place to me. I just moved in," I added lamely.

"Thought so. I heard Mr. Dugan left the place to a nephew. Didn't know the man that well, 'though he did some business with me over the years. Everybody was

23

real sorry about the murder. I hear you're a writer of some sort."

AT&T was a piker compared to the grapevine in a small town. I'd been there twenty-four hours and the first local I run into has my résumé memorized. "I freelance for magazines," I said somewhat warily.

"Investigative journalism, like Wilson and Bernstein?"

I smiled. "Nothing that earthshaking."

The old man studied my purchase for a moment before slipping it into a paper bag and handing it to me across the counter. "I saw that picture on TV, *All the President's Men*. Pretty good, but I'll still take Bogie and Raymond Chandler myself. One thing you learn, though, if you get to be my age."

"What's that?"

"Real life and the movies are two different things," he said, holding me with his eyes. "Take care, now, son."

CHAPTER 4

IT was a few minutes before seven and still bright daylight from the high summer sun. Too early for nightcrawling in the city, but this was that other New York, the rural part, where early to bed and early to rise is gospel and 5 P.M. means supper's on the table.

I didn't want to drink so much as I wanted the society of a comfortable tavern. Too-small tables filled by people chattering to be heard over a Wurlitzer jukebox, a bartender slyly serving pink concoctions to a couple of giggling girls with dubious IDs, a dart match in the back room. It was a daydream for a long-married man and perhaps a nightmare for a longtime bachelor. I fell somewhere in between, so it seemed like merely a good idea to me.

The parking lot at the Lakeside Inn was three-quarters filled with brightly painted vans and shiny new Firebirds. That indicated a young crowd, able to pour their money into flashy wheels because there was as yet no commitment to an adjustable-rate mortgage or shoes for the kids.

I parked the Horizon next to a Ford Bronco with a gun rack in the rear window and headed into the single-story ramshackle building. Clusters of partyers, most in their twenties, stood around under a ubiquitous cloud of gray smoke and sipped Genesee beer from cans. The jukebox was blaring heavy metal to add to the air pollution. Stone-washed jeans and T-shirts with writing on the front were de rigueur. In my tan cotton slacks and herringbone sport coat, I stood out like a Republican in a union hall.

"What'll it be?" A giant cylinder-shaped man with a copper beard leaned across the bar and yelled in my ear.

I ordered a bottle of Labatt's and a glass. He seemed to resent my asking for a glass—real men chug it straight from the bottle—but he gave me one without comment.

"Thanks," I called to his retreating back, but he ignored me. As a matter of fact, everybody was ignoring me, looking over, through, or past me as if I was the chaperone at a high school dance. Which was fine with me. There was plenty to think about.

Start at the beginning. Poker night. Uncle Charlie doesn't show up, doesn't answer Tommy Melnick's calls. That's around nine. By 10:30 or eleven, Charlie's lying on his bedroom floor in his pajamas with a knife buried in his chest. No mess, no theft, no sign of a struggle, no effort made to retrieve the knife. Okay, no significance there. A common fishing knife, no prints, so why not leave it?

I sipped the foam off the glass of Labatt's and signaled the bartender for a bag of beer nuts. He brought the nuts and extracted fifty cents from the little pile of change I had sitting on the bar.

What about Staub's theory, the business dealings and the unholy trinity; Maevis Kendall, Michel Humbert, Gabriel Florio. The coroner's report showed that Charlie had been drinking heavily. Maybe he already planned to skip the poker game or maybe he just forgot about it. He puts on his pajamas and goes to bed with a big head. One of the three shows up unexpectedly and wants to talk business. They argue and . . . no. Charlie was killed in the bedroom. He wouldn't talk business in the bedroom. The killer had to have sneaked in, intending to murder him all along, if Staub's theory holds water.

I flagged down the bartender again and ordered another beer. The din around me was expanding to a steady roar as more and more people tried to elbow close to the bar.

"'Scuse me, coming through!" Not an elbow, but a large and cushiony breast brushed my arm. My train of thought was permanently derailed.

"Hello again." The crush around the bar forced her to lean in close and I could smell a hint of spearmint on her breath. The powder-blue waitressing outfit had given way to faded jeans and a tank top that seemed to be having an anxiety attack faced with the enormity of its task.

"Hi, Sorrel. Nice to see you again." I almost asked her what a lovely lady like her was doing in a joint like this, but a little voice inside talked me out of it. The voice sounded a lot like Phil Donahue.

"It's Sheridan, right? Ralph told me about you. He didn't catch your first name."

"Just call me Sheridan. It saves time." Not to mention a boring monologue on my family history. "How about you? Sorrel what?"

"Brown," she said, tossing her reddish-brown tresses.

Sorrel Brown? It was almost too cute to contemplate. I once knew a girl named Sandy Shore and I'd always wondered what her parents had against her. But I didn't mention that.

"Can I buy you a drink, Sorrel?"

"Thanks, but I just ordered a round. I'm with some people." She pointed vaguely back toward the tables beyond the dance floor. "Why don't you grab your beer and join us?"

"Sure. Thanks."

The bartender brought Sorrel a metal tray with a pitcher and four clear plastic cups on it. She handled it deftly, like the waitress she was, and we snaked our way

27

through the crowd to a table occupied by three people. A skinny young man of about twenty, wearing a large cowboy hat, was smiling fixedly at a ratty blonde who appeared to be talking his ear off. A second man, closer to my age, wearing a cutoff army shirt and a scowl, was leaning back in his chair, large hands resting on what was the beginning of a substantial beer belly.

Sorrel set down the tray and made the introductions. "Sheridan, this is Danny Wade and Rhonda Rossiter." She indicated the younger couple seated across the table and I nodded. "And this is Roy Rossiter, Rhonda's big brother."

He was big, all right, about six feet, with a wide chest and close-set eyes. The eyes stayed on me while we shook hands and followed me as I settled into a chair.

"Sheridan just moved in, to the Dugan place," Sorrel said. "Mr. Dugan was your uncle, wasn't he, Sheridan?"

I nodded. "He left the cottage to me."

"Oh, yeah. The old guy that got killed," Danny Wade said. "Man, that was some kinda bad shit, huh?"

"Really." The ratty blonde, Rhonda, chimed in. "I mean, who'd think of somethin' like that happenin', you know, like here in Mohoca Springs, I mean. I hear it was really gross, right?" She looked eager, hoping I had a few gory, you know, like details to pass along. For sure.

"Murder usually is," I said.

Everyone except Roy Rossiter offered their condolences. He just sat there sipping his beer and staring at me, a bloated Sphinx in olive drab.

Sorrel said, "Ralph told me you were a writer, Sheridan, magazine articles and such?"

"Right. I used to be a newspaper reporter, but now I freelance."

"Gee, I never met like a writer before." Rhonda again. "That's cool. You gonna write somethin' about Mohaca Springs or the lake or somethin'?"

"Hell, what's there to write about 'round here?" Danny Wade asked. He seemed interested, but maybe he was just trying to keep Rhonda out of his face and in mine.

28

"Everyplace has its stories," I said. "For instance, I was thinking of researching a travel piece on all the resort communities that are springing up in the Finger Lakes. Maybe an article on the local wine industry." I was just talking off the top of my head, but it wasn't a bad idea at that. If nothing else, it would provide me with a good excuse to do some snooping around.

The Sphinx didn't like all the attention I was getting. He tipped his chair forward and poured himself some beer.

"Who the fuck would wanna read about that shit? The local goddamn wine industry," he snorted.

I was trying to think of a comeback when Rhonda, bless her heart, jumped in. "Oh, Roy, you're so dense sometimes, I don't believe it. I bet lots of people'd be interested in that stuff." She turned to me. "He does some work for Humbert Winery, y'see, so he don't look at it like an outsider would. I mean, it's just a job, y' know?"

"Oh?" I said. "What do you do there?"

"Seasonal stuff, is all," Rossiter grunted. "Part-time during the spring and at harvest. Pruning and shit like that. I do other stuff rest of the year."

Sorrel said, "Roy drives a school bus and runs a snowplow for the town in the winter. We get a lot of snow here, especially back in the hills."

"Yeah, when he ain't goofin' off, huntin' or fishin'." Wade laughed good-naturedly.

"Fuck you," Rossiter said.

"Danny was only kidding, Roy," Sorrel soothed.

"Yeah, don't be so damn touchy," Rhonda said. She turned to me and began apologizing for her surly brother as if he wasn't sitting there. "He gets pissed whenever he thinks about work. See, if he'd gone back to finish tech school after the army, he coulda been a master tool and die maker, making good money up in Rochester or Syracuse. But after Vietnam, y'know, he just never got around to it."

"I coulda been makin' thirty grand a year by now,"

Rossiter growled. "But I went into the army instead, okay? And the fuckin' brass send me to Nam, with all that crazy shit. So I'm supposed to come home and sit in a classroom after that, right? With a bunch of little pukes who don't know anything about anything, right?"

"Lots of vets did," I said, thinking back to my own days on the GI Bill.

"Yeah, well some of us had to work for a livin'. I didn't have no rich uncle to croak and leave me with a pile of bread, y'know?"

"C'mon, man, lighten up," Wade said.

"Yeah, Roy. I didn't ask Sheridan over here so you could insult—" Sorrel began, but Rossiter cut her off.

"Why the fuck you bring him over at all? You're supposed to be with me, not this hot-shit scribbler. Who needs him or his dead fuckin' uncle?"

"My uncle was almost killed on Iwo Jima, Rossiter, but it didn't stop him from coming home and making a success of himself," I said evenly, feeling the shakes start to work up from my knees. The others might have felt obliged to humor this jerk because he went away to that terrible war in Asia and they didn't. But I'd been to Vietnam, too, and I'd seen too many guys get cut in half by an AK-47 or lose a leg to one of our own claymores to play sucker for every self-pitying slob wearing his old army fatigues like a badge and whining how the war had ruined his life. Most of the guys who served in Vietnam were support troops—cooks, file clerks, mechanics—who never got within shouting distance of a firefight. I had a hunch Rossiter belonged to the majority.

"Meaning what, college boy?" He pushed forward, hands flat on the table.

I knew I should have left it there. But I'd had one too many Rossiters in my life, and one too many beers. So I jumped in headfirst. "I knew this guy once who came back from Vietnam and couldn't hold a job. Blamed it all on the war, right? And everybody ate it up. The only thing is, I knew this guy since high school, and you know what, Roy? He was a loser back then, too."

I saw the punch coming but not soon enough to do anything about it. My head snapped back, my chair tipped over, and I was on the floor, watching little colored balls zip around in front of my eyes. I remember a crowd of legs surrounding me like a grove of blue spruce, and a woman's voice shouting, "No, Roy! Stop it!" Then I felt a boot slam into my side and the dancing balls blurred.

After that, there was distant shouting and scuffling sounds. A pair of arms reached down and pulled me to my feet. I was dizzy, disoriented, but I could feel a familiar soft breast pressing into my back and I heard a pleasing voice in my ear.

"Easy does it now, Sheridan. That's it, you're okay."

The fog began to lift. Sorrel came into focus, a guardian angel in faded denim. Rossiter was gone and so were Danny Wade and Rhonda. The crowd that had gathered for the stampede lost interest and drifted away.

"Are you feeling well enough to drive?" Sorrel asked.

I nodded my head up and down slowly.

"Maybe you can give me a lift home, okay?" She smiled. "You could use a little tender loving care, you know?"

I nodded again, feeling better already.

CHAPTER 5

TIMING is everything.

The room was dark, the bed was bucking, and I was silently humming that tune from *Dirty Dancing*, trying not to speed up the tempo prematurely. Sorrel was urgently mumbling her own two-word refrain. Suddenly we shuddered to the coda. Her body relaxed, my arms bent outward, and I, one knee perched precariously on the edge of the mattress, pitched overboard onto the cold floor.

"Oh, my God, Sheridan, are you okay?"

I looked myself over, spent and bareassed. "Yeah. Was it good for you, too?"

She giggled and peeked over the side of the bed. "I hope you didn't break anything vital."

"Not unless you have an elbow fetish."

"I've got just the thing for a bad elbow." She hopped out of the bed, slipped into a practical-looking maroon bathrobe, and padded out the bedroom door in her bare feet. "Come down to the living room and I'll get us some wine."

It was just too easy, I thought as I put on my pants. One minute I'm trying to pick her up across the counter of a greasy spoon, the next minute she's picking me up off the floor of a honky-tonk roadhouse and taking me home for sex and chablis. No gamesmanship, no cheap come-ons or facile lies. Also no sentiment, no fundamental sacrifices, no exquisite anxieties. Modern romance. It left me with the odd melancholy of a man who wants to have it both ways.

"My dad put it in a few months before he died to save on heating oil," Sorrel explained when I looked askance at the large Klondike wood stove placed awkwardly in one corner of the otherwise tidy living room. An eight-inch pipe ran out from behind the stove and over to a double-sash window. The glass in the upper sash had been replaced with a sheet of plywood to accommodate the stovepipe. It was a Rube Goldberg setup, typical of an old farmer. Pragmatic and utilitarian, and let building codes and aesthetics be damned.

"When was that?" I asked as I settled beside her on an ancient camelback sofa draped with a brightly colored afghan.

"About three years now." She reached for the bottle of Humbert Chenin Blanc on the coffee table. "He died of a heart attack a few weeks after my mother passed away from a stroke. I'd come home from California for my mother's funeral and to take care of Dad. But then he went, too."

"I'm sorry."

"Me, too. I really loved my father, even though we hadn't seen each other for a lot of years. He was a big gruff old dairyman, but he always had a soft spot for his little girl." She sipped her wine. "My mother and I never got along too well. When I was a kid . . . I don't know, it was like we were in some kind of competition for Dad's attention or something. Anyway, we were never close."

"Is that why you moved to California?"

"Yeah, partly that. Also, because I wanted to be Sandra

Dee." She laughed. "I left Mohaca Springs right after high school. I was sick of fighting with mom, sick of small towns. God, that was eighteen years ago."

I refilled our glasses. "You were an actress then?"

"Ha! I was just a kid who wanted to be loved by Troy Donahue, like in the movies. I never really had the drive to stay in acting, not to mention the talent."

"That never stopped Sandra Dee."

"Aw, c'mon, Sheridan. I bet you thought a lot better of her when you were a horny little kid."

"Actually, I was hot for Connie Stevens, but that's another story. So what happened to your Hollywood dream?"

"Not much. I found out in a hurry I wasn't going any farther than the casting couch." She made a dismissive gesture. "So I found some real work, waitressing mostly. I had a little apartment and I met a few imitation Troy Donahues and that was about it. Life, right?"

"Why'd you decide to stay in Mohaca Springs, after your father died?" It wasn't any of my business, but writers ask questions as a reflex and she seemed to want to talk.

"Well, I had the house free and clear. And after I sold off the cattle and the equipment, there was a little money in the bank. With my job at the diner and the extra money from leasing pastureland to other farmers, I had security for the first time. And I like it."

I related my own similar feelings about the cottage and property Uncle Charlie had left me. We were quiet for a moment before Sorrel eased us back into the present.

"You were right on about Roy, Sheridan. I mean, he acts like he was Audie Murphy in Nam, but he wasn't. Not judging by his MOS, anyway."

I was surprised that she knew the term—army shorthand for Military Occupational Specialty, a long-winded way of saying job title. I was even more surprised that she knew all along that Rossiter had been blowing smoke.

34

"What was his MOS?" I asked.

"Personnel specialist," she said. "He did a tour in Nam all right, but I think he was a supply clerk at an enlisted men's club at Cam Rahn Bay. He never actually told me that, but I sort of pieced it together." She put her hand on my thigh, only now it was the maternal instinct rising. "You should be careful with him, Sheridan. He's the type, well, he can be a bully, as you found out. You're better off humoring him, letting him play his little mind games."

I snorted, "Suffer fools in silence, you mean?"

She read something in my voice. "You were over there, too, is that it?"

"Yeah."

"I figured that's why you were so . . . upset." She took a sip of wine. "Anyway, he's a local boy and you're not. People aren't going to just automatically take your side, no matter what the facts, you know? Roy isn't worth the hassle. I'm sure you know the type."

"Yeah, I know the type," I said. "Ham-fisted and windier than Chicago in March. I bet he lives in a rusty trailer on the outskirts of town and punches out his wife every Saturday whether she needs it or not."

"If that's how you sum up my friends, I can guess what you must think of me."

I have a knack for hitting nerves, even when I don't mean to. Sorrel had started a low burn, but I was too far gone with booze and bruises to catch on right away. By the time I did, it was too late. Sorrel was already standing, busily picking up our empty wineglasses and the unfinished bottle. Before I could work my foot out of my mouth, she was halfway to the kitchen.

I tried calling her back with an apology, but she didn't answer. I sat there for a few minutes, listening to her out in the kitchen banging pots and slamming cabinet doors. After a while, she said something about it being "awfully late" and having to get up early for work. I gathered up my jacket, we said a subdued good night to one another from separate rooms, and I left.

It was still sticky warm inside the cottage when I got home, despite the cool early-morning air outside. It was 1:30 and I was tired, but the day's emotional highs and lows ganged up on me and refused to let me sleep.

I stripped off my clothes, put on a robe, and wandered back out to the living room. There was nothing on the tube but unctuous TV preachers and bad B movies. I looked at the pile of boxes I had left on the floor below the shelves housing the stereo system and decided to begin integrating my record collection with the one Uncle Charlie had left me.

I put one of Charlie's albums on the turntable and began to rearrange the shelves to make room for my records. The twin speakers mounted above the shelves emitted a low hiss, then Oscar Peterson began to rap out "Night Train" with Ray Brown's bass filling in all the right spaces. I hummed along as I worked, the music renewing me.

I'd found jazz as a refuge in the late seventies, after the great rock of a decade earlier had mutated into disco and people like Richie Havens were making ends meet singing jingles for McDonalds. Now my favorite oldies list was a mile long, Count Basie and Mel Torme crowding in next to Dylan and The Beatles.

Peterson was halfway through "Honey Dripper" and I was halfway through rearranging the record shelves when I came across the journal. It had been tucked away behind a boxed set of old 78 big band recordings, a hardbound green ledger of a type used for bookkeeping, only without the red column lines. On the flyleaf, Uncle Charlie had written his name and address, along with the inscription, "Melancholy Musings, To Whom It May Concern."

I thumbed through the pages, struggling at first to decipher the odd writing style. Like most left-handers, Uncle Charlie's writing had a pronounced leeward lean to it, the sentences resembling rows of wheat forced backward by a gale. Some of the entries included a date at the top, others didn't. The earliest dated entry was from nearly two years ago, while the most recent was from January of this year.

It was a memoir, of sorts, of all the major events in his life—the Marine Corp during World War II, his business successes, his marriage failures—and anecdotes about the people and places he had known over the years. A few of the entries were humorous—a marathon poker game on Guam during the war, a fishing expedition to Canada that had ended in a freak blizzard. But the majority of the pages reflected the emptiness of a man growing old alone.

"She was the one great love of my life, but I couldn't keep her," Charlie wrote of Monica, his second wife, fifteen years his junior, whom he had married when he was thirty-six and flush with the success of his rental chain. She had been a student at the Eastman School of Music in Rochester, working part-time as a receptionist at Charlie's main store. He had bought her a grand piano as a wedding present, taken her to Vienna for the honeymoon. It had started off well, he wrote, but within five years, the honeymoon was over.

"We were too much alike and too far apart at the same time. Both eager to pursue our own pleasures at the other's expense. Her tastes were highbrow, concerts and champagne. I leaned toward ball games and straight bourbon."

In the end, they had become "like little, spoiled children, fighting over every piddling detail, spiting each other from habit."

"The pity of it is that I still loved her, even after she took me for all she could get and divorced me. It was always more my fault than hers, I know that. I was too old to bend and unwilling to break. So she broke my heart instead."

That had been the last dated entry, made in January. It was followed by two more short paragraphs, each made in different inks and on separate pages. The first was a rambling, disjointed, pitiful confession—no doubt written when Uncle Charlie was deep in his cups. It described "the inevitable grasping of straws when a lapsed Catholic feels the first pains of arthritis creeping into his body and finds newsprint getting smaller."

I almost stopped reading there. The journal had already told me more than I wanted to know. But then my eyes, a bit teary, brushed across the final entry and curiosity broke the spell. Unlike the previous paragraphs, this one was short and unadorned. It read:

> I found out about "T" today. He told me himself. What was I supposed to say? I didn't know his motives, so I did what comes naturally. I denied it all. I hope that's the end of it.

CHAPTER 6

FRIDAY morning was bleak. I woke up at eight o'clock to the sound of rain pitter-pattering against the windows. My side ached, thanks to Roy Rossiter's well-placed kick. The cut on the inside of my lip, though cauterized by Sorrel's bottle of wine, was still tender.

I showered and dressed quickly, determined to follow through on the list of tasks I had set for myself despite the drizzly weather and complaining body. Drop in on my neighbor, Maevis Kendall, to introduce myself and get a read on her. Visit Humbert at the winery for a "scholarly discussion" on the local wine industry. Time permitting, I'd try and track down Gabriel Florio to let him know I just might be interested in a deal involving my newly acquired lakeside property and his bankroll.

And, before anything else, call J. D. Staub and tell him about the journal and the cryptic final entry.

First things first, and that means breakfast. I switched on the television and half-watched it from the kitchen while I fixed a bacon and swiss cheese omelet. A morning show was on one of the Syracuse stations, its host a stylish blond mannequin with an Ultrabright smile. I listened while she led a fidgety city councilman through a somnambulant interview on the city's preparations for the upcoming New York State Fair. I switched channels when Jolly Ollie the Weatherman bounced onto the screen to give "the inside on the outside."

Omelet cooked, coffee perked, and orange juice poured, I settled down at the big oak dining table, with one eye glued to the TV set, a demeaning habit that came from having grown up with a houseful of electronic friends. Beaver Cleaver, Ricky Nelson, Wyatt Earp, Sky King. George Reeves had even inspired me to jump off the garage roof with a blanket for a cape. A cable station out of New York was showing "Bonanza" reruns, one of my favorite examples of revisionist history; rich ranchers selflessly aiding Nevada's oppressed masses. I wolfed down the omelet and watched Hoss befriend an old Indian chief who was being harassed by greedy land speculators. Sure.

I was stacking the dishes in the sink, with a half-promise to wash them before dirtying any others, when the phone rang.

"Hello, Mr. Sheridan?" It was a deep confident voice, but streetwise rather than cultured.

"Speaking."

"This is Gabriel Florio of Florio Development. You don't know me, but I was involved in some negotiations with your uncle over his holdings on Seneca Lake."

"Really? Then you're an agent for Humbert Winery, Mr. Florio?" I decided to play dumb, which came easy to me.

"Uh, no. I'm not with Humbert. I was negotiating with your uncle about a condo project I'm developing."

"I see. I heard he had an offer from Humbert Winery, to buy the place, that is, so I assumed you were with . . ."

"Not hardly," Florio interrupted, then paused to hack something free in his throat. "Excuse the cough. Anyway, Humbert brought your uncle a deal for the place, true. But

40

he rejected it. My offer was something completely different. And a lot more lucrative."

"Uh-huh. So what is it I can do for you, Mr. Florio?"

"First, I'd like to offer my condolences. He was a fine guy, your uncle," Florio said perfunctorily. "But life goes on. I understand he left the property to you, free and clear. I'd like to get together with you to discuss a sale."

"Well, I guess it wouldn't hurt to hear your offer."

"Good. How about we get together this morning, say around ten-thirty, eleven o'clock? I'm at my office in Syracuse right now, but I can be at your place in a little over an hour."

"I'll be expecting you."

The luck of the Irish. I smiled as I hung up the phone. Everyone is so eager to confess, they're calling me up and asking for appointments. Nero Wolfe should have it so good.

I looked up the number for the Sheriff's Department and dialed. It was obvious that Quincy County was rural and lacking the bureaucratic refinements of its more metropolitan counterparts. The switchboard operator took my call and put it through to J.D.'s office with no preliminaries. He answered the first ring.

"J. D. Staub. Can I help you?"

"Morning, J.D. This is Sheridan."

"So it is! And how are you feeling this morning?" The question sounded as loaded as the .38 he carried in his shoulder holster.

"Something tells me you already have an idea how I feel this morning."

"That could be," he chuckled. "One of my road patrols stopped in at a place called The Lakeside last night. That's a standing directive, you know. I have the boys check in toward closing at all the beer joints, just to see everything's quiet. And to let some of the rowdier patrons see that Quincy County's finest are out cruising the streets."

"Very shrewd," I noted dryly.

"Isn't it? Anyway, the bartender at The Lakeside tells my man about a little rhubarb he had in there earlier. Some stranger smart-mouthing one of the local boys. Described the guy as five nine or so, dirty blond hair, kind of preppy-looking, slow reflexes. Sound familiar?"

"And you put all the disparate clues into that computerlike brain of yours and out I popped?"

"Well, that's what I'd like the public to think. Actually, my deputy was in the squad room when you came by to see Areno the other day. He matched you up with the description he got from the bartender and passed it on to Areno, who mentioned it to me."

"And they say the old chain of command method of law enforcement is outdated."

I told him about my encounter with Roy Rossiter, leaving out the part about recuperating in Sorrel Brown's bed. He couldn't place any of the names offhand, although he thought he remembered seeing Sorrel at Ralph and Kay's before and he might know Rossiter if he saw him.

"We have quite a few Roy Rossiter types around here, Sheridan," J.D. said. "Just like anyplace else. Mostly they confine their troublemaking to a monthly brawl in some gin mill. I wouldn't worry about it."

The news about Uncle Charlie's journal interested him, but he was unable to shed any light on who the mysterious "T" might be or what he could have told Uncle Charlie. "The only 'T' I can think of is Tommy Melnick. I can't imagine he'd know anything about a journal, but I'll check it out." He suggested that I comb the cottage for anything else that might tell us more and I agreed to do it as soon as I had the time. Then I told him about Gabriel Florio's phone call and my plan to feel Florio out about his business dealings with Uncle Charlie.

"That's a good break," he said. "Just be sure you take it slow and careful, okay?"

We spent a few minutes more chatting about the lousy

weather, then said our goodbyes. I put some rainy-day music on the turntable and cleaned up the breakfast dishes, waiting for my guest to arrive.

I heard the crunch of gravel when his car pulled into the driveway. When I opened the cottage's front door, he was standing next to a dark-blue Lincoln Continental. The rain had stopped, but there remained a misty grayness in the air.

"Mr. Sheridan? Gabe Florio." He shook my hand as if he was trying to strangle a cat. A short barrel-chested man with the cocky bearing of vintage Cagney. I led him into the house, helped him off with his London Fog rain-coat, and hung it on a peg rack near the door. He was wearing a tan three-piece suit. The vest hugged his torso like an Ace bandage.

"That uncle of yours was a real man's man. I respect that. Mind if I sit down?" Florio spoke in quick short sentences, punctuated each time with an asthmatic intake of breath. While I was hanging up his coat, he staked out a seat at one end of the dining table and took a folded bundle of papers from his inside breast pocket.

"Would you like some coffee, Mr. Florio?"

"No thanks. Had enough at the office to float a crap game. They find the punk that stuck your uncle yet?"

"Not yet. They don't even have a motive at—"

"Motive? Who needs a motive these days? Some hyped-up punk looking for an easy mark. Happens all the time."

"It doesn't happen all the time in my world," I said. "And when it does there's usually a reason for it. Even if it's a lousy reason."

He looked down at the papers spread out before him and wheezed a bit. "Well, anyway, I'm sure the local cops will handle it. Now, what d'you say we talk a business deal?"

"Whoa! You're moving too fast. I'm not even sure I

have the authority to talk business with you yet. I haven't received title to the place from Uncle Charlie's executor."

"That's just a formality. I understand Dugan's lawyer says the whole deal's cut and dried. Just has to go through channels." Florio stopped short, knowing he'd said too much.

"You've already checked with Uncle Charlie's lawyer?" He shrugged his cotton-blend shoulders. "Not really. As it happens, my attorney and your uncle's guy went to S.U. together. Sometimes they do a little kibbitzing over a round of golf." He allowed himself a tight smile. "Okay, I'm interested, I admit it. So, c'mon and have a seat. I want to show you something."

I took a chair adjacent to him and watched as he spread open a sketch of an elaborate housing complex with a series of tiered condominiums, several tennis courts, a building marked "clubhouse," and a semicircular marina.

"This here is Dugan's, er, I mean, your property. Right along here, see? This bank of condos runs up that big hill across the street; here's the lakeshore out front of the cottage and over here is the cove that divides your property from the Kendall place." It was the longest continuous statement I had heard out of him. He paid for it with a coughing fit. As the spasm subsided, Florio began shaking his head.

"Doctor tells me to quit cigarettes. Says it'll help the cough. So I quit. Only the cough gets worse. Maybe it's the cigars." He wiped his forehead with a tissue. "So where were we? Okay, you can see what I'm talking about here. A resort community. Tennis, swimming, boats, the works. Beautiful."

"What about all this over here?" I reached across the table and pointed at the area on the drawing that included the southern half of the project. "That's the Kendall farm, isn't it?"

"Right."

"And you've already bought up that land?"

44

"We're negotiating. The woman's tough, but she'll come around." He reached into his pocket and extracted a long Jamaican cigar, studying me closely as he peeled the silver foil from the cigar with care. "I should probably keep this to myself, Sheridan, but I think I can be upfront with you."

He stood and walked over to the coffee table, lit the dark brown cigar, and tossed the match into the ashtray. He was Edward G. Robinson now.

"See, with your land"—he gestured at me with the cigar—"I can start the project. Downscaled, sure. But enough to satisfy my investors that the project is going to go up. I build maybe a third of the condos and the clubhouse on your side of the parcel, and I dredge out the cove and begin putting in the marina. Right? Then I got some leverage on Mrs. Kendall."

"I don't follow you," I said.

"Simple," Florio said. "I need all your property, plus the hilly property Kendall owns across the road from her house. Without that ridge of hers, I can't make the project cost-efficient because I can't build enough units. But I don't really have to have her lake frontage. It would be nice, but the project will fly without it."

"So? You think she'll be willing to sell you just the back property, the ridge, once you get the rest of the project going on my land?"

"I think so, but I'm not putting all my chips on it." He moved back to the table. "Look at this cove. Right now, it's useless for anything but little dinghies. Shallow, full of cattails, right? So, I take and dredge out this cove for a marina. Nothing she can do about it, once I get title to your place. Then, after I get the marina in shape on your side, I get the state and county boys to go for a public boat launch and picnic ground on Kendall's lake frontage. I donate the cost of dredging the cove and throwing up docks and stuff. In return, the politicians condemn Kendall's land. She gets a fair price, the county get the front half for a public park, and I take the rest off their hands for my condo project. Eminent domain, they call it."

"Are you so sure the politicians will cooperate?"

He snorted. "It's in the bag, kid. Everybody makes out, including you. Let me toss a few numbers at you."

He whipped out a pen and began doodling figures on a sheet of scrap paper. Per-acre-price breakdown, project capitalization, par-value recompense on the cottage, and so on. It was the language of glib speculators everywhere, but what it boiled down to was a sizable six-figure offer, one-third to be paid to me in a lump sum down payment and the other two-thirds to be paid in monthly installments, including interest, over a twenty-four-month period. The twenty-four months was Florio's estimate of how long it would take to complete the project and sell all the condos.

I have to admit, I was tempted. Assuming Florio wasn't just blowing smoke or trying to work some sort of swindle, we were talking a lot of money. After years of barely making ends meet on what I made as a freelancer, I'd finally have a cushion—a big green cushion—to fall back on.

But then, there was Uncle Charlie's murder to consider.

"It's a nice offer," I said. "I'll have to think about it and get back to you."

"Don't wait too long, kid," Florio warned me as I handed him his raincoat. "You have to move fast in this business. If you don't . . ." He let the sentence drop with a shrug of his shoulders. A disquieting grin spread across his face. "Stay healthy, Sheridan. I'll be in touch."

CHAPTER 7

THE sun was beginning to break through the mist by the time Florio drove off. Out on the lake an open-bow boat cruised toward the far shore, a stringer of fish dangling from its side. Fishing was said to be good on a rainy day.

My own fishing expedition had been less successful. Florio was an interesting sort. Flashy, pushy, and single-minded, as you might expect from a real estate hustler. But also careless and imprudent; he talked too much, like a man under pressure. The question was, where was that pressure coming from? And was it enough to push him into murder? I couldn't begin to answer that, not yet anyway. But patience is the chief virtue of a good fisherman, my father always told me. Keep casting out your line and, sooner or later, something will bite. Sound advice, particularly when there are no other choices. Which is why I decided to stroll over to the Kendall place.

Stumbling once on a piece of macadam that had broken away from the shoulder of crumbling West Lake Road, I reached the rutted driveway of the Kendall farm just as a Chevy station wagon with a U.S. POSTAL SERVICE sign on the windshield pulled up to the mailbox.

"Afternoon." The woman sat in the passenger's side of the front seat, her left hand reaching across to the steering wheel while her right gripped a fistful of letters and pulled at the flap on the Kendall mailbox. "Or is it morning still?" She was fiftyish and large, spreading out underneath her paisley muumuu like the proverbial chestnut tree.

"No," I said, glancing at my wristwatch. "The afternoon began officially about ten minutes ago."

"I noticed you walking up the road there," she said with an affable grin. "If you're looking for Maevis, you're wasting a trip. She's usually at work this time of day."

"I was just going over to get acquainted. Guess I'll have to wait until another time." I hoped I didn't sound as relieved as I felt. "My name's Sheridan. I just moved in down the road." We shook hands.

"I'm Norma Wells. Nice to meet you," she said. "I'm the local mailman, in case you couldn't tell for yourself. You know, I was just wondering about you."

"Oh?"

"Yeah." She reached down onto the seat of the Chevy. "I have a couple of pieces of mail here marked for a Sheridan at Charlie Dugan's address. You're living there now, huh?"

"Yes." I thumbed the two letters she handed me. A yellow card-sized envelope I would have recognized as being from Lev Ascher even if he hadn't put his return address in the corner, and an official looking legal-sized envelope from Uncle Charlie's attorney.

"You're a relative of Charlie's?"

"His nephew." I nodded. "He left me the place to me."

"Gosh, that was an awful thing. His murder, I mean. Seemed like a nice sorta fellow, too." Norma shook her jowls. "Getting so you're not safe anywhere anymore."

"Mmm. Did you know my uncle well?"

"I knew him to say hello to, you know. He used to buy maple syrup from us once in a while. My Arnie and me

48

make our own and sell it at the house, sort of a sideline. That Charlie, he'd always tell me how it was me that gave the stuff its extra sweetness." Her fleshy face melted into a demure smile, reminding me of a corpulent Mona Lisa.

"That sounds like Uncle Charlie."

"You know, if you haven't met her yet, I should warn you that Maevis Kendall is, well, real standoffish, if you get my meaning. She isn't easy to get to know."

"It sounds like you know her pretty well."

"I've tried to over the years and I guess I've gotten as close as most. But that isn't saying a whole heck of a lot," she said, frowning. Norma Wells was the type of good-hearted soul who took every problem in her town personally, the Earth Mother of Mohaca Springs. "She's a troubled woman."

"Yeah, I heard about her husband leaving her. And the son's suicide."

"That didn't help matters any." Norma shook her head in agreement. "Ed taking off like that, leaving her and the boy. I shouldn't say it, but he was drinking a lot. Staying away from home, letting the farm peter out. He was a sad man. And then Edward Junior goes and hangs himself in the barn. Goodness, a young boy like that, not even eighteen."

"I'm surprised Mrs. Kendall has stayed on here."

"That's strange, isn't it? Her not being from around here originally, you'd think she'd want to go back to Pennsylvania where her people are, wouldn't you? But you know, she's got her job at the Pinewood, housekeeping. And the boy's buried here . . ." She let the sentence drop, not knowing the answers, unable to speculate any further.

"Maybe she's hoping her husband will come back."

"Possible," Norma murmured. "But, you know, Maevis just isn't the kind of woman a man comes back to. I'm sorry to have to say that, but it's true." She pulled her

49

meaty arm back through the window and centered herself in the passenger's seat. "Well, whatever. I guess I better get a move on if I want to get done in time to fix Arnie his supper. Anyway, nice to meet you, Mr. Sheridan. And have a nice day, as we say in the U.S. Postal Service."

She saluted me as she urged the heavy wagon back onto the road and drove north. I waved her on her way, then remembered the two pieces of mail. I read both on the way back to the cottage.

Lev's letter was welcome, if predictable. Did I arrive all right, how was the weather, have they found Charlie's killer. That sort of thing. The letter from Martin Bridey, Uncle Charlie's attorney, wasn't any better. It was a stilted account of Bridey's effort to "finalize as per agreement" the paperwork on the estate. It was seriously over-burdened with legal jargon and ruptured syntax, but I could decipher enough of it to understand that an amended abstract had been filed with the county office in Geneva and everything was proceeding smoothly.

I wished I could say the same. So far, all I had was an intriguing journal entry, a brief meeting with a man who conceivably could have wanted Uncle Charlie dead, and some hearsay about a mysterious widow who apparently didn't want to sell her land. Put them all together, they spell muddle.

Michel Humbert was the third name on the list and next in line for a visit from T. S. W. Sheridan, boy sleuth. Maybe I'd be lucky this time. Maybe Humbert would take one look at the cut of my jaw and the determination in my eyes and confess right on the spot. And maybe gasoline would go back down to fifty cents a gallon. But I doubt it.

Humbert Winery was located just south of the village of Mohaca Springs, nestled in at the base of a long rolling hill. The main building was a sprawling fieldstone and timber affair, Tyrolean in aspect and three stories high.

Behind it sat a large weathered barn and a series of single-story buildings sided in corrugated metal. Unlike the main building and the barn, these latter structures were relatively new, probably built within the last thirty years.

I followed a sign to the lot designated for visitors and parked next to a pickup truck with a camper mounted on the bed. Several other cars were scattered about the lot, along with a pair of tour buses marked FINGER LAKE TOURS. The free tours offered by a dozen or so wineries in the area were a popular stop, particularly since each included a wine tasting at the end. Humbert Winery was one of the smaller operations, but it apparently still managed to do well with the tourist crowd.

I followed a winding gravel path around to the far end of the main building and stopped at an anachronistic set of modern glass doors. At a reception desk inside, a pretty girl of no more than twenty was studiously working a crossword puzzle.

"Hi. Can I help you?" She looked as if she could help any man with normal drives. She wore a matching green sweater and skirt outfit, the skirt slit high up on the thigh, a deep V neck to the sweater. Her hair was stacked on top of her head like a blond crescent roll, one curly strand running like hot butter down each temple. She had the tiny red lips and swelling breasts of a Vargas girl.

"I'd like to see Mr. Humbert. My name's Sheridan."

"Do you have an appointment, Mr. Sheridan?"

"No, I don't. Do I need one?"

"Well, not necessarily. Some days are busier than others, though. Mr. Humbert is supposed to be going down to Ithaca this afternoon, but I think he's still in the building somewhere. He'll probably stop back here before he leaves. Would you like to sit down and wait?"

"Thanks." I took a seat in a Naugahyde chair across from her desk and made a show of browsing through the dated oenological magazines on the table next to me. She went back to the crossword puzzle. The nameplate on her desk said Wendy Pollock. I envisioned myself dropping in on Janet in Houston with a delicious young Wendy Pollock on my arm.

"What's a five-letter word for 'kingdom'?" she said, looking up at me suddenly.

"What? Oh, a, uh, five-letter word for 'kingdom'?"

"Yes. I think the fourth letter is *l*."

"Let's see. How about 'realm'? R-e-a-l-m."

"Oh, great! Then that must mean eleven down, 'Man with a Gunn', is 'Peter.' Does that make any sense?" She frowned.

"Sure. 'Peter Gunn,' the old TV series. Don't you remember it?" I started to hum Henry Mancini's theme music from the show. She gave me a condescending smile, the kind kids usually save for a senile grandparent.

"I never heard of it," lovely Wendy Pollock said. "I guess it was before my time." Cancel the trip to Houston.

The door to my right swung open and a man in an expensive gray pinstripe suit strode into the room. He was about five foot ten, but so slim he seemed taller. He had a long narrow face, black hair, and a serious tan. Late thirties and handsome, if you like the George Hamilton type.

"Oh, Mr. Humbert," Miss Pollock said, slipping the crossword puzzle into a drawer. "This is Mr. Sheridan. He was waiting to see you."

Humbert's eyebrows peaked a bit at the mention of my name, but that was it.

"Yes, Mr. Sheridan. Is there something I can do for you?" He stuck out his hand. "I'm afraid it will have to be something I can do in the next five minutes, however. I'm guest lecturing at Cornell's School of Hotel Management this afternoon and I'm running a little late as it is."

"I'm a writer, Mr. Humbert. I inherited a place on the lake from my uncle, Charles Dugan. I understand the two of you were acquainted, so I thought I might exploit that connection to get some information from you."

His smile retreated into a straight line, but the deep brown gaze didn't falter. "What sort of information?"

"I'm thinking of doing a piece on the Finger Lakes wine industry," I said. "I thought you might be able to give me some valuable background. You know, the history of local winemaking, your company's history, the changing technologies. That sort of thing."

"I see. Well, as I said, I don't have much time at present but . . . Come into my office for a minute."

It was a large room, paneled in dark walnut planking and carpeted wall to wall with thick green pile. Light flooded in through two large windows in the far wall. The remaining three walls were covered either by floor-to-ceiling bookshelves or framed photos and awards from numerous national and international wine tastings. Humbert stepped behind his desk and began cramming papers into a thick leather attaché case.

"Would you mind my asking who told you I knew your uncle? I'm just curious."

"Not at all. I met the undersheriff yesterday, J. D. Staub, and he mentioned that you and Uncle Charlie were negotiating a business deal for his lake property. It just came up while Mr. Staub was filling me in on the murder."

"That was a terrible thing. You have my sympathies. That sort of random violence seems to be the norm these days, I'm afraid. Has Staub brought anyone in yet?"

"Not yet. But he's confident he will."

"Well, let's hope so. Tell me, how in fact did my name happen to come up?" Humbert didn't look up, instead busying himself with the papers and the attaché case.

"I was telling Mr. Staub that I'd be available if he needed me for anything. I mentioned that I was thinking of doing a story on the local wine industry, so he brought up your association with Uncle Charlie. He thought you might be able to provide what I'm after."

He snapped shut the case and looked at me, self-confidence returning to his voice.

"Of course. I'd be happy to offer whatever expertise I can. Actually, since you are the heir to Mr. Dugan's property, I'd be interested in discussing another matter as well. The business negotiations I was conducting with your uncle. We didn't have a chance to conclude our dealings before his unfortunate death."

"That sounds fair enough," I said.

"But as I said before"—Humbert checked his watch—"I have to run now. I have this lecture on wine appreciation at three at Cornell and if I'm late the students may decide to drink up all my visual aids. Why don't you meet me tomorrow for lunch at the Pinewood? As my guest, of course. Say one o'clock? You know the place?"

I nodded. "I've passed it before on the road down from Geneva. Sounds good to me."

"Fine. Meanwhile, why don't you go down to the tour lobby and avail yourself of one of our tours? I'm sure you'll find our guides highly qualified and instructive."

We were out of the office and into the reception area by this time, Humbert toting his attaché case as he maneuvered toward the plate-glass doors. We exchanged thank-yous and he left. I loitered a few moments longer, shamelessly waiting to get in a last word with lovely Wendy, who was on the phone with someone.

"Hold on a second, Todd," she cooed into the mouthpiece. "Is there anything else, Mr. Sheridan?"

There had to be, but I couldn't think what it was. I suddenly realized how old thirty-five was when seen through a pair of twenty-year-old eyes.

"No, I guess not," I told her, and I went off to find the tour lobby.

54

CHAPTER 8

THERE'S something about a quarter moon in a clear sky and a winding country road. The lake gleaming in the moonlight, I drove up West Lake Road with the windows rolled down and the radio silent. I had left the cottage at 9:30, heading to Geneva to meet with an old friend from my newspaper days. It had been a long day and it wasn't over yet, but the eighteen-mile trip provided a soothing diversion to another place and time.

A couple of centuries or more ago, this land had belonged to the Senecas, largest of the six tribes of the Iroquois Confederacy. The white man's insatiable drive for virgin land had long since reduced the Indians to a shadow existence on a handful of small reservations dotted across the state's western expanse, but the legacy of the Iroquois lives on in the folk stories and place names of the region—Taughannock Falls, Keuka Lake, Canandaigua.

The Finger Lakes is a collection of eleven elongated lakes, each bearing an Indian name, each carved from the earth thousands of years ago when glaciers advanced and receded across this part of upstate New York. To the Indians, the long narrow lakes were a supernatural wonder, pressed into the earth by the hands of the Creator in benediction to the bountiful wilderness. Later, waves of settlers came to clear the land and till the soil and build villages. They brought their own god and, in tribute to their European roots, new place names to the frontier—Geneva, Naples, Waterloo.

"The lake effect," I said aloud as I drove slowly around a dark bend in the road. It was a term used by a teenaged tour guide named Randy who had shepherded a group of tourists and me through Humbert Wineries a few hours earlier.

"The first domestic vines were planted in the region in the 1820s," the boy recited, leading our small congregation along a stony corridor and down a staircase into a cool cavernlike cellar where row upon row of great oak casks were stored. "The settlers discovered early on that the harsh winter temperatures in the area were neutralized somewhat by what is known as the lake effect. In short, the lakes soak up the sun's heat during the summer and fall and release that heat during the winter months, thus causing a moderating influence on the air temperature in the immediate vicinity and protecting the sensitive vines from freeze damage."

Our young guide was tall and very thin, an adolescent skeleton. He was wearing an ill-fitting burgundy blazer, probably inherited from a predecessor who had finished college and gone on to a better-paying job. Tour guides were universal in that respect, like vendors at the ball park. They were invariably either young kids working to pick up some pocket money or oldsters who couldn't or wouldn't settle for a monthly Social Security check and a rocking chair.

"Humbert Wineries was founded in 1878 by Henri Michel Humbert," Randy continued, "who migrated to this country from the Bordeaux region of France. Henri is the great-grandfather of the winery's current owners. Unlike many of the wineries in the area, which have been sold over the years to large corporations and often merged with various California producers, Humbert Wineries has been passed along from father to sons for four generations. Wines bearing the Humbert label are vinted exclusively from grapes grown in the Mohaca Springs vicinity, as has been the case for more than one hundred years." The kid rambled on in a high-pitched staccato, sounding like a bad actor who memorized all the right lines without bothering to learn what the play was all about. When he came up for air, an old lady with suspicious orange hair jumped in.

"What about Prohibition, Randy? How did the winery survive that?" A very good question.

"Okay." The kid looked at her for a few seconds, focusing his reply, then raised his eyes to some ambiguous point a foot or so over her head and began reciting again.

"During the approximately thirteen years that the Eighteenth Amendment was in force, the period from 1920 to 1933 popularly called Prohibition, Claude and Jean-Paul Humbert—Henri's son and grandson, respectively," he added parenthetically, "kept the business alive by producing grape juice for commercial sale, as well as sacrificial wines for religious purposes and medicinal wine derivatives, which were sold to people only by prescriptions from physicians."

"I bet there were a lot of Catholics and hypochondriacs around here in those days," said a fat man in a polyester leisure suit. Everyone laughed except the kid, who probably had heard the line a dozen times before and still wasn't sure what it meant.

Our little group moved on to the bottling area, then packaging, and, finally, the perennial favorite, the wine-tasting room. After a pleasant half hour sampling Humbert's top line—a Chablis Natural, a heavy burgundy, a surprisingly light rosé, and an excellent champagne—we gradually disbanded. Most of the group wandered into the

57

winery's gift shop to stock up on discounted bottles of Humbert wines and assorted souvenirs. I took a quick look through the shop's display window—why would anyone want a beer mug with a wine company logo on it?—and made tracks for the parking lot.

I got back to the cottage around 5:30, my original plan being to do some laundry and then head down to Ralph and Kay's Diner for dinner. But then I remembered the night before with Sorrel and how badly it had ended. I wanted to see her, to let her know I hadn't meant to hurt her, but I knew it was too soon. Better to let it ride for awhile.

Instead, I grilled a steak medium-rare on the hibachi on the deck, tossed a salad, and pulled a couple of Molson Ales out of the refrigerator. After the meal, I put in a call to the newsroom at the *Finger Lakes Daily News* and asked to speak to Karen DeClair.

"Sheridan! How the hell are you? And where the hell are you?" Karen was the metro editor of the *Daily News* now, but I first met her several years earlier while we were both toiling for a daily in Rochester. She had been brought in to work general assignment after a three-year stint as regional correspondent for the paper's Geneva bureau. She was a tiny woman with a round face, frizzy brown hair, and a wry sense of humor. We became friends while working together on a story about a dope-peddling ring.

"I'm fine, and I'm calling from a cottage near Mohaca Springs. So how're things with the *Finger Lakes Daily News*'s first female metro editor?"

Karen left the Rochester paper a few months before I did to take a job as a reporter and copy editor with the much smaller Geneva daily. It seemed at the time to be "a lousy career move," as Karen had put it, but it wasn't totally out of character for a small-town girl from Indiana. "Why chase a career, bouncing from job to job, going to bigger and bigger papers, when I was perfectly happy in

58

little old Geneva?" she had asked me. And it turned out well for her. Within six months after she took the job, new ownership came into the *Daily News* and Karen De-Clair survived a general housecleaning to become metro editor.

I explained over the phone the events that had brought me to Mohaca Springs and my efforts to throw some light on Uncle Charlie's murder. She was familiar with the case from her paper's coverage, of course, but there had been no follow-up concerning the inheritance and, since only the members of the immediate family were listed in the obituary, Karen hadn't known Charlie Dugan was my uncle. I told her I needed some background information on a few people who might figure in the case. We agreed to meet at the paper at ten o'clock that evening, deadline time for the morning daily.

The Friday-night traffic was heavy on Main Street when I pulled into Geneva a few minutes before ten. I found a parking spot about a block down from the *Daily News* building, gently easing the venerable Horizon in between a long shiny LTD and a high-riding Camaro. The sidewalk was busy with clusters of mostly young people roaming from one bar to the next or lining up outside an old theater featuring the latest Chuck Norris punch-out.

The lobby of the *Daily News* was deserted. I checked the building directory mounted on the wall beside a vacant reception desk, then took the elevator to the second floor. A short corridor led to a large bright room with about two dozen metal desks placed around in no discernible pattern and a handful of teletype machines in one corner.

"Hi, can I help you?" A pudgy kid who might have been twenty-two was staring up at me from a desk littered with proof sheets. He was holding a stubby blue pencil in his hand. Probably a rookie or an intern from Syracuse U. getting his first honest taste of the noble Fourth Estate.

"Yeah, I'm supposed to meet with Karen DeClair."

"Sheridan! Over here!" Karen was waving at me from a small cubicle across the room. She was gripping a sheaf of papers in her other hand and pinching a phone to her ear with a shoulder the way Isaac Stern might cradle a violin.

"Geez, I'm glad to see you," she said when I strolled into the tiny office cubicle. "Listen, we've got a fatal up on Route 14 near the thruway exit and I want to try and get it into the final. I've got our night cops reporter on the phone here, calling from a motel near the accident scene. He's ready to dictate, but I've got to run down to Makeup and bump something off page one. Can you take some dictation for me?" She motioned to the video-display terminal adjacent to her desk—a computer console with a keyboard and a small TV screen.

"No problem," I said, taking the phone from her. She hurried out of the office, shouting back as she went, "Slug it 'Fatal 1,' okay? I'll be back in two shakes."

I settled in at the softly humming VDT, the phone receiver scrunched up to my ear, fingers splayed over the keys. "Okay, ready," I said into the mouthpiece.

"Who's this?" a young man's baritone voice asked.

"Sheridan, rewrite man du jour. Who are you?"

"Brian MacKay, ace reporter." He chuckled.

"All right, Brian. Fire when ready."

"Right. First graph. 'Two youths were killed and three others injured last night when the car they were riding in left the road and struck a utility pole on Route 14 near the intersection of . . .'"

It was a typical sad account of boozy teenagers out for a joyride. Two deaths, three serious injuries, and a twisted wreck of an automobile, all reduced to eight column inches and maybe a bad photo for the Saturday-morning paper. I took it all down, read it back to MacKay to check for accuracy and spelling of names, and rang off. Karen rushed into the cubicle a few seconds later and shooed me away from the console.

"Okay," she said, her eyes affixed to the bluish-green lettering on the display screen. "I'll go over this wham-bam and send it along to composing. Be with you in a sec."

It was like that in the newspaper business. Get it first, get it fast, and get it right. If you have to reflect on the tragedy of it all, do it on your own time—over your morn-ing coffee or with a prenoon cocktail at your favorite gin mill. Tomorrow it will be sad. Tonight it's just news.

I wandered over to the kid at the front desk—there were only two other people working in the newsroom at this hour, hunched and squinting at their VDTs and oblivious to all else—and asked directions to the paper's clips files.

"Down the hall and through the door next to the men's room," he said without looking up from the proofs.

His directions led me to a door marked LIBRARY. Inside were a few shelves of reference books, phone directories, periodicals, and three austere rows of gray filing cabinets. There was no one in the room. I found the files marked "Names" and quickly thumbed through the Hs, Fs and Ks, removing three small manila envelopes and taking them to a seat at a long table near the door.

"Humbert, Michel P. (For additional information see Humbert Wineries, subject files.)"

I dumped the contents of the envelope on the table and sorted through a meager collection of newspaper clip-pings, most of them yellowed with age. There wasn't much to learn from them. A few short items on local so-cial events. "The annual Country Club Ball was chaired by Michel Humbert, president of Humbert Wineries . . ." "Guest speaker at last night's Chamber of Commerce din-ner was Michel Humbert . . ." The most substantial clips were a couple of stories on wine production in the area, quoting Humbert as a local expert.

I opened the second envelope. "Florio, Gabriel A." A single clipping fluttered out. It gave a brief mention of a plan to renovate a group of old town houses in Geneva's Historical Preservation District into apartments and condos, crediting Florio as the chief developer of the project. Again, there was nothing in the article that could help me.

The third envelope proved to be no better than the previous two. The files didn't have anything listed for Maevis Kendall or her son, but that wasn't surprising. From what I had learned about Maevis, she wasn't the type who figured to mix in the local social scene. As for the boy, most newspapers have a standing policy not to report suicides unless they have a direct bearing on some issue of concern to the community as a whole. Or unless the victim was famous. The Kendall boy didn't count on either score. The third envelope was for Maevis's wandering husband, Edward. One tattered item from the police blotter about his arrest for DWI about two years ago. It must have been a slow news day for that to have seen print.

"There you are. Find anything of interest?" Karen walked into the room looking relaxed now, if a bit haggard. The next morning's edition had been put to bed.

"Yeah. A fascinating piece on the Horticulture Club's Spring Cotillion. I'm sorry I missed it." I stuffed the clips back into the envelopes and tossed them into a shoe box marked "Return Clips Here."

"Well, those files only go back about three years," Karen said. "Any major stories dated earlier should be on microfilm. You'd need to see our librarian about that, though. She won't be back in until Monday."

"It can wait. I really didn't expect to find out much anyway, not from the clips." I smiled at her. "Journalists don't put half the stuff they know into their stories."

"Yeah, well, you know how it goes, Sheridan. We hear things about people, town gossip, rumors, that sort of thing. But mostly it's nothing we can substantiate. Nothing a responsible newspaper can use."

"Like what?"

"Like the Kendall kid's suicide, for instance. You hear things like the kid went over the edge because of his mother. That she was such a cold fish, that she was a breast-beater. Psychological abuse can be just as destructive to a person as physical abuse. So she drives the husband to drink until he can't take it anymore and he runs away. Then she harps after the kid until he decides to get away permanently, by hanging himself. That leaves her just where she probably deserves to be. Alone in a shabby farm house, reading her bible and cursing out at the rest of the world. Interesting hearsay, yes. Also a sure libel suit if we try to do a story on it."

"What about Humbert or Florio. Got any interesting hearsay on either of them?"

"I don't know too much about Humbert, his personal life, I mean. We travel in different circles. I understand he's something of a snob. One of the local blue bloods, you know. You might want to talk to Art Wirth or Millicent Freeman about him. Art covers the farm beat for us, which around here means either dairy cows or grapes. Millie edits the features section and writes most of the society news. They're both off until Monday, too, unfortunately."

"Now, Florio's another kettle of fish altogether," Karen began. "I recently heard about an investigation that a Syracuse paper is—"

"Hi. Am I interrupting anything?" A man about my size with receding sandy-colored hair and wire-rimmed glasses was standing in the doorway. He had a small paunch and the relaxed open stance of a man who got on well with people, even temperamental reporters.

"Oh, Bob. C'mon in." Karen motioned. "Sheridan, this is Bob Kaufman, owner, publisher, and editor-in-chief of the paper. A jack of all trades."

"Which means we're too small an operation to fill all the key slots." He smiled as we shook hands. "Nice to

63

meet you, Sheridan. Karen was telling me about you earlier. Thanks for stepping in on that car wreck story."

"Glad I could be of use." Kaufman was probably in his late thirties but, aside from the high hairline and the crow's-feet around his eyes, his face was boyish.

"Listen, Karen and I were planning to go next door for a bite to eat after work. We thought you might join us."

"If you're sure I won't be in the way," I said, glancing at Karen. Her easy smile told me there was more than a working relationship between the two of them. I was glad for her. Her "career move" had turned out well indeed.

"Not at all," Kaufman said. "I want to hear more about this investigation of yours."

"Me, too," Karen said, adding, "Besides, don't you want to hear what the Syracuse papers are saying about Gabriel Florio?"

"Lead the way." I nodded. "First round's on me."

CHAPTER 9

THE Sand Bar was an old-fashioned pub tucked into the basement of an aging hotel next to the *Daily News* building. It was paneled in dark walnut with stained-glass doors on the ornate beer coolers that ran across the back of the bar. Someone had marred the natural charm of the place by mounting fishnets and harpoons and other nautical debris along the walls, all in a failed attempt to lend legitimacy to the pub's ill-conceived name. Instead of the salty sea smells of Maine or Cape Cod, the Sand Bar reeked of cigarette smoke and Lemon Pledge.

We slid into a booth near the door and gave our orders to a cheerful cocktail maid who was fifteen years too old and twenty pounds too heavy for the black minidress she was wearing. A turkey club with a gin and tonic for Karen, a draught beer and cheeseburger for Bob Kaufman, and a bottle of Prior's Dark for me.

"So, anyway," Bob continued the story he had begun during our short walk over from the newsroom, "I went into journalism instead of my father's metal-fabricating business. When he died in '81, I got a good offer for the business, which I had no inclination to run, and I used the proceeds to buy the *Daily News*. It's been all I'd hoped it would be. And more," he added, smiling at Karen.

"We're planning on getting married one of these days," Karen said. "It's the best way I can think of for an editor to get even with her publisher."

They both laughed, and I joined in, but not without a tiny twinge of envy. They reminded me of a young Tracy and Hepburn, working together, no doubt fighting together, and then marching up the aisle together just before the credits roll across the screen.

The barmaid brought our drinks and I filled them in on my uncle's case and my own feeble investigatory efforts. They listened quietly, nodding once or twice to show that they were still with me.

"You know, Sheridan," Karen said when I finished my narrative, "you might be wasting your time and talents on this one. You don't really have much to go on."

"True," I agreed, "but then, I don't have anything better to do right now. Besides, I have a hunch about this whole thing, something that's been there since the beginning. I just feel that there's more to it than a random killing."

"I agree with Sheridan," Bob said. "I mean, it simply doesn't add up to your run-of-the-mill break-in story."

"Which is why I have to keep poking around wherever I can, wherever there could be the slightest motive. Like the negotiations on Uncle Charlie's property. And that means Maevis Kendall, Michel Humbert, and Florio."

"Ah, Florio." Karen belted down the last swallow of her gin and tonic. "As I was saying before, we don't have anything on him locally, but I got a couple of calls recently from a reporter with one of the Syracuse papers. Seems that Florio and his company were under investigation by a grand jury up there a while back, along with some of the boys in the planning department of one of the suburban townships. Apparently there were a few irregularities in the bids accepted on a public-housing project that Florio and the others were working on."

"Irregularities?" I asked.

"Yes. According to the reporter I spoke with, a contractor whose bid was rejected for the job started screaming that the fix was in. The papers up there looked into it and found out that all the accepted bids, including Florio's, were quite a bit higher than bids submitted by other firms. The grand jury got involved last winter, my source said. When Florio and the others got wind of it, they withdrew from the project voluntarily."

"That was months ago, then. What's your Syracuse source looking for now?"

"Well, I gather that he's trying to put together an investigative piece showing the connection between certain local crime figures, the contractors that were under grand jury investigation, and various public officials. He called me in connection with Florio's plan to build a condominium resort on the lake. I couldn't tell him much."

"It sounds like the same old story," I said as I signaled for another round. "A little graft here, a bribe there. It makes the world go 'round."

"Hmmph," Bob grunted. "Business as usual in the hodgepodge of municipal government."

"Exactly," Karen said. "Only, looking at it from the point of view of your uncle's murder, Sheridan, it gets a little more interesting. According to my source, Florio's company is in financial trouble. He was hoping that public-housing project would get him healthy again. When he was forced to pull out, his creditors were, as I hear it, extremely dissatisfied."

"Construction interruptus, huh? And his creditors, no doubt, are the very same 'crime figures' that cropped up in the Syracuse reporter's investigation."

"Right. This reporter told me he thinks Florio's company is floating on a sea of laundered mob money. Now that the public-housing deal is snafued, the money's supposed to go into this resort scheme that Florio's been pushing."

67

"The boys with the bent noses fund Florio with a little dirty capital, just to use as seed money." I nodded. "They figure his condo idea sounds like a good way to put the cash to use, so they stick with him despite the fiasco with the grand jury. He's supposed to use the money to get the ball rolling on this resort, only he runs into unexpected trouble while trying to buy up the property."

Bob joined in. "And maybe in the meantime, he's using the money to pay his utility bills. All the while bullshitting his creditors about how everything's under control, proceeding as scheduled."

"Exactly," Karen agreed. "My source figures Florio needs to get that condo deal rolling pronto so he can line up some legitimate credit from the banks, thus replacing the dirty money he's been using to pay his own operating expenses. The infusion of new cash will allow him to pay back the bad guys. But he has to get clear title to the property before the banks will give him a loan."

"Hmmm." I sipped at my beer while Bob and Karen turned their attention back to their food. It made for a pretty decent motive for murder, what with Florio's business—and perhaps his continued good health—at stake. Make Charlie Dugan an offer too good to refuse. When he refuses anyway, remove him from the equation and go after whoever comes next. Who happens to be me. Once I sell, Florio moves on to step two—condemnation proceedings on the Kendall farm.

"Karen, just how solid is the information your guy in Syracuse has? Is he about ready to publish?"

"I don't know for sure, but I'd say it was pretty reliable. He said he had solid information on five different contractors that were involved in the grand jury probe, including Florio, and that all five had various tie-ins with organized crime. My impression is that Florio doesn't carry any special weight as far as this reporter is concerned. He wants to nail down the money men and the grafters at city hall." She began to shake her head, anticipating my next question. "Don't ask me for the reporter's name, Sheridan. You know better. He's conducting a confidential investigation and, when it's ready, he'll publish. I wouldn't have told you as much as I have if you didn't have a newspaper background yourself."

"Okay. I understand, and I appreciate what you've given me." I swirled my finger through the head on my glass of beer. "Just one more thing. Contact this guy, will you? Let him know what I'm up to and ask him to get in touch with me if he comes up with anything else I could use."

Karen sighed. "Every reporter's epitaph should read 'Just one more thing.' Okay, give me your phone number. I'll pass it along. After that, it's up to him."

I borrowed a pen from Bob and jotted my number on a cocktail napkin. Karen and Bob finished their drinks and decided to make it an early night. We shook hands all around. I promised to keep them informed of my progress and they walked out of the Sand Bar hand in hand. I finished off my glass of beer, dropped a handful of change on the table for the barmaid, and slid out of the booth. It was midnight. The witching hour. But not for me, not this night. Watching Karen and Bob together had somehow turned my mood blue. It was simple envy, I knew. But there it was. Two friends go home happy, I just go home.

The traffic on the street had thinned considerably in the last two hours. I walked the two blocks to my car in slow motion, embracing the cool evening air after the closeness of the barroom. I was about to unlock the car door when a reflection in the Horizon's window glass, naggingly familiar, caught my eye. Across the street, a few spaces down, a shiny Lincoln Continental sprawled out over two parking places. It was empty. And it might not have been Florio's car, in which case I would have gone home and forgotten about it. But it was his car. Right down to the Italian flag decal pasted in the lower-left corner of the rear window.

The Lincoln sat in front of a four-story building with a garish neon sign over the ground-floor entrance. MAXI'S FINE ITALIAN AND AMERICAN CUISINE, SINCE 1958. Of course, just because the man's car was parked in front of the place didn't mean he was in there. After all, I was parked next to a Christian Science Reading Room. Still.

I slipped in behind the wheel of my car, turned the key over to accessory, and stuck a Chuck Mangione tape into the player, figuring I'd hang around awhile, just in case.

It didn't take long. Halfway through "The Hill Where the Lord Hides," the restaurant door opened and out came Florio with two other men. The trio stood under the streetlight next to the Lincoln a few moments, exchanging handshakes and laughing. One of the men was average height, around fifty years old, with salt-and-pepper hair and a trim build. I didn't recognize him. The other guy, now shaking hands with Florio and slapping him on the back, was a large man, about six feet tall and weighing in at 250 pounds or more. I remember thinking he looked like Sidney Greenstreet when I first saw his picture hanging in the booking room at the Quincy County Jail. Amos T. Skelly, sheriff of Quincy County and J. D. Staub's boss.

I scrunched lower into the seat of the Horizon as a plain gray Chevrolet sedan pulled up parallel to Florio's Continental. Skelly and the fellow with the salt-and-pepper hair climbed into the backseat of what had to be an unmarked county squad car. The driver, disdaining state traffic codes, swung the Chevy into a wide U-turn and roared past my parking spot. He slowed at the first light and, sans directional signal, turned right and disappeared from view.

Florio got behind the wheel of the Lincoln and pulled away from the curb, heading north. I circled the block and got back onto Main, picking up the distinctive taillights of the Continental two blocks ahead of me. I followed at a discreet distance until we were well north of the city line. Satisfied that Florio was on his way to the thruway entrance and probably going back home to Syracuse, I turned around in a boarded-up gas station and drove back through the city.

Gabriel Florio and Amos Skelly, I mused as I negotiated the succession of stoplights along Geneva's Main Street and cruised over to West Lake Road. Where's the possible connection? I knew from my conversation with Tony Areno that the seventy-four-year-old Skelly was thought of as little more than a benevolent figurehead by the troops in the Sheriff's Department. J. D. Staub handled most of the investigative and administrative duties of the department, while Skelly gladly stuck to the public relations demands of his office. Three decades as sheriff had taught the old man that the most important act of a politician was to get reelected.

But how did Florio figure in with Skelly? And who was the other guy, Mr. Salt-and-Pepper? J.D. might be able to tell me, but would he? "He doesn't take any shit from nobody," Areno had said, "with the exception of maybe Amos himself." If he was Skelly's man, and if Skelly really was tied into Florio's game somehow, could I trust J.D.?

I decided I didn't have a choice. You have to take chances, put your trust in someone if you want answers to dangerous questions. And J.D. was the man who put me on to Florio in the first place. I made a mental note to call Staub at the first opportunity and talk things out with him.

The road was silent and dark at this hour but for the soft moonlight shining down through the breaks in the trees. I was riffling through the AM radio band, hoping to pick up a late score on the Yankees-Red Sox game, when I noticed the headlights bearing down on me in the rearview mirror. Probably another bunch of teenage joyriders, I decided. The idiot behind the wheel had his brights on, too. Finding nothing but static and cross talk on the radio, I switched it off, then adjusted the angle of the rearview mirror so that the speed jockey's high beam didn't glare in my eyes.

The narrow two-lane road was all twists and turns along this stretch. Not a healthy place to try and pass, but I could hear the rumble of the other car's engine closing in, nonetheless. I twisted my neck around to take a look through the skewed rearview mirror. The glowing headlights appeared to be riding on the trunk of my car now.

"Goddamn punk," I muttered. I eased off the gas slightly. Let the idiot pass. Suddenly the lights behind me flickered from high to low beam, then back to high, over and over, rapidly and in concert with a long blast from the maniac's horn. "Jesus Christ!"

There was a metallic crunch and a simultaneous jolt, causing my head to whip back. I adjusted the rearview mirror back to its original position in time to glimpse what looked like the grill of a pickup truck. It rammed the back of the Horizon a second time, harder now, and backed off. For a moment, time was suspended and I recalled the St. Christopher statuette that had been mounted on the dash when I bought the car secondhand. I laughed it off as silly superstition and threw it away. Now, in my millisecond of contemplation, I prayed that act hadn't brought me bad luck.

The relentless pickup was closing in again. I resisted the urge to floor the accelerator and, instead, took my foot off the gas pedal entirely. As the car drifted through a sweeping turn in the road, I turned the steering wheel fractionally to the right until I felt one tire drop off the shoulder and bite gravel.

Whooo-whooo! The truck's horn blared out as the twin headlights continued to rush forward. This time the anonymous machine barely caught the left side of the Horizon's rear bumper. There was a long screech of metal against metal. My head whipped to the right. The car slid sideways, its nose pointing off toward the dark hillside, and stalled to a stop at a ninety-degree angle to the road.

I was swimming in sweat, my legs elastic, when I piled out of the car. The pickup had ground to a stop a hundred yards down on the opposite side of the road. It was dark in color, blue or green, but I couldn't determine the make or the license number. Two heads were silhouetted in the back window.

"You ignorant goddamned son-of-a-bitching asshole!" I yelled as the truck backed onto the macadam and roared off into the gloom. There was a proper time and place for vulgarity, I had always believed, and this was it.

CHAPTER 10

I AWOKE to the frantic high-pitched buzz of a cicada somewhere outside my bedroom window. It promised a hot day.

Lying on my side, not ready to face the morning, I glanced at the alarm clock on the nightstand. How could it be 8:15 so soon? I was used to getting by on six hours of sleep when I had to, but that's assuming it's six hours of unbroken slumber. Last night hadn't turned out that way.

My car, surprisingly enough, started up without hesitation after the incident with the homicidal pickup truck. A quick inspection in the moonlight revealed just cosmetic damage to the rear end of the plucky Horizon. I was back to the cottage by 1:45 and in bed a half hour later, bone weary but unable to turn off the images that darted through my head like tracer bullets. The same dream kept coming to me, tossing and turning me in my bed, twice jarring me awake.

There was a car traveling at night down a straight highway. I was in the front seat with a redheaded woman I didn't know. My wife and her lover were in the back. We were all laughing at some unspoken joke. Then we came to an intersection with a flashing yellow caution light. I wanted to go straight, but the redhead said to turn left, while Janet insisted we go right. I pulled out into the crossroad, determined to go straight through, when a mammoth truck came out of the blackness and broadsided our car. That's where the dream ended.

I tossed off the covers and made for the bathroom and a hot shower. Dreams are like hangovers. Ignore them, drink a pot of steamy coffee, and they go away. Maybe.

The phone rang just as I popped the last bit of raisin toast into my mouth. I picked up the empty plate and coffee mug from the table and carried them to the kitchen sink, then snatched the receiver off the wall phone mounted beside the refrigerator.

"Hello."

"Sheridan?" It was Karen DeClair.

"Um-hmm."

"Your voice sounds funny."

"That's 'cause I have a mouthful of toast." I swallowed. "What's up?"

"Listen, you mentioned last night something about meeting Michel Humbert at the Pinewood today, right?"

"Yeah, at one o'clock."

"Well, on the way over to my place last night, Bob remembered something concerning Humbert that he thought might possibly be useful to you. You know, if he tries to make an offer for the cottage."

"Yeah, go on."

"About a month or so ago, Bob saw an article in the *Wall Street Journal* about how the Regal Bottling Company—you know, the soft drink outfit—was reportedly expanding its operation to include a line of inexpensive table wines. The article said Regal was in the process of completing negotiations on a California winery and that it also had an eye on one or two wineries in our area."

"You don't say." I hopped up onto the kitchen counter and leaned back against the wall.

"So, Bob brought the article to the attention of Art Wirth, the farm reporter I told you about. Art said he'd heard a rumor that Humbert's older brother Guy was sending out feelers to Regal and others to see what price they could get for the Humbert Winery."

"Wait a minute, Karen. Where'd Guy come from?" I pronounced it the way Karen had; Gee, with a hard *g*. "I thought Michel ran the business."

"He does. He's the president, anyway," Karen said. "But his mother is still chairman of the board, even though she lives in New York City now and rarely visits the winery. Guy is on the board, too. Art says Guy pretty much controls his mother's stock, so he has a lot of leverage with the board. The fact that Guy runs his own thriving brokerage firm in New York doesn't hurt, either."

"Did Wirth know whether Humbert Winery was one of the properties Regal was interested in?"

"No, he didn't know for sure. To make a long story short, Bob told Art to look into it and see if there was enough there for a story. Art hasn't gotten back to him about it, so Bob forgot all about it until last night."

"I wonder what Michel thinks about his brother's idea of selling the family business?"

"Well"—Karen sighed—"if he's interested in making money, he might be all for it. Of course, if he's really interested in making wine, I don't think he'd be too pleased. Anyway, for what it's worth, Bob thought you should know."

I thanked her for the information, then told her about the odd twists my evening had taken after she and Bob left me at the Sand Bar. I told her about Florio and Skelly and the man with the salt-and-pepper hair. She dismissed Skelly as "a harmless old windbag who thrived on public recognition and veneration," but she did agree that his being with Florio was curious. Then I told her about the game of bumper cars out on West Lake Road.

She gasped. "Did you get the license number?"

"Nope, too dark. All I know is that there were two people in the pickup, it was a dark color, and it probably has some serious scrapes and dents on the front bumper."

"Jesus, do you think Florio was behind it?"

"Maybe, but I don't see how. I don't think he spotted me and, besides, I followed his car all the way out of town, heading north. I don't know what it was all about."

"It's a good thing you were able to slow down and get off to the side of the road, Sheridan. You were lucky."

"Branch Rickey said 'Luck is the residue of design.'"

"Who's Branch Rickey?"

"Forget it. Look, thanks for calling, Karen, and thank Bob for me, will you?"

I pulled into the parking lot at the Pinewood Lodge at ten minutes to one. It lives up to its name; a sprawling, three-story log building sited atop a small bluff overlooking the lake. No doubt it was built originally as a summer residence by a wealthy downstater back before the Depression. It reminded me of the "great camps" of the Adirondacks, or the many ersatz European minicastles that flourished in the Thousand Islands region of the St. Lawrence back when the century was still young and graduated personal income taxes were socialistic pipe dreams. Since FDR's day, most of these ostentatious play toys had either been left to rot away in wooded seclusion, donated as tax write-offs to universities, or sold to enterprising souls who then converted the cavernous places into tourist hotels and restaurants. Such was obviously the fate of the Pinewood Lodge.

I parked in a space next to a Cadillac Seville and watched as an old man in a blue blazer and polo shirt hopped out of the driver's seat and moved spryly around to the passenger's door. After a short odious glance at my

Horizon, he opened the door of the car for a youngish blonde and the pair of them marched off, arm in arm, toward the main entrance of the lodge.

I surveyed my own outfit and decided it was satisfactory for the Pinewood. Tan slacks, light-blue cotton shirt, dark-blue tie, herringbone jacket. The Harry O. ensemble.

A winding path of crushed white stone led from the parking lot to the entrance of the lodge. Intersecting the path at the halfway point, a stone staircase descended to a second path, which led to a row of a dozen lakeside cabins. A woman dressed in a white uniform was standing on the porch of one of the cabins, removing a stack of towels from a laundry cart. It was Maevis Kendall.

There's no time like the present, I decided as I jogged down the stone steps and followed the path to the cabins.

"Hello. Mrs. Kendall?"

She looked up at me from a pile of dirty linen, startled. Her hair was dark brown overlayed with slate gray, her eyes a probing sea green. She wore no makeup. Tall, rawboned, and leathery, she might have been fifty or sixty-five. The eyes looked as if they had been old forever.

"I just thought I'd introduce myself, Mrs. Kendall. I'm your new neighbor, Sheridan." She continued to stare.

"Charlie Dugan was my uncle." With a little effort, I managed to smile. She wasn't impressed.

"I'm busy. Got to get all these cabins cleaned." She began fiddling with a stack of clean towels.

"I don't mean to bother you, Mrs. Kendall. I just thought we should get acquainted." No response. She merely picked up the towels and turned toward the cabin. Try again, Sheridan. Play your ace. "I was on my way to have lunch with Michel Humbert when I spotted you down here and . . ."

"You planning on selling out to Humbert?" She came at me with those eyes.

78

"Well, I don't really know. He hasn't made an offer yet. I did get a nice offer from Mr. Florio, though." Her eyelids went up a fraction, but the wary eyes didn't waver. "I really haven't decided whether I want to sell the place to anyone. I'm getting to like it here. The people are so friendly."

She didn't seem to take note of the sarcasm. I must be losing my touch.

"You ask me, you'd be a lot better off holdin' on to that place," she said. "Money don't mean everything. I see people with money every day, comin' and goin' through this place like they owned the world. Godless drunkards, fornicators. They will find their reward in the Eternal Fire."

She stopped the spontaneous sermon abruptly, perhaps concerned she had given away too much of herself. It was just as well. Drinking and fornicating are two of my better subjects, but I knew the futility of debating their allure with someone of Maevis Kendall's ilk. Religious zealots, no matter what sect, are the same the world over. Self-righteous, pitiless, humorless, and utterly dogmatic.

I thought back to a few lines of graffiti I once read scrawled on the wall of a Fenway Park men's room. The first line said, "Jesus is the answer!" Beneath it, written by a different hand, was the line, "But what is the question?" This was followed by a third line, penned by yet another washroom philosopher. It read, "Name Felipe Alou's youngest brother." Branch Rickey probably would have loved it. But Maevis Kendall would not.

"Well, anyway, I just wanted to say hello, Mrs. Kendall," I said, sneaking a peek at my watch. It was a little after one o'clock. "Listen, I'm running late. I'm sure we'll have a chance to talk again sometime soon."

Without a word or a gesture of acknowledgment, she turned and carried her bundle of towels into the cabin.

Michel Humbert was well into a second martini by the time I arrived. He was seated at a small table centered in front of a bay window overlooking the lake. The room was octagonal and relatively small, with a stone fireplace and high bookshelves on four walls. It must have been the library in the old days. French doors opened onto a much larger room where several diners were seated, perusing menus and picking at salads.

"Ah, Mr. Sheridan. There you are," Humbert said, saluting me with his martini glass.

"Sorry I'm late."

"Not at all. I was a tad early, actually. Would you like a cocktail?"

I ordered a Dewar's and water straight up from a pretty young waitress who was hovering near our table. Humbert and I exchanged small talk on the weather, the latest Broadway musicals, et cetera, while studying the menu. When the waitress brought my drink, Humbert ordered quiche Lorraine; I decided on broiled sole.

"And a bottle of my chablis, please, Darleen. Vintage 1978. Thank you, love." Humbert gave the girl a matinee-idol smile. He, too, was wearing a blue blazer with a white open-necked shirt and gray slacks. It must be the uniform of the day for the local in-crowd.

"Did you enjoy your tour of our little establishment, Mr. Sheridan?" he asked.

"Yes, it was very instructive."

"Good, good. I hope I can be of help with any other questions you may have. For your article."

"Actually, it's still in the formulative stages," I said. "I thought it might be helpful, though, if I could get you to tell me a little about your own operation, the various types of wine you produce, grape varieties you use, your marketing techniques, that sort of thing. And some insider stuff on the economics of the business, if you would."

I didn't have much of an idea what questions to ask, but I judged Humbert to be the type who could rattle on indefinitely, the unimpeachable expert graciously lecturing a commoner on the finer points of the wine business. He didn't disappoint me.

He talked for nearly an hour, almost mystically at times, stopping only to nibble at the quiche or fill our glasses from the bottle of Humbert chablis. I had only to nod occasionally, throw in an "I see" or "very interesting" to keep him rolling. He told me about the labrusca grapevines common to the area and how they produced a more pungent, heavier wine than the more delicate vinifera vines of Europe and California. He explained the difficulties of growing the vinifera vines in the Finger Lakes, with the region's harsh winters, and he lauded the pioneering efforts of a Russian immigrant named Konstantin Frank who had successfully grafted the vinifera onto native rootstocks in the area in recent years, thus producing "a gentler, more convivial grape." And he complained long and bitterly about the "carping wine snobs" who refused to recognize the distinct flavor and "individuality" of New York varietals.

"But, you know, we're starting to change that thinking," Humbert said. "Already New York's sparkling wines are becoming recognized as world-class. My own champagnes, if you'll pardon my chauvinsism, are nearly the equal of the best French offerings. And our dessert wines, our sherries and ports, are also increasing in popularity."

"Well, I'm no expert," I said, picking up my wineglass, "but this chablis certainly is tasty."

"Mmm, thank you," he said, smiling vaguely, as if a Rastaferian had just complimented him on his grooming.

"The key to improving our table wines, as I see it, lies in a greater commitment to Franco-American hybrids. That is, the crossing of the hardier indiginous vines with the more fragile vinifera. Grafting them," he added patronizingly. I nodded to show him that I understood Franco-American hybrids didn't refer to canned spaghetti and he continued, "Right now, only about fifteen percent of the wine produced locally comes from hybrids. We need to do more of it, much more, committing our best growing sites to the hybrids. Therein lies the future of New York State varietals," he said, pausing. "And that, in compendium, is the reason I'm interested in acquiring your property."

"I see," I said, although I wasn't sure that I did.

The meal was over, the wine bottle empty. Humbert signed the check, placed it on the little silver tray next to the pastel mints, and stood. "Shall we adjourn to the bar and discuss it further?"

CHAPTER 11

U<small>NLIKE</small> the other public rooms in the Pinewood, the taproom was harmonious with the building's rustic exterior. The walls, the curving bar, the tables, and the floors, all were of natural pine.

"Handsome, isn't it?" Humbert asked, sweeping his arm in an arc, the prince showing off his princedom. "A truly masculine room. You can feel the strength and tradition."

We seated ourselves in a couple of macho leather wing chairs near the massive rubblestone fireplace and gave our drink orders to an old black man wearing a red waistcoat. His was the first nonwhite face I'd seen along the lake south of Geneva. He performed his duties with a kind of exaggerated obsequiousness, as if he was having a private laugh at the expense of the taproom's well-heeled patrons.

The place was doing a decent business for a languid Saturday afternoon. A dozen or so people were scattered at the tables, including the silver-haired sugar daddy and his blonde. No one was playing the baby grand that sat in one corner and no one was watching the tennis match on the TV mounted over the bar. No one was listening to the canned elevator music that was being piped into the place, either, but then, no one ever did.

"Now, Mr. Sheridan, shall we discuss your property?" Humbert took a sip of his martini and turned, sort of kitty-corner, in his chair, one arm dangling over the side, a leg crooked casually over the armrest. I couldn't decide whether he reminded me of William F. Buckley or Marlene Dietrich.

"You said you were interested in acquiring prime growing sites," I said. "What makes my uncle's property . . . I should say, my property . . . a prime site?"

"Its proximity to the lakeshore, of course. And the topography, the high ridge, rolling hills. Combine that with the rich native soil and you have splendid conditions for growing hybrids." He finished with a wave of his hand, looking and sounding more like an English public school fop every minute. I wrote it up to the booze. By my count, he'd already soaked up three martinis and half a bottle of wine.

"It's the lake effect, Mr. Sheridan. The closer the acreage is to the water, the greater the effect. It's something to see on a cold winter day, the fog rising off the lake and settling over the surrounding hills. It's like throwing a nice warm blanket on the vines, since the fog bank is warmer than the surrounding air temperature."

"Sounds comfy."

"It is, yes." Humbert swung his body around now, legs tucked back under his chair, head and shoulders thrust forward. "That's what makes your property of interest to me, Mr. Sheridan. Yours and the Kendall parcel comprise the only sizable acreage along the lake that hasn't yet been cut into postage-stamp lots for dismal little fishing shacks. With that land, I can begin to cultivate the grapes that will enable me to make the Humbert Winery into one of the finest small wineries in the country. Not small as in second-rate, but small as in exclusive. And people with taste are always prepared to pay for exclusivity."

"It sounds like a good plan, Mr. Humbert. But I haven't heard your offer yet."

"All right," His tone downshifted. "This is supposed to be a business lunch, isn't it?" He cashiered the gin-induced amiability and slipped on his game face.

"Your uncle, Charles Dugan, received another offer for his property, from Florio Development. I'm well aware of that. I'm also aware that Mr. Florio has been around to see you, presumably to make you the same offer."

"You know about that?"

"Don't be surprised, Mr. Sheridan. This is a small, insular community, Mohaca Springs. Word gets around." He sipped at his drink. "I don't make a practice to listen to gossip, of course, unless it concerns me and my plans."

"Florio made me a very substantial offer."

"I'm sure, just as he made your uncle a 'very substantial offer.' The key point is, your uncle rejected his offer. And do you know why I think he did that?"

I shook my head.

"Because he loved his home and this area, Mr. Sheridan. He cherished the quality of life here and he didn't want to see it diminished by a man of Florio's questionable taste and character." Humbert's next line went well with the schmaltzy string arrangement that was then seeping from the hidden stereo speakers. "Mr. Dugan was a concerned environmentalist and, in my opinion, a noble man."

I had heard Uncle Charlie called a lot of things, but noble wasn't one of them. Humbert was flashing his Achille's heel. Like a lot of other aristocrats, he assumed everyone who didn't make the social register was a congenital idiot. I may have been a rookie when it came to big business, but I was still ready for his pitch.

"If Charlie really did cherish his place so much, what makes you think he'd have sold it to anyone, including you?"

"Because of my intention to use the land for agricultural purposes. And because my offer, unlike Florio's, would have allowed him to stay on in his house."

"Oh?" I wasn't expecting a curveball.

"Yes. You see, I understood his initial reluctance to sell, so I restructured my offer to suit him. I proposed to buy all the acreage he had, with the exception of one acre immediately surrounding his cottage. That way, Mr. Dugan could keep his home, with ample room for his dock, a garden, et cetera, while I used the other fourteen acres for grape cultivation. And your uncle seemed pleased with the proposal," he added unctuously.

"Have you made a similar offer to Mrs. Kendall?" I had a few breaking pitches in my repertoire, too.

"As a matter of fact, I haven't, but that's a different story," he hedged.

"Why's that?"

"Well, because I intend to use not only the fallow land that belongs to the Kendall farm but also the barns, the utilities, the water supply, and so on. The winery has need of more storage facilities for our planting and harvesting equipment, particularly if we expand our acreage. And I had hoped to renovate the farmhouse itself and rent it out to our chief foreman and his family, at a low figure. That would help justify the overall cost of the project."

"I understand Mrs. Kendall refuses to sell," I said.

"So far, yes. And I believe Florio is to blame for that. I began negotiating with Mrs. Kendall some time ago, and I was gradually bringing her around and getting her to trust me—not easy to do with that woman. Anyway, I was making progress when Florio came along with his condo scheme. He began bullying Mrs. Kendall, possibly even threatening her, until she became completely put off by the whole idea of selling." He threw up his hands. "She was difficult enough before, but now she seems to think that Florio and I are two sides of the same coin."

"Which still leaves you without a deal for the farm."

"Yes, for now," Humbert said. "But I'm certain I can win back her confidence, particularly if I'm able to buy your property and begin preparing it for cultivation. She'll see then, despite her paranoia, that my intentions are noble."

There was that word again. I didn't know which was harder to take, Humbert's self-proclaimed nobility or Florio's obnoxious wheezing bluster. That they were both guilty of avarice, I had no doubt. But which one—if either—was guilty of murder?

Humbert was talking again, outlining his proposal. Five thousand dollars per acre for the fourteen acres he wanted, with an additional five thousand thrown in as a "signing bonus." A total of $75,000.

"That may seem low for lakefront property, but most of your land is very steep and lies across the road from the lake itself. And it's the going rate for undeveloped land in this area, Mr. Sheridan. Top dollar. And of course, you would retain the cottage and one acre, to do with as you please. Sell it or move in permanently," he said, adding, "and you'd have the satisfaction of knowing that your uncle's preservationist concerns had been met."

"It's an interesting offer," I said, "but I will need some time to think it over."

"Of course." He seemed satisfied with that, for the moment. I was about to suggest that I buy one last round, when a shrill female laugh shot through the taproom's genteel rumble like a bullet through a beehive.

"Mee-shell! Look, Allison, there's our little Michel now. Speak of the devil."

The speaker was a honey blonde, tall and angular, what the fashion magazines like to call willowy. Mid-thirties and attractive in a fragile do-not-touch sort of way. She was wearing a white suit—pleated skirt and matching jacket—and teetering on a pair of white pumps. Formerly of Radcliffe, I thought, and currently inebriated.

Standing beside her in the entryway to the taproom was another woman, a dozen or so years younger. She had medium-brown hair, worn in a short cut that required little maintenance. She was smaller than the blonde and dressed casually in designer jeans and a brushed-cotton beige blouse.

"Oh, for . . . excuse me," Humbert muttered, rising. He seemed intent on intercepting the women before they made it to our table, but he was too slow. The tipsy blonde was already halfway to the table, with the brunette following close behind. The brunette had her arms out, like the catcher in a trapeze act, ready to grab the blonde, who shouldn't have been working without a net.

"Hell-O, Michel," the blonde said, trying too hard to sound sober. "Who's your cute friend, or is that a secret?"

"Sit down and, please, behave yourself," Humbert said quietly, as he not so gently pushed the blonde into a club chair opposite mine. He then glared at the brunette, who shrugged a general apology and sat down next to the blonde.

"Mr. Sheridan, this is my wife Brooke"—he indicated the blonde—"and my niece Allison. Mr. Sheridan and I have been discussing a business transaction, darling, as I mentioned when I left the house this morning." This time he glared pointedly at his wife, before turning to me. "I'm afraid the ladies have overindulged a bit."

"And we're gonna indulge some more, too," the blonde said. "Where the hell's the water boy? Hey, Gunga Din!"

The old waiter hurried over and took down our requests. Another martini, a scotch, white wine for Allison, and a Manhattan for Brooke Humbert.

"We went up to Geneva to do some shopping and have lunch," Allison explained. "I guess Brooke overdid it with the cocktails."

"It happens." I smiled.

"Happens all the time," Brooke said brightly as the waiter brought her drink. "Bottoms up, huh, Michel?"

"Mr. Sheridan is a writer, Allison," Humbert said. His wife was preoccupied for the moment, playing with the swizzle stick in her glass.

"Really? What sort of things, Mr. Sheridan?"

"Oh, general-interest articles for magazines, some investigative pieces on occasion. And, please, you can drop the mister. Most people just call me Sheridan."

"What s'matter, Sheridan," Mrs. Humbert interjected. "Don't you have a first name?"

"Timothy."

"Timothy Sheridan." She sighed. "Timmy Sheridan. That's Irish. Are you a mick, Timmy Sheridan?"

"Mostly, with a wedge of limey tossed in."

"Oh, then you're a kind of mongrel, aren't you? A crossbreed, between an Irish setter and an English terrier?"

"You could say that. Anyway, I seem to have a knack for attracting bitches."

Allison giggled and Humbert looked as if he wanted to be somewhere else, anywhere else. Brooke Humbert merely stared at my left ear, having missed the point profoundly. It was like a set piece from a Tennessee Williams play.

Humbert recovered first. "Allison is a grad student at Princeton, Mr. Sheridan, studying economics. She's up to visit us for the summer."

"Economics, huh? I'm afraid that's one subject that goes right over my head."

Allison made a face. "It's really not as imposing as it sounds, once you learn the terminology. Kinda like math, I'd say, but it's a lot more interesting."

"In-ter-est-ing." Brooke Humbert cut in. "Very, very inter-est-ing."

"You know," Humbert hurried into the breach. "Since Mr. Sheridan is new to the area, Allison, maybe it would be nice if you two got together for some sightseeing."

"Really, Michel, I'm sure Sheridan has better . . ."

"No," I said. "That's a good idea, if you wouldn't mind. I'd appreciate it."

"Okay, let's do it."

"How about tomorrow afternoon? I can pick you up

around five. We'll take a drive along the lake and then have dinner in Geneva. You like Chinese?"

"Are you kidding? I'd kill for moo goo gai pan. And the drive sounds like fun."

"Fun, fun, fun 'til Daddy took the Volvo away," Brooke sang into the bottom of her glass. "Everybody has fun but me. I don't get anything, do I, Michel?" She was going down for the third and final time. "I . . . don't . . . get . . . diddly . . ."

Humbert stood. "Come along, dear, time to go home." He shoved his hands under her arms and hoisted her out of the chair as though she were a side of lean beef. "I don't know what's gotten into you. I apologize, Mr. Sheridan."

I waved it off.

"Allison," Humbert said. "Will you drive your aunt's car home, please? I'll take her with me in the Mercedes."

"Sure thing, Michel," Allison said. Turning to me, she rolled her eyes and said, "Listen, I'll see you tomorrow at five. Twelve Lakeview Street, okay?"

"Okay."

I watched the three of them zigzag their way out of the bar like a conga line that had lost the beat. If Michel Humbert was a murderer, I told myself, surely the first person he'd kill would be his wife.

CHAPTER 12

SATURDAY night proved to be one of those special times that defined the difference between being lonely and being alone.

I got home from the Pinewood around four, stopping along the way to buy some fresh strawberries and a head of lettuce at a roadside stand. After changing into cutoffs and a polo shirt, I stretched out on the sun deck for a couple of hours until my stomach began making noises. Then I lighted a fire in the grill and slow-cooked a Cornish hen on the rotisserie while watching the sailboats sweep gracefully down the lake.

When the bird reached a tawny brown, I carried it inside, put on one of Uncle Charlie's few classical albums, and enjoyed a quiet supper. Dvořák, I discovered, went well with Cornish hen, a green salad, and sliced strawberries. After the meal, I exchanged the Dvořák album for a Bruce Springsteen cassette and cleaned up the dishes to the beat of "Tenth Avenue Freeze Out." Kitchen back in order, I placed a couple of phone calls I'd been meaning to make and settled in to watch the Yankee game on cable from New York.

By midnight, I was snug in my bed. The cottage was

quiet, the Yankees had won, and all was right with the world.

"Mrrrowww, mrrrr-owwww."

Oh, yeah. I forgot to mention the cat.

I woke up abruptly at six Sunday morning, but not by design. It's just that I couldn't ignore the four-legged alarm clock that was scratching and mewing at my front door.

It was my own fault. I had found it on the doorstep when I got back to the cottage Saturday afternoon, a scrawny mottled orange-and-white tabby, crying louder and with more anguish than Johnny Ray on his best night.

I'm not a cat person. They're aloof; they don't come when you call. If you try to teach them anything, they stare at you as if you're an idiot. And what those claws can do to a piece of furniture would drive Homer Formsby to drink.

But the damn thing was crying and it looked as if it hadn't had a decent meal in weeks, so I figured what the heck. I opened a can of tuna and let the beast eat it out on the stoop while I had my dinner. Then I let it come inside and sleep under my chair while I watched the ball game. But I put it out before I went to bed, and good riddance.

Now it was back for breakfast.

Bleary eyed, I opened the front door and watched the cat promenade in as if it owned the place.

"Morning, William. Did you sleep well?"

I had decided to call it William of Orange, after the English king that invaded and tyrannized Ireland back in the seventeenth century.

William sauntered across the living room with all the royal carriage of his namesake, sniffing and rubbing. There was a drumstick in the refrigerator, left over from the Cornish hen. I stripped the meat onto a saucer, poured some skimmed milk into a soup bowl, and placed both dishes on the kitchen floor for William's consideration while I showered.

When I got back to the kitchen, dressed in tennis shorts and a navy-blue polo shirt, the feline was massaging its face on the corner of the refrigerator. The saucer of meat was empty, but the skimmed milk hadn't been touched.

"Tough luck, pal," I said, dumping the milk in the sink. "That's all you get." William, of course, ignored me. Probably a stray from the Kendall place, I reasoned while I searched the cupboards for a filter for the coffee maker. I promised myself I'd return the little pest posthaste, right after my morning caffeine fix.

But the cat wasn't the only aggravation that morning. The other came when I found that I had two full cans of drip coffee and no filters for the machine. I resigned myself to a cup of tea and plopped down in front of the TV set. The airwaves were cluttered with electronic Elmer Gantrys on Sunday morning, but I managed to find an independent station running a Bullwinkle cartoon.

I was free until two o'clock, which is when Uncle Charlie's second ex-wife, Monica, said she'd arrive. That was one of the two phone calls I'd made the night before. The other had been to J. D. Staub, who, as it turned out, wasn't home. I'd wanted to quiz him on Skelly's connection with Florio and fill him in on my duel with the pickup truck. But that would have to wait.

The call to Monica was more of an impulse. Her number was listed in an old address book I found in the hutch. She had been divorced from Charlie Dugan for nearly twenty years, but when I read about her in the journal, I had to wonder whether she might fit into the picture somehow. I expected a brush-off when I phoned and asked to meet with her at her home in Rochester. Instead, she sounded pleased to hear from me and she offered to drive down to the cottage this afternoon. I was happy to save myself the three-hour round trip.

But she wasn't due for six hours yet and it was a lazy Sunday morning. A little fishing sounded appealing. But first, I decided, I'd drive into Mohaca Springs and hunt up a copy of the *Times* and a package of coffee filters.

The village's three largest churches were bunched together in a one-block section of North Main Street, not a
good arrangement. Scores of cars overflowed the three
small parking areas and spilled out onto the street willy-
nilly, scrunched in beside fire hydrants, double parked,
blocking private driveways.

I sat in my car and waited patiently while the rusted
canary-yellow Rambler ahead of me stopped in the middle
of the street and disgorged two elderly ladies in pillbox
hats. Across the street, a Methodist and a Catholic were
engaging in pyrogenic discourse concerning which had
laid first claim to a vacant spot in a no-parking zone—a
scene that bode ill for ecumenism.

I snaked my way through the traffic maze and continued on to the municipal parking lot next to Ralph and
Kay's. After taking a spot in the half-full lot, I walked a
block south to the IGA grocery store, where I found the
Sunday *New York Times* on sale but no coffee filters. On
the way back to the car, I stopped in at a bait shop and
bought a dozen hyperactive earthworms.

"Hey, Sheridan, how in hell are you this fine Sabbath?"
Ralph Cramer was standing on a wooden stoop at the rear
corner of the diner, a cigarette dangling from his lips.

"Hi, Ralph. Nice to see you again." I tossed the grocery
bag and the carton of worms onto the front seat of the
Horizon and strolled over to the stoop.

"I'm just catchin' a little ciggy break," Ralph explained,
dragging on a Camel straight. "Kay don't let me smoke in
the kitchen. Says it stinks up the home fries, can you
imagine? Well, what're you gonna do after forty years of
marriage, argue?"

"I know what you mean," I said. We gabbed a few minutes about the weather, the price of tomatoes, inflation in
general; a genial small-town Sunday morning kind of
thing. He told me about his arthritic knee; I mentioned
my problem with coffee filters.

"Hell, you don't need those things. They're just a damn nuisance. Wait here a minute." He went inside to the kitchen, returning a minute later with something rolled up in his leathery hand.

"Here you go. Cheesecloth. Just cut 'er up into little pieces and use 'em to line the coffee receptacle."

"Thanks, I appreciate it. By the way, is Sorrel around by any chance?"

"Nope, she's off Sundays and Mondays. Be in Tuesday around eleven. She don't work the breakfast shift."

"Oh." It was probably just as well. "Maybe I'll catch her on Tuesday, then."

"So, Sheridan, how's it going?" Ralph dug another Camel out of the pack in his shirt pocket and eyeballed me appraisingly. "I hear you had an interesting confab with the Humbert clan yesterday. No moss gonna grow on you, I'll say that. Still, you take care, like I told you the other day."

Playing detective in the boondocks is a little like performing card tricks for an audience of professional magicians. Everyone knows what you're up to and no one is impressed. There didn't seem to be much point in trying to hoodwink a Raymond Chandler fan, so I didn't.

"It's in my nature to look for answers, Ralph," I said. "For instance, where'd you hear about me and the Humberts?"

"Ran into Ruly Jackson at Barnett's Grill last night," Ralph explained. "Old Ruly—I call him Blackjack—he's a waiter at the Pinewood."

I nodded; the black guy with the red jockey suit.

"Anyway, Blackjack said there was a scene of sorts with Mrs. Humbert, her being a little tipsy. I recognized you from Blackjack's description. Say, you know who else works over at the Pinewood? Maevis Kendall."

"I know. I met her yesterday on my way in to have lunch with Humbert. She's something."

"Yeah, she's a strange one. Probably worse than ever now, what with Teddy dead and gone."

"Teddy?"

"Edward Junior. Her boy," Ralph said. "Everybody called him Teddy."

The final entry in Uncle Charlie's journal came to me. "I found out about 'T' today." *T* for Teddy Kendall?

"I understand there was never a motive established for the kid's suicide," I said. Ralph shrugged a shoulder, but said nothing. "That's what J. D. Staub told me, anyway," I went on. "There must have been a reason for it, though, don't you think?"

"Well, you know," Ralph drawled, pinching off the burning ash of his cigarette and tossing the butt in the direction of a large green dumpster, "it's really not my place to say one way or the other, Sheridan."

"Look, Ralph, I'm not interested in spreading dirt around about anyone. But the Kendalls were my uncle's neighbors. It's just possible that the boy's suicide could tie in somehow with Uncle Charlie's murder."

"Well, I don't see how the one could have anythin' to do with the other, but I guess you gotta be thorough, right?" He sat down on the edge of the stoop, motioning me to join him, and lit another cigarette. "The Kendall kid used to come by the diner quite a bit, either by himself or with his friend Randy Fenzik. I think they worked together after school up at the winery."

"Wait a minute, this Randy Fenzik. Is he a tall skinny towhead? About six two?"

"Yeah, that's him. You know him?"

"I took a tour of the place yesterday. I think he was my guide."

Ralph nodded. "Musta been him. Anyway, I can't say for sure, but the rumor was that the two of them, Teddy and the Fenzik kid, were kind of sweet on each other. You know what I mean, queers. Leastwise, that's what Kay told me. She got it from one of our waitresses, a girl

96

named Sue Morris. She was in the same class with the two of them at the high school."

"You mean this Sue Morris claimed Kendall and Fenzik were lovers?"

Ralph made a face, the kind you make when you swallow curdled milk. "Yeah, that's what she told Kay. I don't say it's true. I mean, those boys looked okay to me. They sure didn't sound like sissies or act funny or anything like that. I always gave them the benefit of the doubt, myself."

There was a certain sad logic to it. If true, it was the sort of thing that could push a confused teenager to take his own life. A small town, isolated from the big cities, provincial and proud of it. No Gay Political Caucus here. No street-corner drag queens, either. Even the rumor of homosexuality could be catastrophic. In a town like Mohaca Springs, the closet doors remain firmly shut. Where could a seventeen-year-old boy struggling with his sexuality go for guidance in a town like this? Not to a mother like Maevis Kendall, surely. And not to a father who wasn't there.

I thanked Ralph and left him sitting on the stoop, smoking away in the sunshine. Another muggy day on the rise. I was eager to spend a couple of hours out on the blue lake waters, fishing and organizing my thoughts. Besides, if I didn't get back soon, the hot sun was liable to spoil the pint of half-and-half I had bought for William.

CHAPTER 13

"HEY, you! What're you doing out there? That's private property!"

I heard a voice calling from far away, an angry voice, but it was dark outside, and warm. I was too relaxed to move.

Screeeeeeee-eeeekkk!

A piercing scraping noise pulled me awake. I pushed back the visor of my baseball cap, startled by the sunny whiteness, and propped myself up on one elbow. The aluminum boat had drifted into the shallow cove between the cottage and the farm and had grazed a submerged rock. A phalanx of cattails surrounded the boat. It was dead in the water, some fifteen feet from the Kendall shore.

"You hear me, mister?" Maevis Kendall was standing in her gravel driveway beside her Dodge sedan, glaring at me. She was wearing a plain A-line dress, dark blue, and holding in her hand what appeared to be a slim volume. A psalm book, maybe?

"It's me, Mrs. Kendall. Sheridan," I called, removing my cap. "I was fishing. I guess I dozed—"

"You don't own that cove, you know, mister," she bellowed. "Most of it's on my property and you'd better not forget it!" Before I could reply, she pivoted on one heel and marched up the porch steps and into the farmhouse.

I pulled myself into a sitting position and inspected the damage. The hull didn't appear to be leaking. My fishing line, dangling a few feet over the bow, was snagged. I gave it a few tugs, then began reeling it in slowly. The rod was bent almost in half when my hook finally neared the surface, caught up on what appeared to be a length of old anchor chain. Just as the chain broke the plane of the water, the line snapped, nearly toppling me out of the boat. So much for that hook and sinker.

Picking up an oar, I poled the boat out to the middle of the cove where the water reached a depth of about four feet. I pull-started the engine and, slow and easy, piloted through the mouth of the cove and back out into the lake.

The venture had started well, I thought as I swung the bow to port and angled for the dock in front of the cottage. After returning from the village, I loaded Uncle Charlie's fishing gear into the boat and putted out a hundred yards or so from shore, letting it drift while I dragged my line along the lake floor. I hauled in two jack perch on the first drift and a rock bass and a smaller perch on the second, each time starting up the outboard and moving out to deeper water when I got in too close to shore.

By the third pass, the sun was high overhead. I hadn't had a strike from a decent game fish yet and now even the perch were indifferent to the juicy worm on my hook. So I had fashioned a pillow from a flotation cushion and stretched out for a sunbath. Maevis Kendall or no, I was lucky to drift into the cove. I could have as easily caught a current farther out on the lake and ended up a dozen miles south.

I maneuvered the boat to the side of the dock, bouncing it inexpertly against the rubber-tire bumpers nailed to the pilings. My chest and arms were burnt a vivid red. Climbing up onto the dock, tackle box in hand, I tried to recall whether I had seen any Solarcaine in the bathroom medicine cabinet. The sound of tires on gravel brought me around. A blue Volvo was easing its way down the slope of the driveway. I checked my watch. It read 1:45. She was early. I trudged up the incline leading from the dock to the cottage, donning my shirt as I went, and intercepted her on the sun deck.

"Timothy?"

"Yes. How have you been, Monica?"

"Very well, thank you. I didn't recognize you at first. What were you, about fifteen years old the last time I saw you? You've changed a great deal, of course."

"I think I was sixteen." It was a long time ago, a Memorial Day picnic, a few months before she and Uncle Charlie split up. She had changed, too, but not for the worse. She must be forty-five now, middle-aged. And still beautiful. I remembered the wispy young woman with the long black hair that Uncle Charlie had first introduced to the family as his new bride. The hair was shorter now, swept back and not quite touching the shoulders. Her long neck looked leaner, stronger. The dark-green eyes, vaguely Oriental, were still mesmerizing and direct.

"You look wonderful, Monica."

"Well, thank you." She laughed with the confidence of a woman who was used to hearing compliments. "I see you're a Chicago Cubs fan these days. What happened to the Yankees?"

I doffed the baseball cap. "Oh, I'm still a Yankee fan, but I can't help feeling a little embarrassed about it at times. Who was it that said rooting for the Yankees was like rooting for U. S. Steel? Of course, U. S. Steel isn't doing so hot these days, either. Anyway, I started following the Cubs in the National League, sort of as a penance."

"I remember Charlie always pulled for the Red Sox and only the Red Sox, with every fiber of his being. I suppose that was enough of a penance in itself."

"Yes, I guess so." I caught myself staring. It was an odd feeling, meeting a woman you'd had a crush on when you were a kid, then seeing her a couple of decades later and discovering she was as attractive as ever.

"Well, come in the house," I said. "We have a lot to talk about."

She tossed her beaded handbag on the oak dining table and did a slow pan around the room.

"It's homier, a little more lived in than it was. I was down here when he first built the place, the year before we divorced."

"Please, have a seat." I motioned toward the sofa. "Can I get you a drink?"

"A brandy, if you're having something."

I found a bottle of Jacques Cardin tucked away in the back of the liquor cabinet in the kitchen and poured two fingers into a small tumbler. I opened a cold bottle of Molson's Golden for myself.

"Tell me about Charlie's murder," she said when I brought her drink. "How did it happen?"

I sat in the morris chair opposite her and filled in the details as I had heard them from J. D. Staub. I also gave her Areno's theory about a nervous burglar, but left out J.D.'s musings on Kendall and Florio and Humbert and the three-cornered business deal.

"That's ridiculous," she said when I finished my narrative. "It couldn't have happened that way."

"Why not?"

"You said this Chief Areno figured Charlie was on one of his infamous benders and he became so drunk he forgot about the game."

"It's happened before, according to Staub," I said.

"I'm sure it has. Only, as I understand the scenario, Charlie is supposed to have come home, changed into his pajamas, and crawled into bed to sleep it off, correct?"

"Right." I nodded. "Then a burglar came along, maybe

101

someone who knew Uncle Charlie and knew he was supposed to be away. He runs into Uncle Charlie in the bedroom, stabs him, and runs off in panic."

"But there's a major flaw." Monica set the tumbler of brandy on the coffee table. "I was married to the man for five years, Timothy. I knew his habits."

"And?"

"And whenever he came home drunk, which was more often than I care to remember, he invariably went straight to bed, clothes and all. Sometimes he didn't even remove his shoes, for heaven's sake. If he was drunk enough to forego his poker night—and he was a nut about poker—there's no way he would have had the sense to change into his pajamas."

I knew she was telling the truth. She had no reason to dispute the official version of the murder, even if she was in some way connected to it. And her observation about the pajamas fit in with the gnawing suspicions I had felt since the beginning. No matter how you arranged the pieces, they didn't form the picture Areno had drawn.

"So what do you think happened?" I asked.

"I have no idea. A psychotic, maybe? Or someone looking for revenge for some reason or other. I don't know. Only, it seems Charlie must have had a reason for staying home that night. A reason that he apparently didn't want to have to explain to his poker friends."

Monica's speculations were intriguing, especially when set down beside the paltry bits of information I had already collected in the investigation. But they would have to be filed away, like all the flotsam I had gathered on the case, until a clear meaning could be sorted out. For the present, I needed to know about her and Uncle Charlie. I greased the wheels of memory by telling her about the bittersweet entry on her in the journal, the entry dated the previous January.

"I guess he must have heard about my marriage." She sighed. "That was on the fifth of January."

She stood and walked over to the hutch. Her back to me, she stared at the memorabilia on its shelves and quietly reviewed the past twenty-five years of her life. All in all, it was a love story.

"I was only twenty-one when I married Charlie, a self-centered young girl in love with Beethoven and Bach and trendy parties after concerts at the Eastman Theater. And Charlie. He was older, and handsome. He didn't really fit into the world I was trying to build for myself, but he had style and charisma. And enough money to be intoxicatingly independent, if you'll forgive the bad pun." She smiled. "Yes, all the raw materials were there. And I foolishly thought I could mold them into the man I wanted. I was a hopeless romantic in those days."

She turned to face me. "He took me to Vienna for our honeymoon."

"He mentioned that in the journal."

"It was great for awhile. The parties, theater excursions to New York, travel abroad. I started teaching music—I wasn't good enough for the concert hall and I knew it. But I loved the music and I was good at teaching others to love it.

"Anyway, I went deeper into my own world and Charlie began to resent it. He wanted me to follow along on his fishing trips and have stacks of sandwiches waiting for him when he staggered in from one of his all-night card games. He kept at me to quit my job and give up my volunteer work with the orchestra at the Eastman. I wouldn't even consider it. So, you see, he couldn't mold me, either."

She sat on the sofa and tasted the brandy. "He started sleeping around, women he'd meet in bars. Half the time he didn't even remember their names the next morning. The affairs didn't really mean anything to him, I knew that, but it still hurt." She looked at me. "Finally, I found someone else. I asked Charlie for a divorce and he agreed, like a gentleman. I think he thought I'd change my mind

103

and take him back. That I couldn't make it on my own. He was wrong.

"I remarried soon after the divorce went through, a man named Robert Melville. He was older, too; older even than Charlie. He was a banker, on the board of the Philharmonic, the art gallery. A wonderful, thoughtful man who loved me."

I took advantage of the pause to refill her glass. The room was so quiet I could hear William purring under my chair.

"When Robert died three years ago," Monica continued, "Charlie called and asked if he could see me again. I almost said yes, but I knew better. We each had very different lives to lead. Still, he persisted, calling me every six months or so until last January, when I remarried. A younger man this time, not much older than you. Rolf Steiner is his name. He's first violinist with the orchestra."

"Uncle Charlie probably heard about it and was hurt. That explains the timing and tone of the journal entry."

She shook her head, the almond eyes glistening. "It must have been the reason. Maybe he felt . . . used up."

My curiosity about the two of them was used up, too. I changed the subject a bit, telling Monica about the solitary ceremony with Uncle Charlie's ashes out on the lake.

"I wanted to go to the funeral," she said. "But the papers didn't mention anything about a service and, to be honest, I didn't know how Rolf would feel about it. That's why I wanted to meet you here instead of at our home."

I suppose it's the thought that counts. His own children hadn't even bothered to come east from their sunbelt homes to see their old man off. They had long since learned to call my Aunt Maureen's second husband "daddy," as was only right. If they had any feelings at all for their biological father, I suppose they weren't the kind that compelled someone to travel three thousand miles for a last goodbye. Maybe that's why Uncle Charlie had decided on the lonely send-off on the lake, and had picked me to perform it for him. He was afraid no one else would care.

After an awkward silence, Monica said, "Timothy, I was wondering. Charlie and I used to listen to an old record, Sinatra singing Cole Porter. Do you think it's still here?"

"Could be." I got up and thumbed through the scores of albums lining the shelves beside the fireplace.

"That's one of the things we did manage to give each other," Monica said. "I introduced your uncle to the classics and he turned me onto jazz and pop."

"Here it is." I pulled the tattered jacket from the shelf and cued up the record on the turntable. We listened to both sides of the scratchy monaural recording, Monica humming quietly with each cut while I tapped out the tempo on the arm of my chair. All too soon, the big band struck the crescendo for "From This Moment On." Old Blue Eyes soared through the final chorus and the music died.

I put the album back in its jacket and handed it to Monica. "Why don't you take this with you? I'm more of a Stones fan, anyway."

She smiled slightly and took the record, then kissed me on the cheek. "Thank you, Timothy."

We said our goodbyes then, and she left. I watched her walk to her car and slip in behind the seat, gracefully tucking her long legs in after her.

It was getting late and I had a date with Allison Humbert at five. There was still time to shower and change. But first I went into the bathroom and rummaged through the medicine cabinet for the Solarcaine. My skin was quivering with a disquieting warmth. I told myself it must have been the sunburn.

CHAPTER 14

THE Humbert house was an antebellum-style colonial with a colonnade of squared pillars across the front and a circular driveway. It sat on a deep but relatively narrow lakefront lot, hemmed in by a rambling brick ranch house on the one side and a Dutch Colonial on the other. Like all the houses along Lakeview Street, Michel Humbert's home was sparkling fresh, with a well-manicured lawn and an impressive view of Seneca Lake. This was where the upper crust of Mohaca Springs hung their hats.

Allison was sitting on a white wicker settee on the porch when I pulled up. I was running a few minutes late, thanks to the impossible directions given to me by a pump jockey at the Village Gaseteria and Convenience Food Mart.

"I almost called to cancel out," Allison said as I climbed out of the car.

"Sorry, but I had a little trouble finding the place."

"Oh, no, that's not what I meant," she said. "It's just that things are a little screwy around here today."

"What's the problem?"

"It's Michel." She almost whispered the name, as if the

106

surrounding maple trees had ears. "After we got back from the Pinewood yesterday, he and Brooke had a terrible fight. Michel was livid over the scene in the bar and Brooke was just . . . God, I don't even want to think about it. If you could have heard the things they said to each other, Sheridan, the name-calling." She made a clucking sound, like a brood hen. "Well, anyway, just when things were quieting down, Michel told Brooke he had to go out again on business. Brooke began cursing him out and, well, Michel slapped her and walked out. That was about eight last night and he hasn't come home yet."

"What's Brooke say about all this?" I asked. "Has it happened before?"

"I gather it has, only he's never stayed away this long. Brooke was sick most of the morning, you know, from the booze," Allison explained. "She didn't even mention Michel's name until this afternoon, but I could see she was starting to get worried."

"You've checked with the police?"

"Yes. Brooke didn't want me to at first, but I finally insisted on it. I called the Sheriff's Department about a half hour ago. They didn't have anything on him—no accidents reported or anything—but they said they'd alert their patrols to keep an eye out for his car."

"Well, maybe we should . . ." I stopped in mid-thought. Brooke Humbert was standing in the doorway of the house, looking like something out of *The Lost Weekend*.

"Hello, Sheridan."

"Hello, Mrs. Humbert."

She came forward a step, shutting the door behind her. "Please, Sheridan, call me Brooke. I'm afraid I owe you an apology for the way I behaved yesterday. I don't know what made me do it."

Sure she did, and so did I; it was the booze. But I can be gracious, too. "I don't recall anything you have to apologize for," I said.

"Thanks for having such a selective memory." She

smiled, but not without effort. "Allison has told you about Michel?"

"Yes. I was just going to suggest we postpone—"

"I think that's best—" Allison began.

"No, no. Not at all," Brooke broke in. "There's nothing you can do here, Allison. The police are aware of the situation and, anyway, I'm sure Michel will turn up soon. Go with Sheridan and have a good time."

"I still think I should stay here—"

"No, I'll be fine, Allison. Really. Please."

"I'll tell you what," I said to Allison. "We can look around for Michel ourselves, here in the village, then drive up to Geneva and see if we can spot him up there. If we don't run across him, we'll grab a bite at that Chinese place I mentioned and I'll bring you home. Okay?"

"Well, okay. If you're sure, Brooke."

"I'm sure. Go and enjoy yourself. This is supposed to be your summer vacation, remember?"

We cruised all the bars and public lots in Mohaca Springs, then drove up to Geneva and repeated the process in the downtown area. If there was a silver Mercedes somewhere along the route, we didn't spot it.

Allison was somber during our search, spending most of her time squinting hopefully through the Horizon's dusty windows. She did manage to perk up a bit after we settled in at the restaurant. Maybe it was the spicy chicken Hunan dish that we ordered that did it. It isn't easy to keep your mouth shut when your tongue is on fire.

At any rate, she turned out to be an interesting girl. She told me quite a lot about herself—her parents, her friends, her life on campus, horses and skiing, her ambition to join her father's investment firm after Princeton. She described her Park Avenue upbringing with a charming insouciance and a self-deprecating smile.

"Some people think I went into economics just to please Guy," she said, making a face that exaggerated the faint spray of freckles that spanned the bridge of her nose.

"To be the son he never had, or penis envy or something. The fact is, I've always been fascinated by Wall Street and I've always dreamed of working with Guy someday."

It was odd, to me, hearing her refer to her father by his first name. I couldn't imagine calling my dad Tim. But then, I'd been raised a long way from Park Avenue.

"What about the wine business?" I asked. "That would seem to be more of a family tradition, wouldn't it?"

"Well, it always was, until Guy decided to go off on his own. Grandfather Humbert was upset about that until the day he died, I guess, and Michel's never really approved, either. But Grandmother was always supportive of my father. I think, in a way, she's more practical than Grandfather was. I mean, she knows a person has to do his own thing."

"And Michel's thing continues to be making wine."

"Yes, he loves it," she said. "But there really isn't a lot of profit to be squeezed out of a small winery these days. Not without a lot of investment capital to expand and diversify. The large producers, the conglomerates, can undercut and outmarket you so easily it isn't funny. That's something Michel refuses to acknowledge."

"But your father and grandmother, they have a more practical point of view of the business?"

"Well, you could say that." She seemed to grow guarded, as if some special chromosome in her gene pool protected her from discussing family business with strangers. "They've discussed the situation with Michel, with an eye toward possibly selling off the winery to a larger company. But it's all just speculation at this point."

"It's funny that Michel would want to buy my land to plant more grapes, if the family is thinking of selling out," I said, ever the angler. "I mean, as I understand it, it takes several years for new vines to become productive."

"Well, Sheridan, as I said, nothing's been settled," she hedged. "Besides, I imagine additional growing acreage would be a plus for the winery, even if we do sell."

"I suppose so." I let the subject drop, diverting my attention to the last few pieces of spicy chicken.

"I hope Brooke is okay." Allison rerouted the discussion. "I'm still not sure I should have left her. God, what a scene that was last night! My parents have never fought like that in their lives."

I shook my head sympathetically. "Some marriages are better than others." Janet and I had never thrown punches, but we had hurled a few insults in our time, which probably hurt more. "It's just too bad you had to see it."

Allison looked around to make sure the waiter was hovering out of earshot, and said quietly, "Michel called Brooke a drunken slut. So then Brooke starts swearing a blue streak, calling him a . . . well, forget it," she broke off. "I wouldn't even repeat the things they said to each other."

I motioned to the waiter for the check. "Why don't we head back and see if Michel made it home?"

The ride back down to Mohaca Springs was a little cheerier than the trip up to Geneva had been. Allison and I talked about Doonesbury and hiking in the Catskills and Woody Allen's latest film. She squealed with delight when she found a Ry Cooder tape in the glove compartment. I was surprised she'd even heard of him. He was an acquired taste, like bock beer and Buffalo wings. As the miles rolled by, we sang along with "The Bourgeois Blues" and attempted two-part harmony on "Stand by Me," Allison painfully off-key the whole time. It reminded me of my college days and cross-state caravans to the big football game at a rival campus. I tried to recall the words to the school fight song, but they weren't there.

"Sheridan, I can't believe how bad you sing!" She laughed, as the tape ended.

"Me? You sound like somebody's trying to rip your face off, for Christ's sake."

We were still zinging each other on our respective vocal liabilities when I turned down Lakeview Street and pulled into the Humbert's driveway.

"Oh, God," Allison said, her voice a half-whisper.

Two Quincy County squad cars and a gray Chevrolet sedan were parked in a line in front of the house. A deputy stood sentry at the doorway. I eased the Horizon in behind a squad car and switched off the ignition.

"Take it easy, Allison," I said. "This may be nothing to get upset about." But I didn't believe that myself.

The living room was large, although it looked somewhat smaller now, crowded as it was. Brooke Humbert sat on the edge of a long sofa, her head bowed, a tissue in her hand. An older woman, too well dressed for a maid, more likely a neighbor, was sitting beside Brooke and talking to her quietly. Amos Skelly was ensconced on a love seat opposite the sofa, his Buddha belly resting on his knees, a look of professional sorrow on his face.

"There they are now, sir." A uniformed deputy pointed in our direction. He and another deputy had been standing in one corner of the room with their boss, J. D. Staub.

"Sheridan." Staub nodded to me as he came across the room. Stepping up to Allison, he took her by the arm and walked her out to the foyer, motioning for me to follow.

"Miss Humbert, I'm J. D. Staub, undersheriff for Quincy County."

Allison began without preamble, speaking in a gray monotone. "Why are you all here? What's happened?"

J. D. locked onto her eyes. "I'm sorry to have to tell you, your uncle is dead."

"Dead? What happened?" The shock in Allison's voice spoke for both of us.

"One of my deputies found your uncle's car parked up on Beedle Road Extension about forty minutes ago. That's a dirt road up in the hills south of town, not far from the winery. It's used mostly by some of the local kids." Staub

111

glanced at me to see if I'd caught the implication. I had. The local version of Lovers' Lane.

"Your uncle was found in the car, behind the wheel. He had been stabbed."

"Jesus! Oh, poor Brooke. I'd better go to her and see if I can . . ."

"In a minute, please, Miss Humbert." Staub spoke softly but he still held her arm. "I have to ask you a couple of questions. I understand Mr. Humbert left the house at about eight last night to attend a business meeting. Is that correct?"

"Yes, about eight o'clock."

"Do you remember if he said who he was going to meet or where this meeting was to take place?"

"No, he didn't really say." Allison's voice vibrated, on the edge. "I mean, I just heard him tell Brooke he had to go out on business and he left."

"You're sure he didn't say anything else?" Staub pressed. "Where he might have been going?"

"I already said he didn't, damn it!" Allison snapped. "If you don't believe me, ask Brooke."

"I have, Miss Humbert," Staub said. "I'm sorry I've upset you, but I needed to be sure. You can go now."

Allison hurried away into the living room where Skelly, standing now, was saying something to the woman with Brooke. Brooke was leaning back against the sofa, holding a tissue over her eyes.

I said to Staub, "You think you really needed all this manpower, just to tell one woman her husband is dead?"

"What I don't need is a lecture, Sheridan, okay?" Staub snapped. He looked over his shoulder, then added, "Amos loves a parade, especially when he's grand marshal." He pointed a finger toward the front door and I followed him out onto the porch.

"Weisskopf, get on the radio and find out how the chief is coming along out there," Staub said to the deputy standing sentry. When we were alone, he turned to me

112

and said, "Guess what we found sticking in Humbert's chest."

It didn't take much imagination. "A fishing knife with a bone handle and a six-inch blade," I said.

"Bingo. One thrust, right into the heart by the look of it. Sometime late last night or early this morning I'd say. We won't know for sure until the M.E. gets done." He shook his head. "Damn, he was just sitting there in his car, dead as a mackerel, when one of our patrols ran across him."

"It looks like I can cross him off my list," I said. "Unless Skelly decides it was hari-kari."

"Hmmmph." Staub hesitated. "Maybe you should forget about making lists, Sheridan. This thing's not just about Charlie Dugan anymore."

"It is for me, J.D."

He thought about that for a moment. "I have to get back to the crime scene, make sure Areno doesn't miss anything. You want to ride along? Talk?"

"Will Skelly be riding with us?"

"No, Weisskopf'll run him home. Amos wouldn't have come out at all if Humbert hadn't been such a wheel in this county. Now that he's put in an official appearance, I expect he'll want to head back."

"In that case, I'll go with you. Give me a minute to give my regrets to Brooke, okay?"

I got back inside in time to see Brooke being led up the staircase to the second floor by the older woman. Allison was at the bottom of the stairs with Skelly and the two deputies.

"Sheridan, I forgot about you," Allison said.

"Don't worry about it. How's Brooke doing?"

"She's in shock, I think. Thank goodness Mrs. Randall came over from across the street. She used to be a nurse."

"Mr. Sheridan, I'm Sheriff Amos T. Skelly." The old man stuck out his hand. Up until then, I'd been trying to

113

ignore him, which wasn't easy, given his size. I shook hands briefly and mumbled a hello.

"I've been wanting to meet you, Mr. Sheridan. Too bad it has to be under such difficult circumstances." He had a grand speaking voice, full of flourishes and curliques, like Old English script.

"Too bad," I agreed.

"I'm afraid this incident with Mr. Humbert throws a whole new light on your uncle's case, too. Looks like we have a homicidal psychopath on our hands."

"Or an extremely stupid burglar," I said.

"Beg pardon?" Skelly boomed, cocking his head to one side.

"Yes." I raised my voice a couple of decibels. "It doesn't look like a run-of-the-mill break-in anymore."

"Well"—he put one paw on my shoulder and one on Allison's shoulder—"I want to assure you both that my department will do everything in its power to see that this case is solved, you can be sure of that."

"Thank you, Sheriff," Allison said.

Having done his duty, Skelly shook hands with us in turn and trudged out of the house, the two stoic deputies following in lockstep.

When we were alone, I asked Allison, "Is there anything I can do?"

"No, I guess not. There's not much anyone can do now, is there?"

"Listen, don't be discouraged by Skelly. J. D. Staub is the man who'll actually lead the investigation and he's a good man." I took her hand. "You don't have to worry about this thing being swept under the rug with J.D. around."

"Oh, I wasn't even thinking about all that, Sheridan," she sighed wistfully. "I was thinking of Grandmother, actually. Someone's going to have to tell her that her baby boy is dead."

CHAPTER 15

THINGS were quiet in Mohaca Springs on a Sunday evening. What traffic there was traversed Main in spurts, mostly heading north. Tourists from the city wheeling their sensible family sedans back to the Monday wars after a weekend of R&R at the lake.

Staub drove through the village at a crawl, careful to maintain the thirty-mile-per-hour speed limit, automatically scanning the streets for scofflaws despite his preoccupation with Humbert's murder.

"Why do you put up with Skelly?" I asked.

He glanced over dolefully, then turned back to the road ahead. "It's kind of a long story. Maybe I'll tell you about it sometime, when I'm in the mood."

We cruised past the sign marking the village's southern boundary and passed by the Humbert Winery complex. Staub accelerated, urging the unmarked Chevy to fifty-five.

"I do the best I can, Sheridan," he said, eyes front. "I follow the book when possible and I do my job."

"And you do Skelly's job, too."

His only response was to shrug his broad shoulders. "So

tell me what you've been up to. You find any other interesting stuff at the cottage, besides the journal?"

"No, but I may have found out who 'T' is. Or was." I
related what Ralph Cramer had told me about Teddy Kendall. He wasn't overly impressed.

"Could be a reference to the Kendall kid, I suppose," he
said. "But if it was, what does it mean? What could the
boy have told Charlie that Charlie would have to deny? If
the kid really was gay, what's that got to do with your
uncle? Dugan was as heterosexual as any man I've
known." Staub looked over at me again. "And even if
Teddy Kendall is the 'T' in the journal, what're the
chances it has anything to do with the murder?"

He had a point there. The Kendall boy was dead and in
the ground months before Uncle Charlie was killed. Still,
when you're trying to solve a puzzle, you have to examine
every piece you can lay hands on, even the ones that don't
seem to fit. Like cryptic journal entries and late-night
meetings in Italian restaurants. I told him about seeing
Florio and Skelly and the man with the salt-and-pepper
hair, and about the tag team match with the pickup
truck.

"Salt-and-pepper hair sounds like it could be Dick Penrose. He's town supervisor for Mohaca Springs, used to be
on the state Parks Service Board."

"That fits in with Florio's bluster about having the
Kendall place condemned for public use," I pointed out.

"Yeah, Penrose probably still has some juice with the
board. And rumor has it he isn't above accepting a gratuity now and then, for services rendered."

"What about Skelly?"

"Amos may be a lot of things, but he's no petty
grafter," Staub shook his head firmly. "He loves to play
politics, sure, but he's not greedy for money."

We turned off the main highway onto a narrow dirt
road that cut straight through open fields, then snaked
away up into the darkening hills rising ahead of us. A tilt-
ing signpost said BEEDLE ROAD EXTENSION.

116

"Anyway," Staub said as he maneuvered the Chevy over the rutted road, "I happen to know that Amos spoke at a VFW function Friday night. Penrose is a vice commander this year. Could be he and Florio buttonholed Amos there and talked him into a late supper, maybe figuring to get his backing for this public park idea. Amos has a lot of pull with the Republican Committee, and the Republicans run this county. What really bothers me is this business with the pickup truck," he said, adding pointedly, "and the fact you didn't report it to me sooner."

"I meant to," I said. "But I got distracted."

"Hmmph. Well, it could have been a couple of hopped-up juvies, I suppose, but it could have been something else, too. A warning, maybe. Could be you've stepped on a few toes without even realizing it."

The Chevy surged to the crest of the hill. Fifty feet ahead, the road was congested with official vehicles; three Quincy County cruisers with blue warning lights flashing, a bright-yellow ambulance bearing the insignia of the Mohaca Springs Volunteer Fire Department, a gray station wagon with the county coroner's seal on the door. And, off to one side, parked precariously close to a drainage ditch, Michel Humbert's silver Mercedes.

We left the Chevy in the middle of the narrow dirt tract and tramped over to the Mercedes. Tony Areno, a White Owl blunt clenched in his teeth, was supervising as two ambulance attendants hoisted a black body bag onto a gurney.

"We're just about through here, boss," Areno said as we came up. He held out a small plastic bag, like the kind mothers wrap sandwiches in. Inside was a filleting knife identical to the one that killed Uncle Charlie.

Staub paused to look at the weapon through the clear plastic before telling Areno, "Okay, let's get the body down to Doc Gardener's. Tell the driver he'll have to head on through to Town Line Road. There's no point in trying to turn all these vehicles around on this cow path."

Areno mumbled affirmatively and ambled off to speak to the ambulance driver. I followed Staub to the station wagon and a disheveled bald man, who was just then tucking a medical bag behind the front seat.

"What d'you think, Doc?" Staub asked him.

"It's about what you figured, J.D.," the bald man said, slipping in behind the wheel of the wagon. "He's been dead eighteen to twenty hours, I'd say. The wound is nearly identical to the one that killed Charlie Dugan. My autopsy will undoubtedly tell you nothing you don't already know." The coroner started the engine, revved it hard three times, and then poked his shiny head through the rolled-down window and added, "I'll have the report ready by tomorrow morning, but don't get your hopes up."

Staub thanked him with a nod and we walked back to the Mercedes, J.D. leading the way with long steady strides while I picked my way carefully over the hardened tire ruts, dead clumps of sod, and various detritus that littered Beedle Road Extension. A twenty-square-foot area around the Mercedes had been roped off with surveying stakes and twine. A pair of plainclothes detectives were on their knees, grooming the ground, using flashlights to bolster the rapidly fading sunlight. Areno returned from the ambulance and stood alongside as we watched the men search.

"Anything at all?" Staub asked.

"Nah," Areno grumbled. "There ain't nothing here but old candy wrappers, beer cans, and used rubbers. We're double-checking, but what's to find in that mess?" He pointed at the ground, crosshatched from a dozen different tire tracks inlaid one over the other and baked into the earth. "The way that clay sets up in the sun, you can't pick out a fresh tire track, let alone a footprint."

"Photos?"

"Had 'im shoot a whole roll, every angle in the book."

"Okay, get a tow truck up here and impound the car,"

Staub said. Then he was off again, this time to interrogate a couple of deputies who were idling beside a prowl car, awaiting direction.

I was starting to feel as useless as the referee at a pro wrestling match, but I followed along anyway. It was a lesson I learned in college from a sociology professor who was born in the United States but raised in Los Angeles. "Go with the flow," he used to tell us in fluent Californese. "If you can't make it, fake it." Not wanting to waste my education, I now fake it whenever possible.

"Who does the chief have making the rounds?" Staub asked the taller of the two deputies.

"Bates and Walker, sir. Chief Areno told them to split up and hit all the bars and restaurants, Bates heading north through the village and Walker going south."

"Anybody else on it?"

"Not that I know of, Mr. Staub."

"Okay, Torrini, I want you to work your way west toward Penn Yan. Here." He took a photo of Humbert from his breast pocket—he must have picked it up at the Humbert place—and handed it to the deputy. "Flash this in all the bars and diners along the route and see if anyone remembers seeing that face last night sometime. Johnson." He turned to the shorter deputy. "I want you to work your way back to the village from here, stopping at every house between here and the business district. Find out if anyone can remember seeing somebody walk out of these hills last night around midnight or after. Right?"

Staub dismissed the deputies and immediately headed for Areno, who was still watching the plainclothesmen.

"Tony?"

"Here, put this shit in the trunk of my car," Areno told the men, handing each a plastic bag filled with litter. He looked up at Staub. "Yeah, J.D.?"

"I just sent Torrini over toward Penn Yan. Johnson's going to canvass the village."

"Canvass for what?" Areno asked, perplexed.

119

"Tony," Staub lowered his voice. "If the killer rode up here with Humbert—and it looks like he did—then he probably had to walk out of here, right? Which means he could have been spotted."

"Yeah, good point," Areno said. "I shoulda figured."

"No problem. Why don't you head back and get things coordinated at the department. I'll wait for the tow truck."

Areno hurried off toward his squad car, chastened but determined. Staub motioned for me to follow him. We double-timed it to the crest of the hill, "Colonel Bogie's March" playing in my head. Night was closing in from the east and far below us, beyond a series of rolling vine-covered hillsides, Mohaca Springs was beginning to light up. A long slim patch of Seneca Lake was visible through the distant trees and, to the south, I could make out the shadowy silhouettes of scattered farmhouses. One of those houses belonged to Sorrel Brown, I recalled, and the thought made me smile inside and pledge to make things right with her. But my hilltop reverie was suddenly punctured by J. D. Staub.

"Try to picture yourself with a knife sticking in your chest," he said as he stripped the cellophane from one of his panatelas. When he struck a match, I could see the deep worry lines etched into his face, like cracks in the armor.

"I brought you up here for a reason, Sheridan. I wanted you to see what a murder scene is like, the cold clinical details." He drew hard on the cigar. "You've got a stake in this and I know you're good at what you do. But people are dying here."

"People are dying everywhere, J.D.," I said. "I've covered murder scenes as a police reporter. And I've seen death close up, in Vietnam."

"I'm not trying to scare you off. I don't think I could. I'm saying go easy, that's all."

He flicked a glowing red coal from the end of the cigar

and gestured toward the main highway. A pair of head-lights was bumping along on the lower half of Beedle Road Extension. As the headlights drew closer, the outline of a compact car became clear. A couple of horny teenagers, I wondered, making for Lovers' Lane the minute the sun goes down?

The car, a powder-blue Chevette in need of a valve job, chugged the last hundred yards up the hill and parked behind the Mercedes. Staub and I goat-walked down from the crest of the hill and came up behind the new arrival.

"Hey, Mr. Staub, what's happening?" A man in his mid-twenties stepped out of the car. He was wearing jeans and a red and blue rugby shirt. He had a Nikon 35-milli-meter SLR slung over his shoulder and a slim note pad in his hand.

"Christ," Staub said. "How'd you pick this up?"

"From the scanner in the newsroom." The young man smiled conspiratorially. "I hear this weird call a few hours ago alerting all county cruisers to keep an eye out for a silver Mercedes, which I figure belongs to Michel Humbert. Then, not two hours ago, I pick up another call from your dispatcher, a homicide code this time. Put that together with the location, and I figure, hey, one of Quincy County's finest citizens has bit the big one, right? Unless you're up here to hassle teenage nymphos, Mr. Staub." He turned to me and stuck out his hand. "Brian MacKay, *Daily News*."

I smiled. "Sheridan. We spoke the other night."

"Oh, right, on the phone. Rewrite du jour."

"You've lost me," Staub said.

"You had to be there," MacKay said. "So, tell me, it's Humbert, right? You hauled away the body already? Geez, I've got to get the paper to spring for a new car, a Trans Am, something with balls. Can't make any time in that lousy Chevette." MacKay headed for the Mercedes as he gabbed, with Staub and me in tow.

121

"So, what's the MO on this one? It was Humbert, wasn't it, Mr. Staub?"

Staub sighed. "Yes, it was Michel Humbert, Brian. Another knifing, sometime late last night or early this morning. We're conducting an investigation, et cetera, and if you want any more than that, you'll have to get it from the official press release, back in Geneva."

"Aw, c'mon. Gimme a break, huh? My deadline's in less than two hours."

"Sorry, Brian."

"Sheridan, I hear Charlie Dugan was your uncle. Is that why you're up here? What's the connection?" Like most good reporters, MacKay was persistent, bordering on the obnoxious.

"Sorry." I shrugged. "I can't help you. I just happened to run into Mr. Staub at the Humbert place and I talked him into letting me come along for the ride."

"Right," MacKay snorted, not buying it for a second. "So, what've we got, Mr. Staub, another Jack the Ripper running around or what?"

Staub made a production out of looking at his watch. "You better hurry downtown for that press release, Brian. I don't have time to chat."

MacKay made a few more end runs, but he wasn't able to get around Staub. By then, the tow truck had arrived. I watched as the driver and Staub hooked the tow bar to the Mercedes. MacKay snapped a few pictures and scribbled in his note pad. Five minutes later, the tow truck hauled away the Mercedes, with Staub's gray Chevy and MacKay's battered Chevette bumping along behind. Lovers' Lane faded in the rearview mirror.

CHAPTER 16

MONDAY mornings are a curse for a lot of people and I used to be one of them. That's one of the reasons I became a freelancer. No eight-to-five routine, no profane radio alarm clocks and patent-leather disc jockeys yelling you awake with the sun, no dividing and subdividing your existence into coffee breaks and lunch in the cafeteria and happy hour from five to six in the afternoon. Freelancers are truly free.

At least, that's what I told myself as I levitated from bed, took a quick shower and shave, and settled in at the typewriter just as the clock struck 7 A.M. Murder and mayhem in the Finger Lakes not withstanding, I still had to earn a living. A magazine editor in New York was waiting for a rewrite of a profile I had written on an ex-safecracker who was out on parole and living on an organic vegetable farm in New Hampshire—the editor had said it was too long. I liked the piece as written, but it was his money.

I worked diligently for an hour or so, managing to sift out nearly a full page from the piece, then decided to take a break. I had just given William his morning ration of half-and-half and was pouring myself a fresh cup of coffee—the cheesecloth was working out fine—when I saw Maevis Kendall from the kitchen window.

It was an odd sight, even considering the subject matter. There she stood, stock-still and ramrod straight in her side yard. She was turned toward the cove, which means she was facing in my direction, but she was looking up at the sky. She had something held tightly to her chest, but I couldn't make out what it was.

Uncle Charlie had a pair of binoculars stashed in the hutch, I remembered. Digging them out of a cluttered drawer, I popped off the lens caps and took up a new position at the living room window.

It looked like a Bible. And I could see her jaw rising and falling. An early-morning incantation to the god of agriculture? I watched her standing there with her head uplifted, her lips fluttering nonstop, for another couple of minutes. All at once, her head came down, the Bible was tucked away under her arm, and she was off to her car. I continued to watch while she fired up the old Dodge and backed out of the driveway and drove north.

I tried to get my mind back on work, but it was useless. The strange ritual by the cove kept intruding. I decided to put the article aside for another day. I was halfway out the door, on my way down to Ralph and Kay's for breakfast, when the phone rang. I thought about ignoring it at first, then changed my mind.

"Hello, Sheridan?"

It was Florio. Next time, I told myself, trust your first instinct.

"Yes, Mr. Florio. What can I do for you?"

"You hear the news? Looks like you're down to one offer for that place of yours."

"Your compassion is touching, Mr. Florio."

"C'mon, Sheridan. I didn't even know the guy. I'm sorry for his family, okay?" He wheezed. "But I'm a businessman and we need to talk some business."

"I don't need to do anything," I said.

"Okay, so maybe you don't need to, Sheridan. But what's the percentage in turning your back on a good deal just 'cause maybe you don't need the cash right now? Lotta rainy days around here, y'know. So, listen, what do you say we get together later today? Have a little meeting about this. Maybe I can sweeten the offer."

"I'm afraid I'm busy this morning, Mr. Florio. In fact, I was on my way out—"

"Call me Gabe, huh? So, how about this afternoon? You name the place."

"I have to go up to Geneva this afternoon."

"That's fine. I can meet you there someplace."

"Well, okay." I wanted to put him off, but he was a key figure in the investigation. Avoiding him was a luxury I couldn't afford. "How about at Maxi's Restaurant? In the bar, around three o'clock. You know where that is?"

"Maxi's"—he cleared his throat—"sure, I know Maxi's. I'll see you at three." Click.

It was a slow morning at Ralph and Kay's Diner and Outdoor Store.

I bought a copy of the *Finger Lakes Daily News* from a vending machine in the foyer and ambled into the dining room. Ralph Cramer was sitting in a window booth with Norma Wells and a wiry old woman wearing an apron. Otherwise, the place was empty.

"Morning, Ralph. Norma." I nodded to each.

"Sheridan, we were just talking about you," Ralph said. "Pumpkin, this is Sheridan, the boy I told you about."

"Pumpkin" stuck out a gnarled hand. "Kay Cramer, Sheridan. Nice to meet you."

"Have a seat, son," Ralph said.

I slid into the booth next to the rotund Norma, her leather mail sack wedged between us. Three empty coffee cups littered the tabletop. A dish supporting the remnants of a jelly doughnut sat next to Norma's cup.

125

Ralph tapped my newspaper with a finger. "How 'bout this Humbert thing, huh? Can you believe it?"

"Course he can believe it." Kay poked Ralph with her elbow. "He saw it with his own eyes, according to the paper. Didn't you, Sheridan?"

"Not really. I mean, I got up there after the police had pretty well cleaned things up." I opened the paper and read Brian MacKay's front-page account of the murder. It was a straightforward piece, listing the who, what, when, where, why, and how in the first few paragraphs in solid Journalism 101 fashion. The story then stated that I was with Staub at the murder scene, MacKay pointedly describing me as "nephew of Charles Dugan, victim of a similar knife attack." There was the obligatory rehash of the circumstances surrounding Uncle Charlie's death. It went on several more paragraphs with the usual biographical stuff on Humbert and standard comments from "police officials" to the effect that the investigation was continuing at a satisfactory pace. Survivors and funeral arrangements were listed in the last paragraph. A formal obit had been boxed into a sidebar next to the main story but, like most obituaries on prominent people, it didn't tell you the things you really wanted to know.

"Some kind of awful thing to happen in our little town, isn't it?"

"Makes a body wonder whatever happened to common decency."

"Well, I'm making sure my doors are locked tight from now on, I'll tell you."

While the three of them bantered back and forth about murder and morality and paradise lost, I did my best to bury myself behind a menu, shrugging my shoulders or muttering noncommittally whenever necessary. When the waitress came around, I ordered the breakfast special: two eggs, toast, home fries, and coffee for a dollar and a quarter. Proof enough for me that paradise was not entirely lost.

"Come on. What do you think, Sheridan? I mean, really?" Ralph asked.

I munched a forkful of scrambled egg and washed it down with strong black coffee. "I don't know what to think, Ralph. What do you think it's all about?"

"I sure as hell wish I knew," he said.

"Well, I know what I think," Kay said. "I think it's time I got back to work." She slid out of the booth and, with a nod and a smile at me, returned to her kitchen. A few moments later, Norma Wells swigged the last drops in her coffee cup and gathered up her mailbag.

"I guess I better get going, too. Take care, folks."

I watched her go, then turned to Ralph who, with Kay safely away in the kitchen, was lighting up a Camel.

"Ralph, that fellow you were telling me about yesterday, Ruly Jackson?"

"Yeah, Blackjack, the waiter over at the Pinewood. What about him?"

"I'd like to talk to him, away from work if possible. Do you know where I could find him?" I asked.

"Well, sure. He lives over in Harley Corners. That's a little hamlet west of here, on the County Line Road."

"Do you know if he works on Monday?"

"I don't recall. I'll tell you where you might find him tonight, though. Barnett's Grill. There's a big euchre tournament over there at seven-thirty. Me and Kay are going. I bet Blackjack'll be there, too. He's a hell of a euchre player."

"One more thing," I said, chasing a trapezoidal piece of potato around the plate. "This girl you mentioned yesterday, Sue Morris. Is she around?"

Ralph cocked an eyebrow. "No, she only comes in three afternoons a week. Why do you ask?"

"Nothing important." He looked crestfallen, as if he'd just found the last page was missing from one of his murder mysteries. I didn't want to let him down too hard, so I assumed my best Robert Mitchum squint and deadpanned, "It's a tricky business, Ralph. Let's just say I'm keeping all my options open."

He nodded, mollified somewhat at the profundity of my nonanswer. "I understand." He winked. "By the by, Sorrie's here today, if you're interested."

"I thought Monday was her day off."

"Yeah, well, it is," he said. "Only I had to call her in this morning to help straighten out a shipping order."

"A shipping order?"

"Yeah, for the Outdoor Store. Sorrie is sort of my assistant at the store. She helps with restocking and inventory and such as that. She's over there now, in the storage room. I got in a whole bunch of flannel shirts today, only I was supposed to get a bunch of T-shirts with 'Mohaca Springs' printed on them. Hell, I already got flannel shirts coming out of my ears and here we are in the middle of June." He was beginning to work up a head of steam, flailing his arms and shaking his head, piqued at the injustices of the small retail business. "I'll tell you, Sheridan, when it comes to running that little store of mine, I'm not much good anymore. The detail work does me in. I guess I'm just too old."

I assured him he was in the prime of life and thanked him for his help. Newspaper in hand, I paid the check at the cashier's counter and crossed over into the Outdoor Store. The front of the shop was deserted, but I could hear a voice drifting through a curtained doorway in the back. I pushed back the curtain and stepped into the storeroom.

"No, Manny, he doesn't want to keep the flannel shirts, too. We can't use them this early." Sorrel was seated on a stool, a clipboard in her hand, talking on the phone. "Just send the T-shirts and I'll have the parcel service pick up the flannels, okay?" She spotted me in the doorway and gestured for me to come in and sit down.

"Yes, I know that, but it was an honest mistake." She switched the phone to her other ear. "Yes, everything will be packaged and ready to go. I'll put a corrected copy of

128

the invoice in with the packing slip for your records. Okay, Manny, thanks a lot." She gently recradled the phone and let out a short moan.

"Everything straightened out?" I asked.

"Finally!" She made some notes on the clipboard sheet and set it aside. "Poor Ralph. He just can't seem to get the hang of ordering stock for this place. I think the operation has outgrown him over the years."

"What happened?" I asked, pointing to an open box of checked plaid shirts.

"Oh, he decided to order some specialty T-shirts for the summer tourist season, only he couldn't find the right order blanks. So he took out an old order form for flannel shirts and tried to cross out the old order and write in a new one. The supplier couldn't make it out, so he looked up the invoice number and shipped us more flannel shirts."

"And you get to come in on your day off and put everything right."

"Mmm. I started out by giving him a hand back here when things were slow in the diner." She shrugged. "Before I knew what I was getting into, Ralph was dependent on me to keep the inventory under control. Not that I mind really. It breaks up the monotony of waitressing, and he pays me extra for my time."

She busied herself with a stack of invoices. "So, what brings you around today, Sheridan? I thought you'd be out chasing the 'mad slasher,' as Kay calls him."

"I wanted to apologize for the other night. I let my mouth get ahead of my brain, unfortunately."

A hint of a smile touched the corner of her mouth. "Actually, I guess I was mad because you were so smug about it, so sure in a condescending, city-slicker way. And because you were so close to the truth." She laughed. "Roy Rossiter does have a wife and two kids, although he and Pam are separated. And he used to live in a trailer park east of town. Pam and the kids still live there."

I wanted to ask "why?" *Why do you spend your time with Neanderthals the likes of Roy Rossiter? Can't you see your own worth?* But I had just apologized for being quick to judge, and I didn't want to get caught at it again.

"I thought we might get together for a late supper tonight," I said. "I've got a few things to do early, but I could pick you up at . . ."

"Oh, I'd really like to, Sheridan, but I can't tonight. I'm going to a bridal shower for one of the girls who works at the diner."

"Tomorrow night?"

"Tomorrow would be fine. I'd love to."

"Good. What time is good for you?"

"Let's see, I can probably get out of here by six-thirty, seeing that it's a Tuesday night. I'll run home and change." She rapped a pencil against her lips. "How 'bout seven-thirty?"

"Fine. The Pinewood sound okay?"

"Oooh, the Pinewood, classy. Listen," she said, "since we're going in that direction, why don't I meet you at your place? That will save you the hassle of driving down to Mohaca Springs and doubling back."

"Sounds reasonable," I agreed. "I'll see you tomorrow night then, around seven forty-five?"

"Yes." She grinned. "And I'll bring dessert."

CHAPTER 17

I SPENT the rest of the morning at Mohaca Springs High School, trying to find the key to Teddy Kendall. I dropped J. D. Staub's name at the administration office, which was enough to get me a guided tour of the school library. There, I found a dusty back shelf crammed with old yearbooks. I pulled the one from the previous year and began skimming. When I came to Teddy's photo, it jumped off the page at me—the watery blue eyes, the long narrow face, the unruly auburn mane. The steady innocent gaze gave no hint of the tragic end the boy would choose.

After a moment, I glanced down at the list of achievements under the photo. Science club, Future Farmers of America. The usual, I suppose, except now there'd be no future.

I replaced the book on the shelf and was preparing to leave when curiosity reared its head. I thought, Why not? I took an educated guess and pulled down a yearbook dated two years earlier than my own high school graduation. The pages of senior pictures had been black and white back then, but I had no trouble recognizing Sorrel Brown. The hair was shorter, bobbed in a style that some-

131

how made her look older, more mature than her classmates. But the sultry smile was the same. Reflexively, I checked out her list of activities—the field hockey team, Junior Candystripers, cheerleading—then went back to the photo.

A teenage knockout, our Miss Brown. As I stared, I imagined myself in tenth grade, the bittersweet agony of pining from afar for this unreachable senior goddess. With a small grin, I placed the book back on the shelf and forced myself back into the present.

I still hadn't found anything solid, I cautioned myself as I headed back to the administration office to check out some old school records. But I did know one thing. Teddy Kendall, the boy I'd never met, had a face I'd seen before.

The newsroom at the *Daily News* was humming with activity when I arrived. A score of men and women sat hunkered down over VDTs, firing quick questions over their telephones as they typed. Two men I didn't recognize stood in the middle of the room and argued about the size of the news hole allotted for the next eition. It might have been a scene from *Front Page,* except the clatter of typewriters had been replaced by the gentle whir of solid-state word processors.

I found Karen DeClair tucked away in her cubicle, scanning the day's story budget on her VDT. She cleared the view screen and swung around to face me, elbows propped on her desk in the classic let's-get-down-to-brass-tacks pose. "I've been trying to reach you. You could've helped MacKay out a little last night. You know how big this story is?"

"Pretty big, huh?"

"The Rochester and Syracuse papers have assigned reporters to it full-time now. The AP wants all it can get for the state wire. You bet your ass it's big. The biggest crime story we've had since I've been with the paper."

"There's nothing like a little bloodletting to improve one's circulation."

She ignored the sarcasm. "Look, Sheridan, you're on the inside with this story. You could be a big help to us, if you'd only tell us what's going on."

"Karen, all I've got so far is a lot of maybes, that's all. If I really knew what was going on, I'd tell you about it—after I talked to the cops. But, right now, I'm just running on instincts. And you can't print instincts."

"Maybe not, but I've seen your instincts at work before and I figure you'll get a handle on this sooner or later." She paused before adding, "I need this story, Sheridan."

"Tell you what, if you'll give me free access to your newsroom and phones and files, I'll promise to give you the whole story, an exclusive, if and when I sort it all out."

"How about filing a daily piece on the police investigation itself?" she asked hopefully.

"Uh uh, let MacKay cover that stuff. I can't get tied down. I'll file once, when I've got the whole story."

"I can only pay you ten cents a word," she said. "That's our top rate for freelance material."

"Twenty cents, and I'll use a lot of adjectives."

"Okay," she said grudgingly. Then she smiled and added, "I can get some of that back by selling the story to the wire services."

We shook hands on it.

"Now, about that society writer you mentioned."

"Millie Freeman? She's over at her desk."

Karen directed me to the far corner of the newsroom, where a middle-aged woman sat poring over a copy of *House Beautiful*. A brown jar with a rose sticking out of it adorned one corner of the desk. There was an inch of congealed rubber cement in the bottom of the jar. The cement was an anachronism, now that the paper had gone electronic and there was no longer any hard copy to paste together. I took in the society editor's prim face and short frosted hair with its graying edges, wondering whether she, too, wasn't a bit outdated.

"Millie Freeman?" I asked. She slapped the magazine shut and stashed it in a drawer as she looked up.

"Yes, how may I help you?"

"My name's Sheridan. Karen sent me over."

"Oh, yes." She smiled. Her teeth were capped. "I've heard of you through the newsroom grapevine."

"I understand you cover the society beat?"

She nodded. "Among other things, yes. I've been doing my 'Social Notes' column for more than twenty . . ." She turned coy. "Well, let's just say I'm experienced."

"I was hoping you could give me some background on Michel and Brooke Humbert. I assume they were prominent in the local social whirl."

"Very. He'll be a great loss. And Brooke, too, poor dear. I expect she'll go back to Rhode Island now. She's a Bradley, you see. All her people are in the Newport area."

"But Michel grew up here, didn't he?"

"Yes, in Mohaca Springs, the family home on Lakeview Street. Lovely place. Of course, it doesn't have the grounds it once had. Michel's father subdivided the property into building lots back in the fifties, when things were slow at the winery."

"Michel didn't attend public school in Mohaca Springs, though, did he?"

"No, he went to a private academy in Ithaca, as I recall. Then on to Cornell." She poked a finger into her cheek and actually chuckled. "I understand he was a bit of a handful in his school days. A regular roué."

A roué? I hadn't heard that archaic word since reading *Cyrano de Bergerac* in the ninth grade.

"How would you characterize his marriage?" I asked.

"Well, they've been married for twelve years or so. I suppose it's had its ups and downs. There have been occasional rumors . . . that Michel hadn't quite sewn all his wild oats, you know." She sniffed. "But I don't write a gossip column, Mr. Sheridan. I do society news."

I had a few more questions, but I didn't think Millie

134

would approve of them, so I didn't ask. I thanked her for her time and moved across the newsroom to an empty desk with a phone on it. It was nearly three o'clock, the time I had agreed to meet Florio at Maxi's. But I figured it would do him some good to simmer for a few minutes. I dialed a number; Staub answered on the third ring.

"This is Sheridan, J.D.," I said. "How did the autopsy turn out?"

"About as expected, no surprises." His voice was flat. "With one exception. Doc found evidence of recent sexual activity, traces of semen on Humbert's underclothes. Which means the killer could have been a woman, or a jealous husband. Assuming he didn't have relations earlier, before he went up to Beedle Road, which we can't rule out."

"Interesting. Have you turned up anyone who saw Humbert Saturday night?"

"Not yet, but we're still working on it."

I told him of my upcoming meeting with Florio and asked whether he had been able to establish Florio's whereabouts the night of the murder.

"It appears that he was home all night; leastwise, his wife claims he was. For what that's worth." He sounded tired, disgruntled. "Anyway, we can't touch him at this point. Listen, my other line is ringing. I'll have to talk to you later, okay?"

I made it to Maxi's no more than fifteen minutes late. Florio was seated at the end of the bar, wearing another snug three-piece suit. This one was Kermit-the-Frog green. He was busy inflicting a monologue on a younger man in a gray suit who was seated next to him.

"Hey, Sheridan, where you been?" Florio waved me to a stool. "This is my accountant, Sal Minella."

I had been about to make a joke about food poisoning when the guy stood up to shake my hand. He was extremely tall and broad for an accountant, with shoulders Joan Crawford would envy. I decided to exercise restraint.

"You hungry, Sheridan? How about a drink?" Florio asked. He had part of a corned beef on rye in front of him and a glass with something creamy and beige in it. Sal Minella was nursing a bottle of Miller Lite.

"What's that you're drinking?" I asked Florio.

"Amaretto and milk. Great for the stomach. Want one?"

I declined, ordering instead a gin and tonic.

"So," Florio said as he finished off the sandwich. "You ready to do business?"

"You said something about sweetening the offer?"

"Yeah. Sal, gimme the picture." The king-sized accountant took a sheet of cardboard from his briefcase and gave it to Florio. "I want you to take a look at this, Sheridan. It's one of the condos we got planned, a one-bedroom job. Nice, huh?"

The "picture" was an architect's sketch of the interior of the condominium unit's living room—dining room area. There was a modern pyramidal fireplace and sliding glass doors that opened onto a balcony festooned with potted plants. Two small insets had been drawn at the bottom of the sheet, depicting the kitchen and bedroom layouts.

I handed the drawing back to Florio. "Not bad."

"Not bad?" A strangled cough. "That little number'll sell for ninety-five thou, not including options like a garbage disposal and whirlpool bath."

"How about whitewalls?"

"I told you this guy's a card, didn't I?" Florio said to Minella. "Seriously, Sheridan, I got an offer I think you're gonna love. Okay, the original dollar deal we talked before, right? *Plus* you get one of these single bedroom units for your own, free, once the project's built and sixty percent of the condos are sold or in escrow."

"My very own condo?"

"Right. You gotta come up with the maintenance fees

136

and club dues yourself, but that's peanuts. You come out smelling like a Wild Irish Rose."

I wasn't interested in living in a resort condo with a bunch of well-heeled retirees, but I could always sell the place. I'd at least consider the offer, if Florio was still in a position to make it once Uncle Charlie's killer had been discovered. But until then, I had to stall him.

"C'mon, Sheridan, talk to me. Be the first kid on the block to own a Iroquois Shoals luxury condo."

"Catchy name," I said. "But I'll still need some time to check it out—"

"What's to check out? It's cut and dried." Florio elbowed his associate, who bobbed his head on cue. Otherwise, the behemoth just sat there in his gray suit, looking like a 1968 Chrysler Imperial.

I said, "No offense, but I need to have my lawyer go over your financial statement, verify your credit, that sort of thing. Just to be sure this project's going to fly."

"Hell, that's why we got legal contracts, right? You're protected every which way. Tell him, Sally."

"The financing is solid, Mr. Sheridan," Sally said. "There's no possibility of default on our side and no conceivable scenario in which you don't get your cash payments and title to the condo."

"That's very nice." I turned to Florio. "However, I hear you've had some financial setbacks recently. Something about a grand jury probe of an organized crime connection in a housing project you were involved with."

"Jesus H. Christ, I don't believe this." Florio threw up his hands in supplication. "First the county cops call up and make out like I got something to do with Humbert getting knocked off; now you tell me I'm a gangster. Sal, do you believe this?" He coughed a couple of times, then leaned in and poked my chest. "An Italian in the building trades just has to be a mafioso, is that it, Sheridan? Jesus, your name ends in a vowel, you're mobbed up, right?"

"Of course not. Nobody said that."

137

"Damn right, of course not! What about Enrico Fermi? Was he a gangster? Or Giuseppe Verdi or Caruso?"

"Look, Mr. Florio, you're the one who insinuated you had a fix going to get Mrs. Kendall's land condemned, remember? That sounds a little shady to me."

"Fix?" He was perplexed. "So I use a little political juice to get a couple civil servants to vote my way on a lousy condemnation proceeding. This makes me Al Capone?"

Sal became noticeably irritated, particularly when Florio shot off his mouth about using "political juice." But Florio had too much momentum built up to stop there.

"Let me tell you something, Sheridan," he said. "You gotta give a little to get a little. It's a common business practice, that's all."

Right. Business is business and ethics are for losers. The end justifies the means. Come to think of it, there was another name ending in a vowel. Machiavelli.

"Look," I said. "I have a lot to do for the next couple of days. I'll have to get back to you next week."

"I gotta have an answer this week, Sheridan, c'mon. How about I stop by your place Wednesday?"

"Wednesday is no good," I said. Among other things, Michel Humbert was being interred on Wednesday.

"Okay, Thursday then. Say nine o'clock, your place." Florio hopped off his stool, pulling at Silent Sam's sleeve to hurry him out of the bar before I could argue.

"Nine in the morning, Sheridan," Florio barked at me as they went out the door. "And I won't take no for an answer."

CHAPTER 18

BARNETT'S Grill is a two-
story wood-frame building tucked in beside a transmis-
sion shop on Adams Lane, a short alleylike street running
off Mohaca Springs's main drag.

The inside of the tavern had the same shopworn look as
the gray-shingled exterior. A long mahogany bar at one
end of the room and a truncated Formica lunch counter at
the other end acted as parentheses for the dozen or so
scattered tables. Faded photos of an earlier Mohaca
Springs decorated the dark paneled walls and a green in-
door-outdoor carpet covered the floor but failed to hide
the warps and bumps.

It was slow when I walked in at eight o'clock. A stocky
young woman worked the bar, drawing beers for three old
men who looked as permanent as the milk-glass fixtures
hanging from the ceiling. In a lighted alcove at the back of
the room, two kids in jeans were shooting eight ball on an
undersized coin-operated pool table.

I ordered a cream ale from the bartender and asked
about the euchre tournament.

"In the back, in the party room." She pointed to a fire
door at the rear of the room.

The fire door opened onto a corridor. I walked past a pay phone and his and her restrooms and opened the glass door at the end of the hall. A red-faced man was sitting at a card table, counting dollar bills into a cigar box.

"Evening," he greeted me. "You bring a partner?"

"No, I came to watch a friend play."

"Oh, well, just come on in, then. No charge."

The party room was larger and newer than I expected. A fairly recent addition, I thought, as I took in the pine paneling and the dropped ceiling.

Two dozen card tables were set up in the center of the room, each filled with its quota of four players. Ralph and Kay Cramer were seated directly in front of me, matched against a pair of Grizzly Adams types wearing John Deere caps. A few tables over, the waiter from the Pinewood, Ruly Jackson, was slowly shuffling a twenty-four card euchre deck and gabbing with the three elderly men who shared his table.

I scanned the room for other familiar faces and spotted Tony Areno and one of his plainclothesmen. They had a fast moving game going with a fat guy who looked like Oliver Hardy and his skinny partner, who might have resembled Stan Laurel if you squinted and used a lot of imagination. Near the back of the room, standing behind a trestle table laden with Styrofoam coffee cups and bowls of potato chips, was the man with the salt-and-pepper hair. Standing immediately behind him and holding a large cardboard box was Roy Rossiter.

I grabbed a folding chair from a stack along the wall and sat down beside Ralph Cramer.

"Hi, Sheridan," Ralph greeted me. "Hey, Blackjack is here, like I said he'd be. You seen him?"

"Yeah, thanks. Say, Ralph, who's the guy in the back, the one in the red blazer?"

Ralph looked up from his cards and focused in on the man with the salt-and-pepper hair. "Oh, him?" He snorted. "That's Dick Penrose, town supervisor and a

140

horse's ass, you ask me. He's supposed to hand out the prizes later."

I watched the Cramers play for a few minutes. They were well ahead on points and Ralph had the deal. Kay called for hearts trump and was about to lay the coup de grace on the boys in the John Deere caps when I noticed Ruly and his partner tossing in their cards and getting up to stretch before starting the next match in the round-robin tournament.

I excused myself and got up to follow Jackson. He was next to an open window, lighting a cigarette, when I caught up to him and introduced myself.

"You're the young fellow was with Mr. Humbert up to the Pinewood t'other day," he said slowly, crinkling his eyes at me. "Ralph say you wanted to talk at me 'bout somethin'."

"I'm trying to get a line on Humbert, what kind of guy he was," I said, not sure how to explain. "It has to do with a business deal we were discussing before he died."

"I don't much like talkin' ill of the dead."

"I just asked for your impression of Humbert, Mr. Jackson. Good or bad."

"Yeah, I know what you axed me," he said. "But I figure you mean did he fool around with womens and the like."

"Did he?"

"Not at the Pinewood. Oh, he'd get hisself high sometimes and make a little scene, maybe. But he didn't do no heavy breathin', leastwise not at the Pinewood."

"Not at the Pinewood," I repeated. "But maybe someplace else? Is that what you mean?"

"I don't mean nothin'." He shook his head. "Oh, I hear stuff, too, you know, 'bout fancy white boys and all. But I don't go spreadin' rumors. That ain't my way."

"Rumors about Humbert and fancy white boys?"

"That ain't up to me to say," Jackson said, tossing away his cigarette. "I gotta get back for the next game."

141

Jackson returned to his table, leaving me standing there with a dissatisfied frown. The room was growing noisy and filling up with cigarette smoke as pairs of card players continuously changed opponents. Dick Penrose was still standing behind the trestle table, watching the crowd and smiling the predatory smile of politicians and used-car salesmen. I looked around for Roy Rossiter, but he was gone.

I worked my way across the room to Areno's table. He and his partner, the plainclothes detective, were paired up against a man and woman, Laurel and Hardy having moved on to another table.

"Hello, Tony," I said, taking a chair next to Areno. "I'm surprised to see you here. I thought J.D. would have you out chasing leads."

"Leads? You gotta be kiddin', Sheridan," Areno snorted as he shuffled the deck. "We don't have any damn leads."

He dealt the cards with a nimbleness that belied his slow manner and stubby hands. When he was finished, he turned up the opening trump card, the ten of clubs.

"By me," said the little man to Areno's left.

"Same here, partner," said Plainclothes, giving Areno a meaningful shrug.

"Pass," agreed the chunky woman on Areno's right.

Areno turned the ten of clubs facedown and said to the man on his left, "Me neither, Billy. Name your poison."

"Nope, I can't call trump." Billy shook his head.

"By me, too, I guess." Plainclothes nodded.

"Hearts," the woman declared cautiously, adding, "with a little help from my partner."

"Hearts it is," Areno said, leading off with the ace of diamonds. Billy followed suit with the queen, followed by the nine of clubs from Plainclothes and the king of diamonds from the lady.

"That's one for the good guys," Areno crowed as he raked in the trick. He led off again, this time with the king of spades. The others followed suit, Plainclothes capturing the trick with the ace.

"C'mon, Esther, for Christ sake," Billy groaned. "You're the one called hearts trump."

Plainclothes led back with the queen of clubs. Esther, looking determined, trumped him with the ten of hearts. Areno flipped out the ace of clubs and Billy offsuited with the nine of diamonds.

"Now you're cooking, Esther," said Billy.

Esther led with the left bower, the jack of diamonds. Areno, no trump cards in his hand, offsuited with the ten of diamonds. Billy followed trump with the queen of hearts, and all three turned to look at Plainclothes, who was grinning like the Cheshire cat.

"Ta da," Plainclothes intoned, stylishly tossing on the table the jack of hearts.

"Hah! Way to go, partner," Areno said. "That's a euchre and that means the game."

"Esther, how in hell can you call for hearts trump when you don't have the right bower?" Billy lamented.

"I had the ace and the left." Esther pouted. "Told ya I needed a little help from my partner, didn't I?"

"Yeah, well," Areno cut in, "anyway, you owe us each a buck and a half to cover the side bets. Nice work, Koenig." He winked at Plainclothes.

Billy and Esther paid up, stood up and walked off, each grumbling about the other's shortcomings at cards. I smiled at Areno and said, "Tony, an officer of the law making side bets at a neighborhood euchre tournament? I thought gambling was illegal."

He laughed. "Yeah, but playing those two isn't gambling. It's stealing." He took a swig of beer from a clear plastic cup. "So, what brings you here tonight, Sheridan? Slumming or just lonely?"

"I'm trying to absorb some of the local culture," I said. "I bet you'd like some of your card-playing luck to rub off on your murder investigation."

"Shit, you don't know the half of it."

"Which half is that?"

143

Areno looked over at his partner. "Hey, Koenig, why don't you go get us some beers."

"Sure, Chief," Koenig said, picking up the loose bills from the table. When he was out of earshot, Areno turned back to me.

"Wait'll you hear this," he said quietly. "Amos and J.D. had a big argument this afternoon about something, right? I don't know about what, but I could hear 'em going at it in J.D.'s office. So then Amos comes storming out and he tells me that from now on, he's running the Dugan-Humbert investigation himself and I should deal only with him."

"Where's that leave J.D.?"

"That's what I wanted to know, so I went in J.D.'s office and asked him. He says Amos took him off the case, just like that, and assigned him strictly to administrative duties until further notice. Can you believe it?" He fanned the deck of cards absently. "Christ, with Amos heading the investigating team, we'll never catch this loony tune. Hell, Amos hasn't run an investigation in fifteen years."

"What the hell can Skelly be thinking of?" I asked. "Did J.D. tell you why the sheriff dumped him?"

"Nope. He just said Amos was in charge of the investigation now and I should just follow orders."

I wondered if J.D. had gone to Skelly with what I had told him, about seeing Florio and Penrose and Skelly together that night. Maybe it wasn't as innocent as J.D. had thought, and maybe Skelly decided it was time to stonewall the murder investigation. And the best way to do that would be to take J. D. Staub out of the picture. But I didn't want to go into all that with Areno, so I changed the subject, picking up on something he'd said earlier.

"Tony, you said the killer was a loony tune."

He nodded glumly. "Yeah. So what?"

"What if the killer isn't a nut? I mean, couldn't he be a professional, just doing a job for someone?"

"What, a hit man? You mean like a mob contract?"

"Possibly," I said. "There have been rumors that Florio, the land developer, could be connected."

"So he has your uncle and Humbert whacked over this business deal he was trying to swing?" Areno ruminated for a few seconds. "I guess it's an angle worth looking into, but I don't figure this for a mob hit."

"Why not?"

"Well, it just ain't, I don't know, splashy enough for the mob, you know? I mean, wise guys are into overkill, like car bombings and stuff. Hit men don't use knives." He paused as Koenig returned with the beers. Picking up a glass, Areno took a sip and added, "Knives are strictly for loony tunes, broads, and fags."

Loony tunes, broads, and fags. I kept going over what Tony had said as I drove home to the cottage. He was right; the killings did lack the usual flair of a mob hit. Still, if Florio and his shadowy backers were behind it, they wouldn't want to advertise their involvement. So why not make it look as if a knife-wielding psychotic was on the loose? But how did they get Humbert alone up on Beedle Road Extension? Humbert's body showed signs of recent sexual activity, but how—if at all—did that figure in?

I passed the Kendall house—no lights were on—and gently pumped the brakes while I strained to locate the entrance to my driveway. The night was dark and moonless, a heavy cloud cover obscuring the starlight.

Cruising slowly, I found the graveled effluence of the driveway and wheeled the Horizon to the right. The headlights swept across the lawn and the darkened cottage for only an instant, but it was long enough. A large stocky figure was standing in the backyard, next to the bulkhead door that covered the well pump.

I nosed the Horizon to the left, slammed on the brakes, and jumped out of the car. The figure, head and shoulders still in darkness, stood motionless, like a deer temporarily mesmerized by the headlights. Cradled in the intruder's arms was a large bundle.

"Okay, hold it right there," I called out as I advanced onto the dewy grass.

To be truthful, I was hoping he wouldn't hold it right there. I wanted him to be as afraid of me as I was of him, so that he'd turn and run off in the other direction. Instead, he ran straight at me, a silent juggernaut, the bundle clutched to his chest until the final moment, when he suddenly thrusted it at me like a huge bean bag.

"Oooofff." I had braced for his charge, but it was no contest. He ran over me without breaking stride, the New York Giants versus the Maryknoll Sisters. I landed on my back in the high grass, all the air slammed out of my lungs. Only a few seconds passed before I could catch my breath and stand up, but it was too long. I could hear heavy feet pounding away down the road, deeper into the inky night. A moment later a car door banged, an engine whined, and I could see a pair of red taillights receding up the highway.

I watched until the lights disappeared, then tried to calm the trembling in my legs. My back was wet with dew and my pride was crushed, but other than that, I was unmarked.

I turned toward the cottage then and almost stumbled over the bulky battering ram my antagonist had used to flatten me. I nudged it carefully with a toe, then I dragged it into the light provided by the Horizon and read the label.

I had been steamrollered with a fifty-pound sack of insecticide.

CHAPTER 19

FIRST thing in the morning, I inspected the well pump. I thought I'd arrived home in time—the bag of insecticide the intruder left behind was unopened—but it doesn't hurt to make sure.

I flipped back the wood bulkhead door and climbed down into the tiny subterranean pumphouse. As far as I could tell, the pump and its numerous galvanized appendages hadn't been tampered with. The only footprints on the muddy concrete floor were my own. Whoever had tried to pollute the cottage's water supply had run off before he could do any damage. Except to my psyche, I thought, as I returned to the cottage.

"Somebody in this burg doesn't want us to stick around, William." I sighed as I filled the coffee maker. The cat was lying in a patch of sun on the kitchen floor, uninterested.

While I waited for my coffee to brew, I went into the living room and put on a cassette. It was loud enough to send William scurrying to the bedroom for sanctuary. Jackson Browne reverberated through the house, "Running On Empty." It was a fitting anthem for me that Tuesday morning. Things were happening, things that I couldn't understand, and I was inexorably caught up in them like a man riding out a flood.

I wandered around the living room, dust rag in hand. One by one, I wiped down the knicknacks on the hutch. Dusting completed, I filled an empty Windex bottle with water and spritzed the hanging plants. Then I tossed the old newspapers into the trash and ran the vacuum cleaner through the house, chasing several dust bunnies and one irritated cat out from under my bed in the process.

It was a stall tactic, this housekeeping fit of mine. The fact was, I had a long day ahead and more questions to be asked, but I wasn't in the mood. What I really wanted to do was to forget everything for twenty-four hours, stay home, and fish the calm lake waters. But I knew I wouldn't.

The Quincy County Sheriff's department is headquartered just off Main Street in Geneva in a curious hodgepodge of a building; half Gothic cut stone and gargoyles, half tinted glass and structural steel. The squad room and administrative offices occupy the modern half, while jail cells and holding tanks comprise the bulk of the original edifice.

I gave my name to an efficient female deputy who cleared me on the intercom and then directed me down a long civil-service-green hallway to the last door on the left.

J. D. Staub was seated at his desk, his long thin face looking even longer and thinner as he stared morosely at an in-basket overflowing with yellow and white sheets of paper.

He glanced up. "Sheridan. Have a seat. What's new?" His voice packed all the tone of a ten-dollar guitar.

"Not much. I caught some guy trying to poison my well with a sack of insecticide last night, but other than that, nothing's new. What's new with you?"

"Wait a minute." He seemed to be hearing me through

a seven-second time delay, like on radio. "Somebody tried to . . . Did you see who it was?"

"Too dark. He laid me out with the bag of bug killer and took off. No harm done," I added, "to me or the well."

"Son of a bitch. You want me to send a man out to the cottage to check things out?"

"I'd rather you tell me what's going on between you and the sheriff."

"You do get around, don't you," he said.

I shrugged. "I hear Skelly took you off the case."

Staub leaned back in his chair, studied the arrest reports piled on his desk, and sighed. "You asked the other day why I put up with Amos, remember? I told you it was a long story and maybe I'd tell you someday if I was in the mood. Well, I guess I'm in the mood now." He sat up straight, arms behind his head. "I started here twenty-nine years ago, signing on when I got out of the service, after Korea. I was an M.P. in the army and I figured that would give me an edge getting into police work. That and belonging to the right political party.

"Anyway, I had a good background from the army, my people were all registered Republicans, and I got high marks on the civil-service exam. So I became a deputy. Amos was in his second term then, very popular. And why not? Things were quiet, not much crime; it was pretty much a closed community. Didn't take much to be sheriff then."

He stopped long enough to strip and light a cigar.

"The department was a lot smaller. Everybody knew everybody else; it was homey. I did my patrols, chasing speeders, jiggling door handles, that sort of thing. And I took night courses in sociology and police science at the community college, figuring to get ahead that way."

He blew a smoke ring across the desk. It caught a draft from the air conditioner and floated to the ceiling.

"One day, after I'd been with the department for four

149

years, I happened to do something that caught Amos Skelly's attention. There'd been a rash of car thefts, all stolen from dealerships here and in the three surrounding counties. Based on the patterns of the thefts and the delivery schedules for new car shipments to the dealerships, I had a notion where the thieves might strike next. So I took my idea to Amos. We staked out this one place for three days, but the jokers finally hit it, and we nailed them.

"After that, I was on my way. I was promoted to detective junior grade, then full shield, then chief of detectives, all under the protective wing and approving eye of the old man. About ten years ago, when the previous undersheriff retired—he was eight years younger than Amos, I should add—I became the new second in command."

He prodded the air with the cigar stub. "I deserved each and every promotion, Sheridan, don't get me wrong. But I'm enough of a realist to know I wouldn't have made it this far if Amos hadn't backed me all the way."

I said, "So the man is a good judge of talent, and smart enough to hang on to anyone who makes him look good."

"Yeah, until yesterday anyway."

"What happened yesterday?"

"I'm getting to that," he said, motioning for me to have patience. "Before the last election for sheriff, I sat down to have a serious talk with Amos. There was scuttlebutt around the department at the time that maybe Amos should step down and I should run, seeing how he was seventy years old. I didn't initiate the talk, but I heard it. And I have to admit, I liked what I heard. So I went to Amos about it. He asked me to hang on, back him for another term. In return, he promised to bow out this year and endorse me for the job."

"And yesterday he had a change of heart," I said.

Staub nodded. "He came in here all worked up about the murder investigation, complaining how having a big unsolved case made him look bad. And jeopardized his reelection."

He flipped a cigar ash off into the wastebasket.

"So I called him on his promise to me." His face was stony, but I could hear the hurt in his voice. "He acted like I was crazy, like he didn't know what I was talking about. He accused me of plotting behind his back to run against him. Well, I let him have it. I told him how it felt to spend twenty-odd years cleaning up after him while he kissed ass on the local banquet circuit."

"And he retaliated by taking you off the case?"

"Yes. He assigned me to doing paperwork because he didn't want me to get the limelight. Says he can crack the case without me." He paused a half-beat. "That's when I gave my resignation. I'm gone at the end of this month."

That was a news flash I hadn't anticipated, although I should have. Even a dog can get his fill of leftovers. And J. D. Staub was no dog.

"What will you do now, J.D.?" I asked. "You plan to challenge Skelly in the primary, I hope."

"No. Why should I? He's got these voters in the palm of his hand. He has had for thirty years."

"But he's incompetent. And too old to get any better. You could defeat him on the age question alone."

He shook his head. "I don't need this anymore. I'll be fifty-five next week. That qualifies me for a full pension."

"You're just going to retire?" I stood up. "What about this department? Who's going to keep it running the way it should be run? Skelly? And don't forget Uncle Charlie, J.D. Or don't you give a damn anymore who killed him?"

Staub ground his cigar to a stub in a metal ashtray on the desk and looked up at me, his voice calm now. "I still care, Sheridan. I told you, I'll be here until the end of the month. If Tony feels he needs to talk to me about the case, we'll talk. But other than that, I'm out of it."

I walked to the door, then turned. "Yeah," I said. "I guess that says it all."

Tony Areno reminded me of an over-the-hill fullback, as I watched him quickstep his way through a maze of scattered tables and chairs in the squad room. He was aiming toward his desk in one corner of the room, a manila folder clenched in his fist. I was able to get the angle on him, intercepting him just before he touched down in his chair.

"Hi, Chief," I said. "How'd the tournament turn out last night?"

"Not too bad." Areno said, tossing the folder on the skewed pile already obliterating ninety percent of the desktop. "We took second place overall, good for twenty-five bucks and a tin trophy. We picked up another ten or twelve bucks on side bets."

"Who took first prize?"

"Ah, a couple of old geezers from down around Watkins Glen. I think they were using signals." He squatted on one corner of the desk and hitched his pants. "So, you been in to talk to J.D.?"

"Yeah."

"How'd it go? He tell you anything?"

"Yeah. Did you know he's resigning, effective at the end of the month?"

"I heard about it this morning." He wagged his head from side to side, then carefully scoped out the newly vacant squad room. "I can't believe Amos would stick it to J.D. like this," he said, his voice subdued.

"You know about the reason for the argument, the election thing and all?"

"I heard rumors. That was it, huh? Amos won't step aside for J.D.?"

I nodded. "And J.D. won't run against him."

Areno pivoted off the desk and plopped down in his chair. "Just between you and me and the lamp post, J.D. would get just about every vote in this department if he did run, including mine."

"Maybe you should tell him that."

He shrugged his heavy shoulders. "Maybe I will."

"How's the investigation going? Anything turn up?"

"I thought we might have something this morning, but it didn't turn out to be much use."

"What was that?"

"Look, Sheridan, I like you and all that. You're a good kid, far as I can tell, but if Amos found out I was passing out information on this investigation to you . . ."

"Come on, Tony. You said it wasn't anything useful."

He checked again for eavesdroppers, found none, and relaxed. "One of my guys got a name last night from a part-time bartender at the Lakeside Inn, a guy named Peterson. He says he was going off shift Saturday night about a quarter to nine and he sees a silver Mercedes idling in the back of the parking lot. I don't know if you've seen the Lakeside, but they don't get too many Mercedes in their lot."

"I've been there," I said.

"Yeah, well then you know what I mean. Anyway, this guy Peterson was on his way to his car to go home when he sees the Mercedes. He says he didn't recognize Humbert, but he did know the guy who was sitting in the passenger seat. A kid named Randy Fenzik."

"Have you brought him in yet?"

"Yeah, we sent a squad car down to his folk's place in Mohaca Springs first thing this morning, brought him in for questioning. He admitted to being with Humbert Saturday night. He says Humbert picked him up hitchhiking and gave him a lift to the Lakeside. After that, the kid says Humbert took off again. Claimed he had a business meeting to go to."

"You have the kid next door now, Tony?"

"Uh huh, but not for long. We're releasing him."

"Just like that?"

"What am I going to do with him? We checked out his story. Koenig talked to two people who swear they saw Fenzik at the Lakeside Saturday night after nine and that he stayed late. Besides, it turns out the kid works at the winery, so his story about Humbert giving him a ride makes sense."

"I'd like to see him."

"Well, you better hurry, then," Areno said. "He's being cleared over at the booking desk right now."

I crossed the squad room on a diagonal and rushed down a short hallway that connected the new building to the old. The booking desk is located in what once was the central foyer of the old building. I was a little late.

"What happened to the Fenzik kid?" I asked the desk sergeant. He gave me a bellicose stare, so I added, "Chief Areno told me I'd find him here."

"Oh." He looked up at the big Elgin wall clock. "You missed him by about four minutes."

"Did you have someone run him back home?"

"No, he said he didn't want a lift." The sergeant shrugged. "He just walked out, heading toward Main."

CHAPTER 20

I SPOTTED him twenty minutes later standing at the junction of South Main and West Lake Road, wagging his thumb in the direction of Mohaca Springs. He was wearing faded jeans, a T-shirt with a Billy Idol decal on the front, and a sullen expression that seemed to typify a generation of self-proclaimed punks.

"Hey, thanks, man," he said as he climbed into the passenger's seat. It was a different persona today, removed from the burgundy blazer and studied articulation of the tour spiel. "You going as far as Mohaca Springs?"

"Sure thing," I said, adding casually, "You're Randy, from the winery, aren't you?"

"Yeah. Do I know you?"

"I was in one of your tour groups the other day. My name is Sheridan."

"Oh, yeah, right. I remember now." He stared straight ahead, seemingly fascinated by the view through the Horizon's dusty windshield. Curiosity would never kill this cat.

"I was just in to see Chief Areno. He tells me he had you in for questioning this morning, Randy. Did they give you a hard time?"

155

"Hard enough," he said warily. "What's it to you?"

"Charlie Dugan was my uncle."

"Look," he said, swiveling around to face me. "I told the cops I don't know anything about those murders. Okay? I just happened to catch a ride with Mr. Humbert Saturday night, that's all."

"Relax, Randy. I'm not out to do you any harm," I said as I rummaged through the tape caddy resting on the seat between us. I picked out an Elvis Costello recording and inserted it into the cassette deck, turning the volume low. "But I do have a couple of questions you could help me with."

"What questions?" he asked.

"I understand Teddy Kendall was a good friend of yours. You worked together at the winery."

"Yeah, we were friends." He took a crumpled pack of Kools from his pants pocket and depressed the cigarette lighter in the dash. "He was about the only friend I had in high school."

"That was a tragedy, his suicide," I said. "His mother took it very hard, I understand."

"You must be shitting me," he snorted. "He never would have done it if that bitch didn't treat him like dirt."

"Lots of teenagers think their parents are tough on them because they don't love them. Usually, they're wrong."

"Yeah, well, not this time." He touched the lighter to his cigarette and puffed a series of shallow drags. "She was always telling Teddy he was going to hell, just like his old man. She used to say he was born wicked and he'd die wicked and that if he didn't love Jesus and pray all the time like she did, he'd burn. She was always preaching at him."

"What did Teddy do that got her so convinced he was going to hell?" I asked.

"Not a fuckin' thing! That's what was driving him up

156

the wall! I mean, she didn't want him going out at night, to dances or parties or anything. She didn't want him to bring anybody home. She didn't even want him to work at the winery at first, because they make alcohol there. 'A den of iniquity' she called it."

"That's pretty extreme," I agreed. "But maybe she was worried about the company he was keeping."

"What . . ." he started to ask, then lapsed into a brooding silence.

I tried again. "Look, I'm not interested in gossip, but I am interested in finding out what happened to my uncle and I think Teddy's suicide ties in somehow."

"You think . . ." He stopped and turned back to the view out the windshield. "Hey, I'm sorry about your uncle, but I didn't know the man, okay? Your giving me a lift doesn't mean I gotta play twenty questions."

I didn't particularly like having to prod the kid's personal demons, but I didn't have much choice. There were things I needed to know and I was willing to bet Randy Fenzik could tell me. Circumstances had led me back to the angular young tour guide; circumstances that made it essential I dig into things that were none of my business. I'd met other teenagers like Randy. They protected themselves from an adult world they didn't fully understand by building a carapace around their emotions; a hard shell of cynicism and bravado designed to keep fear and confusion and disappointment at bay. Sometimes the only way to break open that shell was to hit it hard, over and over, until the shattered pieces fell away and the person hiding inside emerged.

I switched off the tape player and stared at my passenger. "Not twenty questions, Randy. Just one. The rumors about you and Teddy Kendall, are they true?"

"I don't wanna hear about any bullshit rumors!" He sat up, rigid, the cigarette sticking from his clenched fist like a weapon. "Just let me off here. I don't need this."

"Then what about Michel Humbert, Randy?" I was winging it now, playing a hunch. "Is that bullshit, too?"

"Michel?" He turned toward me, face flushed. "How'd you—?" Then he broke off again and looked away. "You're not a cop. What gives you the right?"

"You and Teddy and Humbert." I recited it like a mantra, then added quietly, "Two men are dead, Randy. That's all the justification I can give you."

A fragile silence filled up the car and began nagging at me like a backseat driver. I began to think I had played it all wrong, pushing him into a reticence I wouldn't be able to crack. Then, slowly, he started to let it out.

"I still don't see how Teddy figures into any of it." He sighed as he reached over and ground out his cigarette in the console's ashtray. "Or me and Michel, for that matter."

"I don't know either, Randy," I said, eyes on the road. "I'm just trying to cover all the possibilities."

"I guess"—he shrugged, then continued softly—"you don't know what it's like in a little town like Mohaca Springs. I mean, if you've got different feelings than everybody else." He looked at me, an ember of defiance still smoldering in his eyes. "I'm gay, okay? I'm not ashamed of it anymore. I'm not alone. I know that now."

"Was Teddy. . . ?"

"It wasn't like that." He shook his head. "We . . . experimented a little, I guess is the word. But Teddy wasn't . . . he was undecided about himself. Couldn't commit either way, you know? He was my friend, that's all."

"And Michel Humbert?"

He gave up a small resigned smile. "Yeah, Michel was a player. Almost wiped me out when I found that out. I mean, who would've figured? He's one of the big deals in this town, right? Got a fancy wife, a big rep as a ladies' man." He was animated now, his hands punctuating every word. "I ran into him up in Geneva one night and he said he'd give me a ride home. He was a little high, on booze I mean. Man, when he started coming on to me it was like . . . a revelation, you know?"

I nodded.

"After that," he went on, "we got together once in a while, nothing regular. Sometimes he'd bring some weed for me. But it didn't have anything to do with my job at the winery. I got that on my own, before I knew about Michel."

"Did the two of you ever drive up to Beedle Road?"

"Yeah, we went there sometimes. But, listen, we didn't go up there Saturday night. I mean, it happened like I told the cops. He saw me in town and I asked him for a ride up to the Lakeside. That was it."

"He didn't say where he was going from there?"

"No, only that he had a little 'moonlight business meeting' to go to. That's exactly what he said. So I figured maybe he had something lined up. But, hey, that was okay with me. All I was looking for was a ride."

We passed by the cottage and the Kendall farm. I turned Elvis Costello on again and continued driving toward Mohaca Springs.

"What about Teddy?" I asked. "You both worked for Humbert. Did he ever come on to Teddy?"

"I think he hit on him once. Teddy wouldn't talk about it, but I'm pretty sure they got together one time. At least, Michel hinted that they did."

"Why wouldn't Teddy tell you about it, Randy?"

He shrugged. "Like I said, Teddy wasn't really sure what he wanted. He was always serious and . . . mixed-up kinda, 'specially since his old man took off."

"Did Teddy talk to you about his father?"

"Not much. He told me he couldn't understand why he ran out on him like that, that's all."

"When was the last time you saw Teddy?"

"I guess it was about four days before he . . . you know. We stopped off in town for a sandwich after work on a Friday night. I didn't see him after that. He didn't go to

159

school on Monday, and he called in sick for work. Next day they found him in the barn."

"Who found him?"

"I don't know. Crazy Maevis, I guess. Anyway, she called the cops and that was that."

"And you don't know why he did it," I said.

"Like I told you, he was really mixed-up. And his old lady was always on his case." He shrugged.

We were into the village now. Randy asked me to drop him at the end of his street.

"My parents are pissed about me being picked up this morning. I'd just as soon they didn't see you, no offense."

"That's fine with me. What about your job? Don't you have to go to work?"

"Mrs. Humbert canceled all the public tours until after the funeral. I'm off until next week."

I pulled over to the curb at the head of a quiet residential street a few blocks west of Main. Randy got out of the car, then leaned back in again.

"Listen, Sheridan, about what I told you . . ."

"Like I said, I'm not out to cause any trouble."

"Well . . . thanks." He nodded once and headed up the street. I drove down a block, turned left, and backtracked to Main. It was getting late. On the way through the village, I stopped at the bait shop near the Big M market and bought some crayfish. They came in a square white carton, like Chinese takeout food. I checked the inside of the carton before paying the counter man. All six of the little lobsterlike crustaceans were alive and active.

The drive back to the cottage was easy. Traffic was light and what cars there were on the road hadn't heard of speed limits. I slowed as I pulled abreast of the Kendall place. Maevis's Dodge wasn't parked in the driveway.

I pulled into my own drive and hurried into the cottage to change, slipping on a pair of cutoffs and a worn set of tennis shoes. Picking up the carton of crayfish, I went outside to the storage shed near the dock. The old metal minnow bucket I was looking for was resting atop a case of motor oil. Dumping the contents of the carton into the bucket, I headed down to the edge of the cove.

"Ahhhh!" I exclaimed as I dipped first one, then both feet into the water. It was cold this early in the summer, a frigid reminder of New York's harsh winters. The mucky bottom sucked at my feet as I worked my way around the perimeter of the cove. The water was shallow along the rim of the cove, only up to my knees in most spots, but the consistency of the mud seemed to change with every step. I had to keep my toes curled tight to keep from losing a sneaker.

Eventually, bucket in hand, I made it to the Kendall side of the cove. Slowly, bent in half like a coolie in a rice paddy, I waded the length of the shoreline, pushing back cattails and clearing the muddy water with one hand as I went. The floor of the cove was the same here as along the other side. Plenty of mud and muck, virtually no rocks.

I moved farther out into the cove, the water rising nearly to my crotch, and worked my way back in the same coolie fashion. The muck was still there, oozing from beneath my shoes to cloud the surface. I waded half the length of the Kendall shoreline before I literally stumbled across the submerged rock that my boat had struck two days earlier. I went down, one knee in the muck, the one bucketless hand plunging into the water. I steadied myself, then began feeling around the rock for the old piece of anchor chain my line had snagged. Just as my freezing digits were about to fall off, I latched on to a few rusty links and began to tug.

Beeeeeeeep!

"Uh-oh." I dropped the chain and looked over at the farm. Maevis Kendall's sedan swept down the driveway, horn blaring, and jerked to a halt. Out of it on the fly came Crazy Maevis, her slate hair floating in her wake.

"Didn't I tell you to stay off my property, mister?" She stormed to the edge of the cove.

"Well, yes, but I . . ."

"Have you heard of property rights, mister? Do you know that property rights are sacred?"

"Look, I was just . . ." I began again.

"I could shoot you for trespassing, do you believe that? Or don't you believe in anything?"

"Hallelujah!" I screamed at the top of my lungs. It produced the desired effect. She stopped yelling at me for a second, long enough for me to get a word in.

"All I was doing, Mrs. Kendall, was collecting some crayfish for bait." I smiled, innocent as a choirboy.

"Aren't no crayfish in this cove."

"Sure there are." I angled the bucket so she could look into it. "See?"

She sniffed at the bucket, unconvinced. "You best be off my land by the time I get back with my scattergun, mister," she hissed. Then she turned and double-timed to the house, slamming the door behind her.

I made my back along the perimeter of the cove and stepped up onto terra firma. Six ravenous leeches were dining on my calves and thighs. Dropping the bucket, I ran to the cottage and grabbed a box of kitchen matches from the mantel. Once outside, I began burning off the ugly parasites one at a time. William crawled out from under the deck and strolled over to watch, just as the last leech loosened its hold and dropped on the lawn.

"You know, William," I said, "I wouldn't send anyone back to live with that old crone. Not even a cat."

He stared at me for a moment, then padded up to the porch and began scratching the hell out of the front door.

Chapter 21

If a woman hasn't got a tiny streak of the harlot in her, she's a dry stick as a rule.

That's according to D. H. Lawrence, who should know. Ordinarily, I don't accept other people's rules at face value but I had to admit, Maevis Kendall fit comfortably into that aphorism. And, for opposing reasons, so did Sorrel Brown.

We arrived at the Pinewood at eight o'clock and were seated, at my request, in the small library-cum-dining room where Humbert and I had eaten lunch on Saturday.

"You're spoiling me, Sheridan," Sorrel said as the waiter handed out the menus. "Most of my dates think a big night out is dinner at a Ponderosa."

She was wearing a white sun dress with lacy short sleeves and a scooped neckline that had nearly cost me my composure when I first saw her standing at the cottage door. It was having a similar effect on the other male diners, who stared openly while the maître d' led us to our table.

"Any night with you is a big night," I said, somehow not feeling the least bit foolish.

"You're not too hard to take, either," she smiled.

For awhile, I forgot all about dead men and killers and relaxed into the pleasure of being somewhere special with an attractive mature woman, a woman who didn't hold back her emotions like they were the hole card in a game of stud poker. Too many of the women I had known had treated a simple date as if it was a sort of contract negotiation. A fifty-dollar dinner was a standard perk.

We talked and laughed our way through cocktails, appetizers and soup, Sorrel detailing the tribulations of waitressing, while I countered with the trauma of writing on deadline. By the time the waiter brought on the main course, we had moved on from a mishandled one-nighter to something warmer and more comfortable.

"Mmmm, this is wonderful," she said, tasting the veal marsala. "How's the lamb?"

"Simply marvelous, as Julia Child would say."

"You know, Sheridan, when Ralph heard we were going out tonight, he made me promise to pump you for all the dirt on the murder investigation."

I took another bite of the lamb. "Ralph's a nice old guy, but he tends to overdo the Philip Marlowe bit."

She grinned. "Mystery novels and whodunits on the late show are his passion, not including lake trout."

"Actually, he's been helpful to me," I admitted. "I haven't been able to put all the bits of information I've picked up into anything concrete. But without folks like Ralph, I wouldn't even have the bits themselves."

"Well, don't let it get you down." She patted my arm. "And, whatever you do, be careful, Sheridan. I know you want to find out what happened to your uncle. But you could be putting yourself in danger, and it's not worth that."

"Don't worry," I said. "Uncle Charlie would probably tell me the same thing. 'Never go looking for trouble and never turn down a pretty girl or a free drink.' That was his motto. He was quite a character."

"I never really knew him, I'm sorry to say," she said.

"He came into the diner once in a while, of course, but he was just a face in the crowd, you know?"

Uncle Charlie would be sad if he heard that, wherever he was. He had always done his best to leave an impression with every pretty woman who crossed his path, and Sorrel was certainly the type to catch his eye. But then, even Ted Williams struck out once in a while.

"Listen, Sorrel," I began as I refilled our wineglasses. "I don't mean to bring up any sore points, but I wonder if you'd mind answering a few questions for me. About Roy Rossiter, for one."

She sipped her wine before answering. "All right."

"Good. First, do you know what kind of car he drives?"

"He doesn't. He drives a pickup truck."

"What color is it?"

"Umm, I guess you'd call it forest green. Dark green, anyway. Why?"

"Because someone in a dark pickup truck harassed me on the road down from Geneva the other night."

"And you think it was Roy?"

"It occurred to me. Among other things, he probably resents me for taking out his girl."

"I am not Roy Rossiter's girl," she huffed. "And I told him so the other day, after that stupid scene at the Lakeview. Not that I should've had to. God, you go out with a guy a couple of times and he thinks he owns you."

"Well, anyway, he can't be too pleased about my cutting in on him. Tell me," I said, "what's Rossiter's connection with Dick Penrose, if any?"

"The town supervisor? The guy who likes to wear white shoes and matching belts?"

I laughed. "That's the guy."

"Well, I don't really know. . . . Oh, I guess you could say Roy works for Penrose, in a way. Roy drives the snowplow for the town in the winter, which sort of makes Penrose his boss. And it's possible that Roy works odd jobs or seasonal work at Penrose's business, like he does for Humbert Winery and a few other local businesses."

"What business is Penrose in, outside of politics?"

"He owns a farm-supply store in the village," Sorrel said. "But what's Dick Penrose got to do with anything?"

"I don't know yet," I said, which was mostly true. "Look, Sorrel, would you mind if I bounced a few other names off you, just to get your comments? Then I promise I'll leave you alone."

"Well, I wouldn't want you to promise that." She squeezed my leg under the table. "But, all right, a few more questions. Then you finish your dinner before it gets cold."

"I promise. First name, Teddy Kendall."

"Teddy Kendall?" Her face dropped. "Why do you want to poke around into that poor kid's life? Didn't he have to put up with enough grief when he was alive?"

"I don't know," I said. "Did he?"

She looked disappointed in me. "This investigative reporting thing really gets sleazy sometimes, doesn't it."

It was a rhetorical question, but I answered it anyway.

"When you set out to dig something up, Sorrel, you have to figure that you'll get your hands dirty." I nodded. "Yes, it's sleazy to solicit gossip about a boy's suicide. But there's a possibility that Teddy had some connection to my uncle, and I have to find out what that was."

She shrugged her shoulders and sighed. "I think you're on the wrong track, but I'll give you what I have." She took a few seconds to organize her thoughts, then continued. "Let's see, what can I tell you about Teddy Kendall? Well, he was a local high school kid who used to come into the diner once in a while with a friend of his. He was a little short for his age and he had a mild case of acne, but he was kind of cute anyway. He was always polite and quiet—not like most of the teenagers that come in—and he impressed me as being intelligent, but too shy to express it." A frown pulled at the corners of her mouth. "I suppose everybody was as shocked as I was to hear he'd killed himself."

"The kid he came into the diner with, was it Randy Fenzik?" I asked.

"His name was Randy, but I don't know his last name," she said. "Tall, skinny. A little sullen, maybe?"

I nodded, "That's Fenzik. Did you ever pick up any rumors about the two boys being homosexuals?"

"No!" She was indignant again and the little frown tightened, as if it had just bitten down on something distasteful. "Is that what this is all about?"

"There was some talk that he might have been gay, that's all," I said lamely, not wanting to get into what Randy had said about Teddy and Michel Humbert.

"Talk from who?"

"Ralph, for one. He didn't really believe it himself, but he heard rumors to that effect after the kid died. From one of your co-workers, Sue Morris."

"Christ, Sheridan. Sue Morris? That bitchy little ditz?" Sorrel laughed derisively. "She barely made it out of high school herself, she's such a bubblehead. And a vicious gossip. I wouldn't believe a word out of her gum-snapping little mouth."

"She sounds like a winner," I said. "But why get so worked up about it?"

"I just hate people who try to make themselves more important by putting down others unfairly, that's all." She picked up her spoon and rubbed it back and forth across the tablecloth, calming herself in the process. "Sheridan, remember what it was like to be in high school, how cruel kids could be?"

"Sure. The cliques, the in-crowd. To be honest, I'd figure a beauty like you was one of the ins."

"The poor farmer's daughter? Forget it. White trash all the way. God, I used to dream I'd leave this town and make a success of myself, then come back to rub a few

167

high-and-mighty noses in it. But it didn't work out that way," she ended with a sigh.

"Hey, you took a shot, went out to Hollywood," I said. "You could still rub it in a little. Make up a couple stories, flash your old SAG card around for credibility."

"Flash my what?" she asked indignantly.

"Your Screen Actors Guild card."

"Oh. I'm afraid I never even got that far. The casting couch scared me off, remember?"

"Okay, so let's forget about the Sue Morrises of the world," I suggested. "Next question; what can you tell me about Maevis Kendall?"

Sorrel grinned slyly. "Uh-oh. Now you've backed me into a corner. It would take a Sue Morris to do justice to Maevis Kendall, from what I hear."

"Such as?"

"You know, the whole holier-than-thou trip. Like she invented Christianity herself and anybody who doesn't think the way she does is a heretic. If this was Salem three hundred years ago, she'd be the one carrying the matches."

"What about her husband, Ed? Did you know him?"

"Oh, yeah. Everybody knew poor Ed. He used to come into the diner all the time, up until he took off. He'd come staggering in every two weeks or so with a real snootful. We'd fill him up with coffee and send him home to Maevis and her fire and brimstone." She tilted her head to register her puzzlement. "You know, I asked him once why he even bothered to go home to her and you know what he said? 'I have to stay on for the boy's sake.' Makes you wonder what made him decide to finally desert them, doesn't it?"

"Yes, it does," I said. "But I have one more question, okay? And then we'll finish our meal."

"Fire away."

"Michel Humbert," I said flatly. "Your impressions."

"Another guy who could booze it up pretty good. And a toucher."

"A what?"

"A toucher. That's a name I use for guys who like to put their hands on a girl, like they're just being friendly. Only what they're really doing is trying to cop a feel."

"Michel Humbert was like that with you?"

She nodded. "And not just with me. He didn't come into the diner very often, but when he did, he usually had been drinking some and he tended to get friendly with the waitresses. Like we were supposed to get really turned on by him or something."

"And did he follow through with it?" I asked. "I mean, did any of the girls take him up on it?"

"Not that I know of." She shrugged. "I think everyone saw him as pretty much all talk and no action. A lot of married guys act like that when they're out on their own."

"Well, did he—" I began, but Sorrel cut me off.

"Uh, uh. You've had your 'one more question.' Time to finish our dinner." The accusing finger she had been pointing at me now reached over and tickled my ribs. "Don't you want to get back to your place? For dessert?"

Back at the cottage, there were no more questions. In fact, there were very few words of any kind.

I opened a chilled bottle of Liebfraumilch, which we drank while the Modern Jazz Quartet played on the stereo. We sat quietly, looking out at the moon and the lake, stirred by John Lewis's piano and our own vibes. After an hour or so, we adjourned to the bedroom and made another sort of music.

"Sheridan? Psst, Sheridan?"

"Mmmm?" I curled up defensively and wondered why someone was jabbing me with a blunt instrument.

"Sheridan, wake up."

"Wha. . . ?" I rolled over in the bed, languid, and blinked at the darkness. Sorrel was sitting up, her bare breasts protruding above the sheet.

"I heard something," she whispered. "A thump, kind of. Maybe your cat is trying to get in."

"William?" I muttered, then added a four-letter expletive and rolled over again.

"Well, I'm going to let him in, okay?"

She interpreted my grunt as an affirmative and slipped out of the bed. I heard the sound of a wire coat hanger clattering, followed by soft footfalls fading from the room. Like little cat feet, I thought dreamily, sliding back into the fog.

"Sheridan!" Sorrel shrieked out my name.

I leaped from bed and rushed into the living room, relief and confusion stopping me cold as I saw Sorrel standing transfixed by the front door. She was wearing one of my shirts, looking gorgeous and terrified at the same time. I was about to ask what was wrong when I saw for myself.

The heavy oak-batten door was swung halfway open. In its upper panel, just below the old brass knocker, a bone-handled fishing knife was sticking out chest-high, its six-inch blade gleaming coldly in the moonlight.

CHAPTER 22

A DRIZZLING rain shrouded the lake in mist. It was a lousy morning for a funeral.

I talked Sorrel into staying for breakfast; French toast Napoleon, my own recipe. It should have been romantic, and it might have played that way, if not for the memory of that stainless-steel blade plunged into my front door.

"You don't like the food?" I asked Sorrel, pointing to her nearly full plate.

"It's just that I'm not very hungry this morning." She pushed the plate away with finality. "I keep seeing that damn knife, Sheridan, thinking it could easily have been sticking out of you."

"I don't think so," I said. "I think someone was just leaving a message, trying to scare me." I shrugged and added flippantly, "Comes with the territory."

"God, spare me that gung ho crap, Sheridan," she snapped. "This isn't one of Ralph's paperback novels. The good guys don't automatically win in the end."

"They don't automatically lose, either." I stood and picked up my plate. "I guess I better feed that damn cat before he shreds the kitchen cabinets to splinters."

Sorrel left around ten o'clock, in a hurry to get home and change before starting work at eleven. Or maybe just in a hurry to get away from an ugly memory. The agitation was still there when she drove off, but her goodbye kiss had been warm and we had made a date for Thursday night, cheese fondue at her place. I pledged to bring the wine.

The fishing knife lay on the kitchen counter wrapped in a piece of wax paper. I planned to drop it off with Tony Areno when I could get around to it. Not that I expected anything to come of it. The other knives hadn't given up any fingerprints and this one probably wouldn't, either.

I was running hot water over our dirty dishes when the phone rang.

"Hello, is this, uh, Tim Sheridan?"

"Yes, what can I do for you?"

"Tim, my name is Ray Donafrio. I'm with the *Syracuse Times-Express*. I think Karen DeClair talked to you about a story I'm working on."

"Oh, right. You're putting together a piece about the contractors' scandal up there."

"Yeah. Karen called the other day and told me about you. She said you're looking into the knife murders down there and you thought there might be some connection with one of the guys I've been investigating."

"Possibly, yes. Gabriel Florio."

"Uh huh." His rich baritone voice sounded amused. "He's one of the boys, all right. I've managed to link him to a laundering operation the wise guys are running up here. Florio and half a dozen other contractors," he added.

"Listen, Ray, I wonder if you could give me a read on him. Just how deep is he into organized crime?"

"Well, deep enough to have gotten himself into some hot water, according to my sources. Apparently he's into the mob for a couple of hundred thousand. The way I heard it, they were looking to lay off some of the profits from their gambling operations with a few of the so-called legitimate businesses in the area. Florio had already been tied in with some bribes that various contractors had paid to local officials and some union types in order to get contracts for a big public-housing project up here. When that deal went under following a grand jury probe, Florio was hurting for cash, and the mob bosses knew it.

"Anyway, Florio started circulating this condo project of his, figuring he could get healthy fast if he could put the deal together. The wise guys probably thought it looked like a good way to launder some of the dough they bring in while at the same time putting the cash to work for them. Only it's been several months now and Florio still hasn't got the thing off the ground. So now, my source says the wise guys are starting to wonder where their cash has been going. I figure he's been using it for operating expenses all along, while trying to put together the condo deal on a wing and a prayer." He added, "And if he's trying to con these boys, he'll need all the prayers he can get."

That would explain why Florio was pushing so hard to buy up our land, Kendall's and mine. Two hundred thousand wasn't a lot of money to the mob, but that wasn't the point. You don't borrow from those gentlemen and then welsh on the deal. It sets a bad precedent and gets the boys upset. Which isn't a good thing to have happen when your arms and legs are the collateral on the loan.

"Tell me, Ray," I said. "In your investigation, have you run across a guy named Dick Penrose? He represents Mohaca Springs on the Quincy County Board of Supervisors. I think he's Florio's point man down here."

"No, I can't say that I have," Donafrio said. "But I'll sure run a check on him and see what I can turn up. A county supervisor, huh? That would be a plum for my story."

"How close are you to publishing?"

"Well, my editor wants to start the series on Sunday,

provided I can pull a few loose ends together over the next few days. This bit about Penrose might help."

"One more thing, Ray. A guy named Sal Minella. Ring any bells?"

"Sure does. Minella is a C.P.A. and his biggest clients are reputedly these same wise guys who're handing out the dirty money. Minella also happens to be Florio's brother-in-law, which is probably how Florio got involved in the first place. Gives 'family' a whole new meaning, huh?"

We talked for a couple more minutes, Donafrio giving me the details on the other contractors and mafiosi implicated in his story, while I filled him in on the high points of the Humbert-Dugan murders. After we hung up, I hurried to the bedroom to dress for Humbert's funeral. I had to settle for a corduroy sport coat and a pair of chocolate brown slacks. There was no getting around it. I needed to buy myself a dark-blue suit.

The Mount Holly Cemetery sits atop a high hill just west of Mohaca Springs. It wasn't difficult to find. It's the only sizable hill in the area that sprouts headstones instead of grapevines.

A crowd of mourners stood in a semicircle around the grave while a priest in white vestments sang a canticle and sprinkled holy water on the coffin. A fine rain was falling still. A rainbow arced across the horizon and disappeared into a storm cloud. It might have been a movie set, I thought, as I studied the assembled cast.

I counted fifty heads bowed over the grave. Dick Penrose was there, standing beside a small woman I assumed was his wife. Amos Skelly was off to one side, head hanging, looking like a dozing polar bear. Humbert's pretty young receptionist, sniffling and chaste in an appropriate charcoal-gray dress, held the arm of a young man I didn't know. Allison stood beside a distinguished middle-aged couple, her parents no doubt. Brooke Humbert, a black veil shielding her face, was being propped up by the neighbor lady who used to be a nurse.

The coffin was lowered into the muddy grave. Brooke tossed a handful of earth in after it, as did the man I assumed to be Guy Humbert. The assemblage began to break up, a few mourners gathering in small groups and talking in low tones, others making for the narrow access road and their cars. Brooke stayed on beside the grave. Guy Humbert, his wife, and the priest moved a few feet away, allowing Brooke a few private moments.

Allison noticed me standing alone beside a huge stone cross and came over.

"Thank you for coming, Sheridan." She looked much too young for the black dress and petite black hat that she was wearing. The spray of freckles were undetectable in the dull light of the cemetery.

"How is Brooke taking it?" I asked.

"She's been terribly quiet. But calm, really," Allison said, glancing back at the grave site. "She hasn't been drinking at all, which is a good sign."

I nodded in agreement, then swiped at the raindrops dripping down my brow. "Allison, I'd like to talk to you for a few minutes, if I could. I realize this isn't a very good time, but it's important."

"All right, Sheridan. I guess there's time."

I took her arm and led her up the hill to an ornate gazebo. We stepped inside and shook the rain from our clothes. I wasn't sure how to begin. She began for me.

"I meant to call you and let you know about the services, but I've been so busy the past two days," she said. "I've been working at the winery, taking care of a few of the administrative chores that couldn't wait."

"That's okay. Were you able to keep things under control down there?"

"Yes, to my amazement, I was." She smiled. "Actually, I feel guilty admitting this, but I enjoyed it. I suppose I'll stay on in some capacity until Guy and my grandmother decide what they want to do about the place."

"Is your grandmother here today?"

"No, she's back at the house. She's confined to a wheelchair," Allison explained. "We didn't think it was a good idea to have her come out in this weather."

"Probably just as well," I mumbled. "Listen, I got you up here because I want to ask you about something."

She turned away, looking off at the rainbow.

"I need to know about the fight Michel and Brooke had that night. What was it she said to him?"

"I told you. She was drunk. She said a lot of things, things that weren't very nice."

I walked over beside her. The rainbow was fading away, barely more than a memory now.

"I need specifics, Allison."

She turned to face me, eyes glistening. "My uncle is lying over there in a fresh grave and you're asking me to smear his memory. I'm sorry, Sheridan," she said, struggling to control her rising anger. "But I don't think this is the time or the place for guessing games."

She turned abruptly to leave, then stopped dead and said, "Oh! Daddy! I was just coming."

Guy Humbert stepped up into the gazebo. He was shorter than his younger brother had been and lacked Michel's polished good looks. Still, there was a family resemblance in the chin and a shopworn handsomeness in the steady brown eyes. Eyes that now appraised me with solemn resignation.

"She's right, Mr. Sheridan. Your timing isn't the best." He patted Allison's cheek and nudged her gently. "Princess, why don't you go down and wait in the car with your mother and Brooke? I'll be along in a few minutes."

Allison glanced back at me, then nodded to her father and walked out into the misting rain. We both watched her go. When Humbert finally turned back to me, he said neutrally, "Allison told me about you. Your uncle's murder. Your background as a reporter. She also told me about the fight Brooke and my brother had the night he was killed."

"And?"

"And, frankly, I think it's none of your business."

"I wish it weren't," I said.

He sighed. "I could threaten you with a slander suit, but that would only create more publicity. Besides, I think you've formed your own opinion of what was said that night."

"I could guess." I nodded. "Michel was homosexual. Brooke knew about it and about his philandering. That's why she drank herself into stupors. It's also why she didn't want him taking any 'business trips' on a Saturday night."

Humbert stared at me for a few long seconds; long enough to come to a decision. I could see it in the way his shoulders suddenly relaxed and the brown eyes softened.

"Actually, my brother was bisexual," he began. "I've known about it for years, since he was in prep school in Ithaca—an incident with another boy caused a minor scandal. I suppose I thought he'd grow out of it, naive as I was in those days." He smiled mirthlessly. "I took his marriage to Brooke as a good sign. More folly, I'm afraid. Perhaps it was his drinking that brought it out in him; I don't know. At any rate, there were several other incidents over the years—some involving other men, some with women, always a drunken binge. We both—Brooke and I—tried to get him to stop, to seek professional help. He refused."

Humbert paused and shook his head. "Poor Brooke, I don't know how she could stay with him for so long, frankly."

"I suppose when you really love someone . . ."

"Yes," he nodded, "she must have loved him a great deal." He drew himself up straight. "So, Sheridan, now you know about the skeleton in my family's closet.

177

Maybe it will've been worth it, if you manage to find out who killed my brother, and your uncle. I suppose 'justice' would make it so. But I'm not certain of anything anymore."

"I'm not either, Mr. Humbert," I said.

There didn't seem to be anything else to say to each other. With a terse nod, he left, jogging back down the hillside to the waiting black limousine. I sat awhile in the gazebo, watching as a pair of workmen filled in Michel Humbert's grave. They were smiling, cracking jokes, laughing out loud. It wasn't a proper scene for a graveyard, but I understood it. When you've been at it long enough, you forget about other people's sorrow. Tomorrow you'll have to dig another hole. It's just a job.

CHAPTER 23

EVERY traffic light on Main
Street seemed to be waiting for me to pull up so it could
turn red. There were six in all, and by the time I braked
for the fifth one in as many blocks I'd had my fill of watery Wednesdays in the friendly city of Geneva.

I caught a green arrow and made my left turn onto West
Lake Road, headed for home. The route between Mohaca
Springs and Geneva had become so familiar in the last
few days, I was able to switch my brain to automatic pilot
and let the car find its own way.

The bulk of my afternoon had been spent chasing
around the labyrinthine corridors and file rooms of the
Quincy County Office Campus, a loose collection of
vaguely Federal-style buildings surrounding a strip of
green lawn adorned with two huge weeping willows and a
Civil War cannon. The county courthouse is one of the
main buildings clustered around the green, as is the
county's Bureau of Records.

An investigation is like a collage. Bits and pieces are
studied, turned this way and that, studied some more,
then pasted onto a canvas one at a time until an image
begins to take shape. Sometimes the image becomes clear

179

as each piece is added; sometimes it merely grows more abstract.

My amble through the halls of county officialdom wasn't a waste of time, despite the gauntlet of prickly civil servants who did their best to make it so. For one thing, I ran across a site plan and development proposal for a lakeside resort community, filed by Florio and his attorney; step one in the plan to ease the county board toward an eventual eminent-domain proceeding against Maevis Kendall. Florio was carefully assembling his team, just waiting for the time when he could begin playing hardball against Maevis. More significantly, I found a few of the pieces I needed to reconstruct the short and un-happy life of Teddy Kendall. A pair of birth records, a sealed court document, an address for an old Victorian house in Geneva that was now a real estate office but, in years past, had served a different sort of clientele. My col-lage was beginning to come together, but I can't say I liked the picture it was forming.

After two hours of thrust and parry with the county's clerical staff, I stopped by the *Daily News* to place a long-distance call to the Pentagon on the paper's WATS line. Old military files are public record, but army bureaucracy being what it is, the average citizen can spend months trying to get his questions answered. Luckily, I had my own service record and the power of the press to fall back on. My call was rerouted three times before I found a cap-tain with the Army Information Office who was able to expedite my request. I had a short list of names for him to check out, looking for any military service that included the kind of training that taught how to kill efficiently with a knife. The list was another shot in the dark—Roy Rossiter, for one, didn't seem to have the guile or the temperament to be the assassin—but even a shot in the dark will hit its target once in awhile.

The captain asked me call back at noon the following day—1200 hours, to quote him exactly. I hung up the phone and was about to evacuate the newsroom before Karen DeClair spotted me, but my luck ran out.

"Calling ahead for a pizza, Sheridan?" she asked wryly. "Or might your presence here have something to do with the murder investigation you're supposed to be covering for me?"

"Why, Karen. Hello. I've been looking all over for you. Where have you been?"

"I was in a budget meeting with the other editors, not that you care. Seriously, Sheridan, how's it going?"

"All I can tell you is that things are beginning to fall in place just a bit and that you may have a big story coming your way in the next day or two." I held up my hands to ward off the questions that were forming on her lips. "That's all I can say for now, Karen. I have to run."

She decided to leave it alone. Smiling now, she said in a raspy stage whisper, "Got a hot date lined up, huh?"

"No," I whispered back, glancing around the room conspiratorially. "I have to get home and feed my cat."

I got back to the cottage just before six. William greeted me when I came in the door, rubbing obscenely against my calf and crying for his supper.

"I've brought a present for you. Look." I took the thing out of the paper bag and jingled it in William's face. "It's a flea collar."

William stared at the little white plastic strip with those cat eyes of his, then looked up at me. Without so much as a meow, he pranced back to his favorite roost under the morris chair. I got down on my knees in front of the chair and tried applying child psychology.

"Look, it's just an itsy-bitsy kitty collar," I gushed, holding the thing up to my neck. "It won't hurt you, see?"

William seemed embarrassed for both of us. I got up, disgusted with myself. I tossed the collar on the couch and went over to the stereo and put on an album. Eine kleine rock musik was just the thing to ward off premature senility and surly felines. I cranked up the volume and smiled wickedly as the Steve Miller Band exploded into "The Joker." The speakers throbbed and, true to form, William lit out for the bedroom.

"To each his own," I said as I went to the kitchen to fix our dinners.

I was back on the road by eight o'clock. The cottage was somehow too quiet, too safe for me that night. I was tense, anxious. I needed to burn off the excess energy; I needed to find a place where people were alive and sudden death only happened in the NFL.

The Lakeside Inn was jumping when I arrived. Kids in jeans were everywhere, crowded up to the bar, overflowing the game room in the back, stomping their feet and clapping as a flat-chested girl in cutoff shorts did a drunken breakdance while Southside Johnny belted out white R&B on the jukebox.

I managed to pantomime my drink order to the bartender and slide off to a corner booth next to the game room. The beer was cold and the action that swirled around me served as a tonic for my mood. By the time I'd drained the first bottle, then made the round trip to the bar and back for a second round, I was feeling downright congenial.

"Hey, man, got change for a buck?" The voice belonged to a teenager with bright-red hair and thick Buddy Holly glasses. "Bartender's all tied up. I need some quarters." He gestured toward a machine in the game room, where another kid was joyfully zapping incoming nukes with a laser beam.

Amazing what a difference a decade makes, I thought as I dug into my pockets for change. In my time, you protested a war. Half a generation later, you contested one on a video screen at twenty-five cents per battle.

I handed the redhead his change and took his dollar. He

said, "Oh, wow," in lieu of thank you and hurried back to the front. I watched him go, then turned back to my beer and cogitated until another young voice broke in.

"Hi, Sheridan, how's it goin'?" Danny Wade stepped out of a forest of swaying bodies and edged up to my booth. He had a bottle of Utica Club in his hand and an uncertain look on his face.

"Hello, Danny. Have a seat?"

"Uh, well, okay." He slid in opposite me. "I, uh, saw you sittin' over here and I kinda wanted to talk to you."

"Sure," I said easily. "Where's your girl tonight?"

"Rhonda?" He shrugged. "We broke up the other day. That's sorta why I wanted to talk to you."

"If you're looking for advice to the lovelorn, you picked the wrong guy, Danny. Ann Landers I'm not."

He shook his head. "No, what I mean is, I been wanting to talk to you about Roy Rossiter. I was gonna look you up before, only I was still goin' around with Rhonda and I didn't want any hassles with her brother, y'know?"

I nodded. "So, what did you want to talk about?"

"About the other night, Friday night. Somebody gave you a hard time drivin' down from Geneva, right?"

"Yeah," I said. "Rossiter tried to run me off the road with his pickup truck."

"You already know?"

"Not enough to prove anything. You were the one who was with him?"

"Yeah," he admitted. "Only I didn't know he was gonna do it, really. I mean, me and him were just up in Geneva cruisin', you know? And he sees your car drivin' down Main—I didn't even know it was your car, but Roy recognized you. Anyway, he says, 'There goes that son of a bitch Sheridan' and he says he's gonna teach you a lesson. Bust your balls a little." He stared remorsefully across the table, like a man asking for dispensation. I wondered whether I should assign him an Our Father and three Hail Marys.

"Go on," I said, almost adding "my son."

"Well, I didn't know what he had in mind, understand. But I couldn't stop him anyway, not unless I wanted to get out and hitch home. I just wanted you to know what went down, that's all. So you can watch out for that asshole."

"I appreciate it, Danny," I said. "You guys didn't happen to stop off at Maxi's Restaurant that night, did you?"

"Yeah," he said. "We had a couple at the bar there. How'd you know that?"

I answered his question with one of my own, in the best Socratic tradition. "Was Dick Penrose there, too?"

"Yeah, he was there with Sheriff Skelly and some other guy. In fact, Penrose and Roy were talkin' together when I come outta the men's room."

"Talking about what?"

"I dunno, work maybe. Rossiter works for Penrose sometimes, down at his farm-supply store."

"I'll bet Penrose stocks a lot of insecticide at his store, right?" I asked.

"Yeah, I guess so." Danny was lost now, and rapidly losing interest in the conversation. "Anyway, I just wanted to let you know what happened and tell you I didn't want no part of it. I also figure you should know Roy's here tonight. Came in a couple minutes ago."

I scanned the room, craning my neck to see past the forest of bodies that peopled nearly every square inch of floor space. I didn't recognize him on my first pass, but there he was, all the way across the barroom next to the jukebox. The big cowboy hat had thrown me off at first, but there was no mistaking the broad-beamed Roy Rossiter. He was downing a can of beer with one hand and fondling a bottle blonde with the other.

"Thanks for the warning," I said.

Danny tossed me a casual salute and headed for the door. I figured I'd do the same. Maybe call J.D. in the morning and have him pick up Rossiter for questioning about running me off the road and the incident with the bug killer. But it would be difficult to prove anything without involving Danny Wade and I didn't want to do that. He had already gone out on a limb and I didn't think I should pay him back by sawing it off. I decided to go home and sleep on it.

Sometimes it's best to leave well enough alone, but that's a lesson not easily learned. As I cut a diagonal across the Lakeside's gravel parking lot toward my car, I spotted a dark-green pickup. I glanced over my shoulder, then went over to inspect the truck. It was a late-model Ford, splattered with mud along the wheel wells and moronic bumperstickers on the back bumper—IF YOU CAN READ THIS, YOU'RE TOO DAMN CLOSE.

I was more interested in the front bumper. I was standing there, leaning down to inspect a series of dents and scrapes along the bumper when I felt a stubby finger tap my shoulder like a jackhammer taps concrete. I turned halfway and looked up into Rossiter's watery eyes, just visible in the shadow cast by the brim of his ten-gallon hat. The little bottle blonde was standing beside him.

"Hello, scribbler," he said, a feral grin distorting his fleshy face. "Find what you're lookin' for?"

"Yeah." I nodded. "Looks like you've been playing bumper cars, Roy."

He shrugged. "Hit a deer up on County Road the other night. Huge fucker with a eight-point rack." The grin expanded. "Speakin' of big racks, where's Sorrel tonight? She turn off the pussy machine or what?"

"Leave it alone, Rossiter."

"You wanna be real careful snoopin' around other people's vehicles, boy. You wouldn't wanna get your nice new clothes all dirty." He reached out with one finger and flipped at the sleeve of my sport coat. "What's with the little leather patches here, shithead. I guess you musta worn holes in the elbows pickin' your ass up offa floors,

185

huh?'' He glanced at the little bottle blonde, who giggled her approval between snaps on her gum.

I took in his hat, his plaid shirt, and suede vest, his denims and pointy boots. Dodge City chic.

"We can't all be fashion mavens like you, Roy," I said. "Last time I saw you, you were wearing your soldier suit. Tonight it's a cowboy outfit. What're you going to be tomorrow? A clown?"

The grin ran off his face, replaced with a glassy rage I'd seen before. "You're still a mouthy son of a bitch, aren't you, shithead."

I just smiled pleasantly and waited for the inevitable. Back in Basic Training, the army had taught us a few things about self-defense. I never did master shoulder throws, but I got an A in groin kicks.

Rossiter stepped back, giving himself leverage to throw the big roundhouse right he was planning in his paleolithic brain. He was large, but he was also slow, and, unlike our first encounter, I was ready this time.

His arm came around in an arc wide enough to encompass Rhode Island. I stepped inside of it, deflecting it with a forearm, while at the same time driving my knee up between his legs. He let out a prehistoric howl and clamped his legs together, dropping both hands to his crotch. I shot my left fist into his burgeoning stomach and followed up to the side of his jaw with a short right as he was going down.

Rossiter was in the fetal position on the ground, sucking oxygen like a chain-smoker climbing Everest. The bottle blonde was appraising me with a jeweler's eye. A small crowd began streaming out of the Lakeside, led by the beefy bartender, who was hefting a truncated Louisville Slugger. It seemed like a good time to make my exit, but first I kneeled down beside the retching Rossiter.

"You fight like you drive," I said amiably. "Say hello to Penrose for me, okay?"

186

CHAPTER 24

GABRIEL Florio didn't show the next morning for our nine-o'clock meeting, which both puzzled and disappointed me. As much as I disliked the man, I knew I had to confront him one last time. Now that would have to wait. I had too much to do to spend the day hanging around the cottage. First I had to see Tony Areno to give him the knife I found sticking out of my door two evenings past. I meant to do it sooner, but other things had got in the way and, besides, I was sure he would find no prints.

Second on the agenda was a brainstorming session with J. D. Staub. I was beginning to get a tenuous hold on the case; a spider's web of circumstantial evidence and hunches. I needed to bounce a few ideas off J.D. to get a second opinion.

Item number three was a return call to my contact at the Pentagon. If the captain followed through as promised—and if the information I'd requested bore fruit—I'd know I had the story right. But those were a couple of big ifs.

I waited at the cottage until 9:45. Florio didn't show and didn't call, so I fired up the Horizon and headed for

187

Geneva. As things turned out, I made it only as far as the Pinewood.

My stomach did the Fosbury Flop as I pulled even with the rustic resort's roadside parking lot. Two county squad cars, their red and blue pursuit lights flashing silently, were parked nose to nose at the far end of the lot, near the Pinewood's front walk. Resting next to them was Amos Skelly's official gray Chevrolet.

I parked behind the Chevy. A throng of people—the Pinewood's kitchen staff, judging by their white uniforms—was gathered below the slope leading to the resort's housekeeping cabins. Their attention appeared to be directed to one cabin in particular, the entrance to which was being guarded by a deputy sheriff.

I sidled up to the edge of the pack and attempted an end run at the cabin. No such luck. The deputy cut me off with a sharp command and ordered me back to the herd.

"Hell-ooo."

I was searching the crowd for a sympathetic face when I spotted an old woman sitting in a white wicker chair on the front porch of another cabin, two doors removed from the action. She was watching me and smiling contentedly.

"Hello." I strolled over and bowed. She was even older than I had first judged. Her face was heavily fissured and, despite the warm June morning, she was wearing two cardigan sweaters over her simple blue dress.

"Are you a guest here at the lodge?" I asked.

"Yes. I come here every year, with my daughter, don't you know. She's having breakfast in the lodge, I think. I've already had mine."

I motioned toward the cabin with the deputy standing in front of it. "It looks like you've had some excitement here this morning."

"Oh, my, yes. There was a body in there." She pointed to the cabin. "The police took it away in an ambulance. I don't know why they needed an ambulance, though, because the poor man was already dead."

"Sorry to hear that. What happened, I wonder?"

"Well, I don't really know. The maid found him; says there was blood everywhere." She tossed her bony hands in her lap. "My land, the poor young thing was scared half to death."

I didn't figure she was describing Maevis Kendall. Not even a nice old lady's tired eyes could mistake Maevis for a young girl. Besides, I recalled seeing Maevis's sedan at the farmhouse when I drove out.

"Did anyone say who the man—" I started to ask.

"Sheridan?" A male voice cut me off. It was Koenig, the plainclothes euchre player. He was hailing me from the porch of the cabin where the body had been found. I said my goodbyes to the old woman and walked over to meet him.

"How'd you find out about this so quick?" he asked me as I stepped onto the porch.

"I haven't found out much of anything, yet. I was just passing by on my way up to Geneva."

He nodded. "Well, it looks like we've got victim number three for the ripper."

"Anybody I know?"

"That guy Florio. He was sliced up pretty bad. The killer didn't leave the knife behind this time, though."

Off to our left, a couple of uniformed cops were interviewing a small Hispanic-looking man in a white cook's smock, while other members of the Pinewood's staff listened in. I turned and looked inside the cabin. A police technician was dusting a nightstand for prints.

Koenig waved me in and made the introductions. "Sheridan, this is Stevens from Forensic." We nodded to each other and Stevens resumed dusting the table.

The cabin was a bloody mess. A white bedspread on one of the double beds had a dark-red stain across it, shaped like the African continent and nearly as large. Another huge stain had fouled the carpet and there was a crimson archipelago splattered on the wall behind the bed. A chair lay on its back in the corner.

189

"Come up with anything, Earl?" Koenig asked.

"Nothing usable here," Stevens pointed to the night-stand. "But I got a clear set off one of the glasses in the john. Maybe just the maids, though."

"You never know," Koenig said. He turned to me. "Maybe we'll catch a break this time."

My mind was racing, trying to take it all in and fit these new pieces into what I thought I already knew.

"When was Florio killed?" I asked.

"Coroner says probably late yesterday afternoon, around dinner time, while most of the guests were up to the lodge."

"Was he registered here?"

"No." Koenig scratched his jaw. "The manager says this cabin wasn't rented to anyone."

"Who found the body?"

"Girl named Kelly Morse, one of the housekeeping maids. She was up here to open it up, let it air out because the cabin is reserved for the weekend." He looked at the bloody bedspread. "She found Florio sprawled on the bed."

"Is Tony Areno around? I'd like to talk to him."

"He's up at the main house with Sheriff Skelly, checking out the staff schedules."

"And Staub?"

Koenig shrugged neutrally. "Haven't seen him."

Just then, Areno entered the cabin.

"Good morning, Tony," I said.

"What's so good about it?" he grumbled. "Koenig, you just about through here?"

"Another few minutes, Chief."

"Okay." Areno motioned me to follow him out onto the cabin's small porch. "How'd you happen to turn up so fast, Sheridan?"

"I was on my way up to Geneva when I spotted all the commotion."

"Hmph." He ran a hand through his thick black hair.

190

"Well." He exhaled. "It looks like we're on to something this time. Maevis Kendall was assigned to work this cabin yesterday. One of the other maids saw her over here, going inside with a guy who fits the victim's description. And she didn't show up for work today. We got a coupla men down at her place now to pick her up."

I started to speak, but he cut me off.

"Looks like it's all tied in with that land deal with Florio and Humbert and your uncle, like J.D. figured. Don't ask me why that'd set her off like this, though."

"Actually," I said, "I was on my way up to see J.D. this morning to kick around a hunch I had about that."

"What sorta hunch?"

"Well, I . . ." I began to explain when Skelly came blustering down the walkway. Following in his wake were three uniformed deputies, a gangly photographer wearing a necklace of Nikons and lenses, and the ubiquitous Brian MacKay of the *Daily News*.

"What's the status here, Chief?" Skelly bellowed.

"Just wrapping things up now, Sheriff. I got a squad car down to the Kendall place, oughta be bringing her back anytime."

"What's this civilian doing here?" Skelly demanded, peering at me.

"Uh, he was on his way up to see us at the department, Amos," Areno said. "Something about . . . what was it you said, Sheridan?"

"I wanted to drop off a bone-handled knife that someone stuck in my front door Tuesday night."

The corpulent sheriff jumped on it. "Tuesday night? You took your time about reporting it, didn't you."

"I've been busy," I said. "Besides, I figured it was clean, like the others."

"Next time leave the figuring to the authorities, young man," Skelly scolded. "Had we known about that incident, we might've gotten on to the Kendall woman sooner." Pivoting back to Areno, he said, "Tony, be sure

191

to get his statement. This could be key. Living next door like that, the Kendall woman had plenty of opportunity to—"

"Sheriff Skelly!" A boyish deputy with buckteeth stuck his head in the door. " 'Scuse me, sir, but Deputy Clemens just radioed from the suspect's house. They were fired upon, sir, and Esterhaus was hit."

"Good God!" Skelly paled. "Christ, Tony, get a move on. Radio for backup, all available units to the Kendall place pronto!"

"What about J.D.? You want me to—"

"Forget about J.D. He had his chance. Now let's get on with it."

Suddenly it was Keystone Kops time. Areno running for his car radio, deputies sprinting off in all directions, Brian MacKay writing furiously in his note pad, grinning ear to ear, while the photographer's autowinder whirred nonstop.

Everyone was moving. Everyone except Sheriff Amos T. Skelly, that is. He posed motionless for a few seconds, balled fists resting on his hips, jaw jutted out squarely under a steady gaze.

He, too, had heard the camera clicking.

CHAPTER 25

BY the time I got back to the cottage, the carnival across the cove was in full swing.

I got out of the Horizon and stood there in my driveway a few minutes, watching the show. Five squad cars and the gray Chevy were deployed around the farmhouse in a loose semicircle. Skelly and Areno were huddled behind the Chevy, no doubt planning the assault on Fortress Kendall. The rest of the troops—seven uniforms and two plainclothes detectives—were hunkered down behind squad cars, trees, and various other bullet-absorbing objects.

Brian MacKay was keeping a respectful distance from the house, sitting in his car along the shoulder of the road, pen poised. The industrious photographer from the *Daily News* was another story. He had managed to work his way to a spot behind Maevis Kendall's Dodge and was busy mounting a telephoto lens on his Nikon.

I jogged down the road to Kendall's driveway and crabwalked over to the gray Chevy.

"What're you doing here, Sheridan?" Skelly challenged me. "This is official police business. No place for amateurs."

I held back the rejoinder that came to mind, but just barely. "I'm here to cover the story, Sheriff," I said. "I have an exclusive deal with the *Daily News*."

That lit up his eyes, as I thought it would.

"Well, okay. Just make sure you keep down. We already had one man hit."

"Nothing serious," Areno interjected. "Esterhaus caught a little buckshot in the hand. That crazy bitch fired her shotgun right through the screen door at him when him and Clemens came to pick her up."

"Any more shooting?"

"Not since we got here," Areno said, pushing himself up to peek out over the hood of the car. "Not a sound out of her. She took that potshot at Esterhaus, then broadsided his cruiser with a second blast, but that's been it."

Torinni popped up from behind a squad car and scampered over to us. He was carrying a bullhorn, which he handed to Skelly.

"Here you go, sir," he said. "Batteries are okay."

"What about the tear gas?"

"It's on the way down with the tac team, sir."

"Outstanding." Skelly rotated his thick neck around to Areno. "Tony, I'm going to try and talk her out of there. If I can't, we'll wait for the tear gas. Make sure the men are covering all the windows."

"Right." Areno picked up his walkie-talkie and ran a check with his troops. Satisfied that everyone was in place and ready, he nodded to Skelly, who struggled to his feet.

"Mrs. Kendall," his voice boomed through the bullhorn. "This is Sheriff Amos T. Skelly speaking. I order you to come out with your hands upraised. Leave the weapon in the house. You won't be harmed."

I had to give Skelly points for guts, if not brains. Standing there beside the hood of the Chevy the way he was, he was exposing at least two hundred pounds of blubber to the line of fire. But not for long.

He had barely finished his spiel when a shotgun blast rang out from the farmhouse. A spray of buckshot whistled across the roof of the Chevy and, a nanosecond later, the sheriff hit the ground as if he'd been dropped from a helicopter.

"You okay, Amos? Amos?" Areno crawled over beside Skelly. The massive body rolled over slowly.

"I'm fine," Skelly puffed. "Fit as a fiddle."

From the house came the unmistakable screech of Maevis Kendall. "Cursed are those who serve the Devil Satan! Woe is the defiler of the Kingdom!"

The two lawmen looked at each other. "I think we better wait for the tear gas," Areno suggested.

Skelly nodded. "I concur."

We settled in and waited in the shadow of the gray Chevrolet. Meanwhile, up along West Lake Road, the curious and the bored were beginning to gather, lining up along the shoulder of the road: farmers, businessmen, locals, tourists, kids on bikes. There must have been two dozen vehicles crowded end to end along the apron of grass bordering the highway, including a blue van with a large eye painted on the side; a news team from one of the Syracuse TV stations. Everybody loves a circus.

The gathering didn't escape the notice of Skelly, either. He ordered Torinni to take two uniforms up there to help keep the public at bay, adding, "But be courteous about it. We don't want to alienate anyone."

Areno was busy studying the farmhouse from behind the Chevrolet's rear end. After awhile, he gave it up and crawled over beside me.

"Lotta fuss for one loony tune, huh?" he said, his voice low. I murmured my agreement.

"So, Sheridan, you might as well give me your theory on all this bullshit. What the hell got into Maevis Kendall?"

"It's just conjecture," I hedged. "But my guess is she

couldn't risk having anyone get this property away from her. And I've got a pretty good idea why."

"Yeah? That's one we still haven't figured," Areno said. "A motive, other than she's nuts. Tell me."

I glanced at Skelly, who was now listening in, and forged ahead. "I think she killed her husband, Ed, and hid his body in that cove over there," I said, all in a breath.

The two cops pivoted their heads around in unison and stared at the placid cove. After a moment, Areno turned back to me. "How d'you figure?" he asked.

"Several things. First, there's the fact she refuses to sell the farm for any amount of money, even though she's all alone here now. Why wouldn't she want to sell and move back with her own people in Pennsylvania? Why is she particularly protective of that little cove? She caught me out there a couple of times and nearly chewed my head off. Then there's Ed Kendall himself. The word around Mohaca Springs was that Ed stayed on and put up with Maevis all those years because he felt he owed it the boy, Teddy. So why did he take off two years ago, with Teddy still a fifteen-year-old schoolboy?"

Skelly grunted, "Just reached his breaking point, that's what people assumed."

"If it wasn't for the way she's acted over this land deal, I'd agree with you," I said. "But when you put the two together, along with another bit of information I lucked into, you get a different reading."

"What other information?" Areno asked.

"I was fishing out on the lake one day when I dozed off. My boat drifted into the cove and banged into a submerged rock. And my fishing line got fouled on a length of heavy anchor chain that seemed to have been wrapped around the boulder. It didn't register at the time, but later, when I got to thinking about it, I decided to wade out there to check it out. I was able to locate the boulder again, but Maevis came along and chased me out before I could bring up the chain."

196

Skelly started turning it over in his mind, finally seeing the possibilities. "It could be that Ed Kendall's body is at the other end of that anchor chain. Maybe he came home one night with a snootful and got into a row with his teetotaling wife. Maevis goes a little crazier than usual and kills him—maybe accidentally with a fry pan, or maybe on purpose, with that shotgun. She then dumps his body in the cove, weighting it down with a boat anchor and chain and securing it to the boulder." He looked at his chief of detectives. "She's a big strong woman. Bigger than her husband, as I recall. She's physically capable, surely."

"So," Areno summarized, "she hides the body and lets everyone assume that Ed finally got fed up and took off."

"And it worked," I said. "Until Florio and Humbert began trying to buy up the property. She couldn't sell out and risk having the body discovered." I added, "Florio, for one, was planning to have the cove dredged out for a marina."

"I like it." Skelly nodded. "Of course, we've already got her nailed pretty good for Florio. But motive was a bit sticky. Now, if we can come up with Ed Kendall's body in that cove, we can tie her in with the whole shebang. Florio, Dugan, and Michel Humbert. Case closed."

"Except for—" I began to say, but the wail of an approaching siren cut me off. The tactical team had arrived with the tear gas. Skelly poked me in the chest with one of his plump fingers.

"You stay around, Sheridan. I'll want you to point out that rock." He started to get up, grabbing Areno's arm for support. "C'mon, Tony. Let's go get our killer."

Fifteen minutes later, it was all over. Areno deployed the tac team around the house while Skelly again spoke to Maevis through his bullhorn—careful this time to stay well concealed behind the Chevy. When Maevis refused to respond, Skelly gave the signal with a dramatic sweep

197

of his arm and the assault was on. Tear-gas canisters were fired through the first-floor windows. Deputies in bulletproof vests and gas masks broke down the front and rear doors, shotguns at the ready. In seconds, they were inside the house.

The crowd along the highway loved it. Grandmothers and preschoolers, middle-aged men and youngsters in jeans, all oohed and ahhed. Minicams whirred; reporters scribbled frantically while jockeying for a better view; plumes of dirty white billowed out the broken windows of the house.

And through it all, Sheriff Amos T. Skelly, bullhorn to his lips, directed the action like a poor man's De Mille.

No shots were fired. After a long minute, Maevis Kendall, bent but unbroken, was led out onto the front porch by two deputies, her hands cuffed behind her, her mouth running full tilt.

"Satan's children," she raged at the cops and the crowd. "You will know the wrath of the Lord! You will burn forever in the pits of Hell!"

The crowd booed lustily, eating it up.

"Woe is he who partakes of the demon rum!" Maevis screeched, her eyes wild and unfocused, as the two uniforms half-carried her to the waiting cruiser. "For the Lord God protects the Righteous and vanquishes the Sinner! The Kingdom shall come to those who . . ." On and on she raved, in capital letters, until the deputies pushed her down into the backseat of the cruiser and climbed in after her. The thrillseekers along the road honored the performance with a standing ovation, but there would be no curtain calls.

"Torinni, get her downtown immediately," Skelly directed. "We'll be along shortly."

"Sir." A deputy with a gas mask tipped back on his head ran up. "We've got another body inside. A shooting victim. Looks to have been dead a day or more."

I joined in the general stampede to the house, as curious as the cops to learn the identity of the latest corpse. The place was a mess. Chairs overturned, window glass scattered about the floor, curtains torn and dangling from their rods. My eyes began to water uncontrollably, even as a lake breeze was rapidly blowing the house clean of the acrid tear gas. But there was a stronger smell to contend with now; the unmistakable stench of decaying flesh.

The body was stretched out along the sofa, arms folded across the chest. It would have looked almost peaceful if not for the bloodsoaked shirt and the gray wasted face. A crimson cross had been fingerpainted in blood on the wall above the sofa. The last rites according to Maevis Kendall.

"It's Dick Penrose," Areno gasped. He was standing over the body, a handkerchief pressed over his nose and mouth. "Shotgun blast got 'im point-blank."

Skelly was stunned. I didn't feel too well myself.

"Where did he come from?" the sheriff asked, but no one answered him.

I worked my way back out to the front porch and sat on the railing, gulping down fresh air by the cubic foot. A couple of minutes later, I was joined by Areno and Skelly.

"God, what a stink!" Areno spit over the railing.

"She must've had him in there for at least twenty-four hours," I said.

"Yes," Skelly interjected. "But the question is, what is Dick Penrose doing here in the first place?"

I stared at the sheriff, searching his fleshy face for guile and finding none. Maybe J.D. had been right; Skelly got his kicks from pomp and circumstance, not graft. In any case, I decided to spell things out for him.

"Penrose was Florio's front man on that condo project," I said. "Florio probably promised him a big cut of the profits if Penrose would use his clout to get Maevis off her land."

"What're you saying?" Skelly blustered. "That Dick Penrose was on the take? I don't believe it."

"You should. Florio was planning to use Penrose's leverage with the state Parks Commission and the county board to push through a condemnation proceeding on this place. Some of the preliminary paperwork is already on file at the courthouse. Penrose's job was to convince everyone what a good idea it would be to put a public park and boat launch here. That was the carrot Florio was offering. The real purpose was to free up the rest of the acreage, across the road, for his condo deal."

"Now that I think about it, Penrose even spoke to me about some public park idea of his," Skelly said, somewhat sheepishly. "I'm afraid I hardly gave it a thought at the time. I never connected it up with the Kendall property."

Areno said, "You think maybe Penrose got a little antsy about his cut and came by here to pressure Maevis some more?"

"Could be. That would account for the timetable. He tells Maevis she might as well sell, because the state and county were going to take the land anyway. Maybe he explained the condemnation proceeding to her. She panics, goes berserk, and pops Penrose with the shotgun."

Areno finished it for me. "Then she arranges to meet Florio up at the Pinewood later in the day and she slices him up, too. In for a penny, in for a pound, huh?"

"Something like that." I shrugged. "You saw her when they took her out of here. She's gone way past any kind of rational behavior at this point."

"Well," Skelly said, rapidly returning to his usual overbearing self. "That's how I see it, too. The woman was obviously a psychopath. She killed her husband, then, in order to keep her secret, she murdered four other men. That's assuming, of course, we find Ed Kendall's remains in that cove. I think we better get a scuba team in there immediately, Chief. Meantime, we'll want to get back to town ASAP, get this thing nailed down. I'll deal with the press. You try to get some kind of coherent statement

200

from the Kendall woman. Koenig can take over down here. Sheridan here can go as soon as he points out where that rock is."

I had been dismissed as far as Skelly was concerned. He had his killer, her motive, and an eager audience to play to, which is all he ever wanted. And he wasn't about to share the limelight with me.

"I'll need to have Sheridan come downtown," Tony protested. "He'll have to give a statement."

Skelly wouldn't hear of it. "It'll be a madhouse down there when this news breaks. He can come by in the morning to make his statement. No rush, now that we've got our killer."

When I got back to the cottage I made three phone calls. The first was long distance, the Pentagon. It was a short conversation. My cooperative captain had at hand the information I'd requested. I listened carefully, then thanked him for his efforts and rang off. When the dial tone sounded, I made the second call.

"*Finger Lake Daily News*, Karen DeClair." She was out of breath, rushed off her feet with trying to pull together the Maevis Kendall story for the next morning's edition. But she found her voice quickly enough when I told her I couldn't file anything yet. Hell hath no fury like an editor scorned.

"Is this some kinda goddam joke, Sheridan? I've got MacKay out at the sheriff's office, trying to piece things together; I'm sitting here waiting to hear from you and you tell me—"

I cut her off, told her to have MacKay file what he had, and added that I'd try to get back to her before the final deadline that night. Then I hung up.

My third and final call was to J. D. Staub. I reached him at his office and compared notes on the Florio-Penrose murders.

"Maevis was brought in a few minutes ago, raving like

a lunatic," he said. "Doesn't look like we'll get much out of her for awhile, if ever."

"Did you see Florio's body?"

"No, I'm still being kept out of the investigation for the most part. I got the details from a couple of the uniforms, though. She slashed him up pretty good."

"It doesn't jive too well with the way Uncle Charlie and Humbert died, does it?" I asked.

"She used a knife," Staub said without conviction.

"Yeah," I said. "Skelly's on his way back with a parade of newsmen on his heels."

"Figures. By morning, he'll be the biggest hero in the state, knowing how he'll play it up."

"Maybe." I hesitated. "J.D., have you given any thought to challenging Skelly in the primary?"

He cleared his throat. "Actually, I have. I wouldn't stand much chance in a primary, but I was thinking, if I ran as an independent in November . . ." He paused. "Of course, now, with the publicity he'll get on this Kendall deal, I don't know if I'd just be wasting my time."

"Think positive," I said. "You planning to be home later tonight?"

"Sure. Why?"

"I may have something for you. I don't want to say right now."

There was another pause on the line, then Staub said, "This thing isn't over yet, is it, Sheridan?"

"No."

CHAPTER 26

". . . For 'Eye Witness News,'" this is Marcia Westerby reporting from Geneva." Click.

I switched off the television using the remote control and slumped deeper into the chair. Eyes shut, I willed my mind free of distractions and listened to the quiet comfortable sounds of the cottage. William purred beneath my chair. The refrigerator compressor hummed in the kitchen. A windowpane shuddered under a gust of wind. For a few precious minutes, I was able to close out the world's cruel ironies. But only for a few minutes.

Amos Skelly had been the star of the six-o'clock news. Camera crews caught his wide-angle body and telegenic smile on the steps in front of the Sheriff's Department. He posed with Maevis's shotgun cradled in his arms and held forth for the army of reporters that had flocked to Geneva to cover the story of the "Seneca Slasher," as one overenthusiastic TV reporter had dubbed the killer. An hour earlier, the skeletal remains of Ed Kendall had been fished from the little cove beside the farm.

"Ladies and gentlemen." Skelly raised his arm for silence. "A press release has been prepared and is available at the watch commander's desk inside. Beyond that, I can only say that I have arrested Maevis Kendall of Mohaca Springs and charged her with three counts of second-degree murder in connection with the deaths of her husband, Edward Kendall, Mr. Gabriel Florio of Syracuse, and Mr. Richard Penrose, supervisor of the Town of Mohaca Springs."

"Sheriff! Sheriff Skelly!" Cries and hands went up simultaneously from the crowd of journalists. Skelly acknowledged a particularly persistent young man from a local radio station. The kid thrust a portable tape recorder in the general direction of Skelly's face and asked him, "Are you satisfied in your own mind, sir, that Maevis Kendall is also responsible for the two previous stabbings? The Dugan and Humbert murders?"

"In answer to that, I can say only this . . ." Skelly paused. "I believe that the good citizens of Quincy County can now put aside their fears and stop concerning themselves with the so-called 'Seneca Slasher.' And you can quote me."

The camera zoomed in for a tight shot of Skelly as he deftly fielded a dozen more questions, none of them particularly penetrating. Then the "Eye Witness" coverage cut to some artfully edited footage of the tactical team and its assault on the Kendall place. At that point, I had turned off the set.

As I sat there in the chair, the afterimage of Skelly still burning, I remembered a neighbor of ours from when I was a kid, a man named Arnson. One time, during the annual Great Lake Fishing Derby, this Arnson joined my father and me for a day's fishing out on Lake Ontario. Like Skelly, Arnson was a large blustery type, a guy who bothered to wet a line maybe once a year but still acted as if he knew how to fish like Fred Astaire knew how to dance.

The three of us sat out on that boat for more than an hour, without a single significant strike, when suddenly Arnson's pole bent nearly in half and he began to reel in.

"This is the one, by God, I've got the prize winner here, for sure!" Arnson crowed as he struggled with the fish. Then, as suddenly as it had first bent in half, his pole straightened, the line went slack, and Arnson fell back heavily onto his butt. My father looked down at the crestfallen man and said, "There's an old Irish proverb, Arnson. 'It isn't a fish until it's on the bank.'"

Sorrel Brown had outdone herself.

She greeted me at her door, thick red-brown mane brushed back and free-flowing to her shoulders, white blouse silky and revealing. Her slacks, a pretty lilac shade, hugged her hips and thighs like a jealous lover.

"Right on time, eight o'clock," she said, leading me inside and kissing me deeply once the door was shut. "I thought you sophisticated city slickers were always fashionably late."

"Only in paying the rent," I said, stepping into the living room.

The fondue pot was set up on the old pine coffee table. A dish of cheeses and cubed meats sat next to it. Two plates and a pair of long thin forks were lined up along one side of the crowded table, fronting the sofa. Soft music played on the stereo and soft light bathed the room from a single floor lamp.

I handed Sorrel the bottle of wine I was carrying in the crook of my arm. It was an Humbert chablis.

"Oh, great, it's already chilled," she said. "Why don't you open it while I bring out the glasses?"

We sat close on the sofa, sipping wine, nibbling bits of cheese, and dipping the chicken and beef into the spicy bubbling fondue pot. A concert of Chopin's finest played on the radio over a public-broadcasting station in Rochester. For a long while, as if by an unspoken compact, neither of us mentioned the turbulent events that had happened earlier in the day. Until I broke the truce.

"That was quite a scene out at the Kendall farm."

"Mmm, I heard all about it at the diner," she said as

she reached for the wine bottle and refilled our glasses. "Unbelievable, isn't it? Ralph was so excited, he was chain-smoking Camels and interrogating anyone who came in the door. Kay finally sent him out to the parking lot." She laughed.

"Maevis Kendall really flipped out," I said. "She was raving like a lunatic. I'd say she was destined for a padded cell someplace. Probably for the rest of her life."

"Good." Sorrel nodded tersely. "At least she won't be able to hurt anyone ever again."

I took a deep swallow of the chablis and placed the glass on the table. "That must be a great relief to you."

She stared into my eyes, her brow wrinkled. "Well, of course. It's a relief to the whole town."

I nodded. "But especially for you. She was the last one, wasn't she?"

She stood and crossed to the other side of the coffee table, hands clenched. "What are you talking about?"

"Why don't you sit down? I think it's time you told someone about it, don't you?"

"What are you talking about?" she repeated, her hands on her hips now. "I don't understand."

"I think you do, Sorrel. I'm talking about Uncle Charlie and Michel Humbert. I'm talking about why you killed them and why Maevis Kendall had to be next on the list."

"That's . . . You're crazy! I heard all about it on the news," she said, pointing to the stereo. "Maevis is the one. She killed her husband and then killed the others to cover it up."

"Yes," I said quietly. "She killed Ed. And then she murdered Florio and Penrose after they backed her into a corner. But you killed the others."

"I don't believe this! Why would I kill anyone?"

"You blamed my uncle and Humbert for Teddy Kendall's suicide. And maybe deep down somewhere, you blamed yourself, too." I paused, felt my heart racing. Sorrel's eyes were brimming with tears.

"You were Teddy's real mother," I said, my voice a whisper. "And Charlie Dugan was his father."

My indictment melted into the silence of the room. Sorrel closed her eyes, her shoulders quivering. After a moment, she walked slowly to a low bureau along the wall and pulled open the top drawer. For an eternity, she stared down into the drawer and said nothing. Just listened.

"I saw Teddy's yearbook picture," I continued quietly. "I saw the resemblance to one of my cousins. Uncle Charlie's son. I also looked up some old school records. You dropped out three months before graduation and moved to an address in Geneva. I traced the address, Sorrel."

"They destroyed him, Sheridan," she said finally, her back to me. "He was just a confused little boy, needing so much love and understanding, and they gave him indifference and scorn. They had to pay for that, Dugan and Humbert. And Maevis." She reached into the drawer, then turned to me. In her hand was a bone-handled fishing knife.

"I was saving this for her," she said as she studied the gleaming blade. "But it doesn't matter now."

She came back to the sofa and stood over me, the knife clenched in her fist, her face a blank. Gently, I reached up and took the knife from her, placing it on the coffee table.

Sobbing, head bowed, she sat on the sofa and picked up her glass. She trembled as she brought it to her lips. A single drop of wine spilled from the side of her mouth and streaked down her cheek, like a dry white tear.

"It seems like such a long time ago," she murmured. "My senior year. It should have been a wonderful time, but it wasn't. I couldn't do anything to please my mother. I wore too much makeup, she'd say. My sweaters were too tight; I stayed out too late. Always something. But I didn't want to hear it. The boys liked me the way I was. The other girls at school were jealous of me, like mother.

But I didn't mind. I was always more comfortable around men. They were nice to me, like my father was."

"And Charlie Dugan?" I asked softly.

"He was nice, too, I thought. I met him in a bar one night, in Geneva. We were both a little drunk. He took me home to his cottage and we . . ." She looked at me, pleading. "He said it would be all right, that he only wanted to give me pleasure. He was older, like my father, and I thought I could believe in him.

"It was just that one night. I never saw him again. A couple months later, when I found out I was pregnant, my parents tried to get me to tell, but I couldn't. I couldn't tell Daddy that I'd slept with a man his own age, couldn't explain it. They never found out that it wasn't just a high school boy I'd been with."

"They took you out of school and sent you away to have the baby," I said.

She nodded. "I stayed in Geneva at a home for unwed mothers. After I had the baby, I gave it up for adoption and moved away from here."

"You joined the army."

"Yes. I passed a high school equivalency test and they sent me to nursing school. I was a good nurse, too. I stayed in for ten years and I even served in a field hospital in Vietnam. But then I . . . I left and took a job in Los Angeles, waiting on tables. I never even came back to Mohaca Springs for a visit in all those years. Until my mother died and Daddy needed me again."

"When did you find out about Teddy?"

She sighed. "Last summer. Teddy came into the diner one day after school and mentioned that it was his birthday. July the tenth, seventeen years to the day since I'd had my baby. And he had my hair coloring.

"After that, I tried to get closer to him. He needed a friend. Things weren't good at home. Maevis was a witch; his father had run out on him, so everyone thought. Teddy wasn't fitting in very well at school. He was so lonely." She stopped for a moment, lost in Teddy's pain. I poured the last of the wine and waited.

"One night last February," she continued with new resolve, "he met me in the parking lot at the diner when I came off shift. He was crying. We sat in my car and talked for a long time. He told me about his boss, Humbert . . . how they had driven up to Beedle Road and parked. He told me what Humbert did to him up there."

She grabbed my arm, digging in her fingers desperately.

"He was so confused, Sheridan, so lost! No one would help him. He was treated like a leper in his own house." She let loose her grip and began to cry again. "I only wanted to help him. I took him home with me and I . . . I told him the truth. I hoped it would help him somehow, to know about me and his real father. But I was wrong, terribly wrong. He came apart completely, called me a liar. He said he'd go to Dugan and find out the truth. The next day, Teddy called me at home. He said Dugan denied everything but that it didn't matter anymore." She wiped away the tears. "The day after that, he killed himself."

I put my arms around her, held her close. She rested her head against my chest. I could feel her heart pounding in rhythm with my own.

"They had to pay for what they did to him, Sheridan. I had to make them pay."

"It's over now, Sorrel. You understand?"

"Yes." She sniffed. "I know."

"You'll have to come with me now and tell your story to the police. You don't have to be afraid, Sorrel. There are still some good people out there, people who can help you."

"I'm not afraid anymore." She looked up at me, a tiny smile on her face. She was a child again, huddled up on the old living room sofa, safe and warm inside a man's embrace. In a little-girl voice, she said, "But will you hold me now? For just a little while?"

We sat there, my arms around her, and listened to Chopin. After awhile, she went to sleep. I eased myself off the sofa and covered her with the afghan.

The telephone was waiting on the bureau. Reluctantly, sadly, I picked it up and dialed.

"Hello, J.D. This is Sheridan."

CHAPTER 27

FRIDAY is a busy day for most taverns and the Sand Barn was no exception. It was well past two o'clock in the afternoon, yet the place was still crowded from the lunch hour.

We found a vacant booth in a relatively quiet corner and ordered a round of drinks; bourbon and water for J. D. Staub, gin and tonic for Karen DeClair, Budweiser for Bob Kaufman, and a bottle of Labatt's for me. It wasn't really a celebration. More like an Irish wake.

I sipped the head off my beer and looked at J.D.

"How's she holding up?"

"Fine, considering," he said. "She asked about you."

"I was planning to stop in later, before I head back to the cottage. If that's all right."

"I'll see that you get in to see her."

"What about Maevis Kendall?" Karen asked. "I understand she's in pretty bad shape."

"Yeah," J.D. said. "We had to pack her off to the state hospital in Rochester. She's totally out of it."

"Your press conference this morning caught a few people by surprise, J.D.," Kaufman said, smiling.

"Yeah," Karen interjected. "Skelly, for one. He looked

211

like he swallowed a quart of Mexican mineral water. Really got caught with his pants down." She glanced at me. "We would've been, too, if Sheridan hadn't spent the wee hours in our newsroom, filing the story."

I shrugged. It was the best piece I'd ever done, but it didn't make me feel any better. "If you think Skelly looked sick this morning," I said, changing the subject, "wait'll he hears that J.D. is going to run against him this fall."

"Is that right, J.D.?" Kaufman asked.

"Yep. Going to give it a shot as an independent. And I think my chances are pretty good now, thanks to Sheridan." He hoisted his glass in my direction.

"You know, Sheridan," Karen said, "I'm still not clear on how you put it all together. Up until Maevis did him in, I figured Florio was behind the murders."

I shook my head. "Florio was just another greedy businessman who got himself in trouble by bending the rules. His big mistake was taking that mob money in the first place. The pressure got to him, made him careless."

"But how did you get on to Sorrel Brown?"

"It's a long story," I said. "From the beginning, J.D. and I were convinced there was more to my uncle's murder than a bungled burglary attempt. Too many inconsistencies. Nothing taken, no ransacking. Then there was the fact he didn't answer his phone that night when his buddies called. Why not?" I looked into each of their faces, then answered my own question. "Because he was with someone at the cottage, someone he didn't want his friends to know about beforehand. And since he was found in his pajamas, it made sense that he was there with a woman."

"What about the theory that he simply came home drunk and went to bed to sleep it off?" Karen asked.

"His ex-wife, Monica, shot that one down," I said. "She told me he wouldn't have had the wherewithal to change into his pajamas, not if he was drunk enough to miss his poker game."

"Okay," Karen said. "I can follow that. But where does Sorrel Brown figure in?"

"She didn't at first," I admitted. "I suppose I should have been a little suspicious that night when we first met. After all, she gives me the cold shoulder at the diner, yet a couple hours later, she picks me up in a bar and takes me home with her. Why the sudden interest, if it wasn't the fact that Ralph Cramer told her who I was? But I didn't really pick up on that until later."

I took a pull on my beer and settled back in the booth.

"The key to everything was the assumption that the 'T' mentioned in Uncle Charlie's journal was Teddy Kendall. In itself, it didn't necessarily have anything to do with my uncle's murder, but it was curious. Then Humbert was killed, and, thanks to Randy Fenzik, I was able to connect Teddy to Humbert as well. Two murdered men, both killed in exactly the same way, and each apparently tied in with a young man who had committed suicide.

"Humbert's relationship with Teddy was obvious, once his bisexuality had been established. But where did Uncle Charlie fit in? In the journal, Uncle Charlie had written, 'I found out about "T" today.' What had he found out? I went down to the high school, looking for any sort of a lead, and I ran across a picture of Teddy. He looked just like my cousin, Charlie's son. He had the Dugan eyes."

"So you suspected your uncle was the Kendall boy's real father," Kaufman said. "Wouldn't that point you at Maevis?"

J.D. spoke up. "Not if you knew Charlie. Drunk or sober, he had an eye for a pretty lady. No way he'd ever go to bed with Maevis Kendall, and I can't imagine her ever committing adultery. Murder, yes, but not adultery."

I nodded agreement. "So I went down to the county offices and checked out a few things. I found a birth record for a baby, a little girl, who was born to Maevis and Ed Kendall eighteen years ago, on June 29. She was premature, though, and died of complications four days later. But there was another birth record, this one for Edward

213

Kendall, Jr., born July 10. Only this time, the clerk wouldn't let me see the complete file, just a revised birth certificate. The rest of the data had been sealed by court order."

"Obviously, Teddy had been adopted," Kaufman said. "But it still doesn't connect to Sorrel Brown."

"It does when you lay it alongside other things," I said. "There was the story she told me about going out to California after high school, to try her hand at acting. But, when I was at the high school checking up on Teddy, I happened to take a look at Sorrel's yearbook, too, just as a lark. And it made me even more curious. Here she was supposed to have been an aspiring actress and she didn't even belong to the school drama club. But she did belong to the Junior Candystripers, which was a club of sorts for kids who wanted to go into nursing." I took another hit of beer. "At that point I was still resisting the idea that Sorrel could be mixed up in the murders. But I did think to take a look at her school records while I was there and I found out that she had left Mohaca Springs High with three months remaining on her senior year. Her transcripts had been forwarded to an address in Geneva. I looked up the address in an old city directory at the county office campus. There's a real estate office there now, but way back when, it was a home for unwed mothers. When I put that together with a few minor things, I had to take another look at Sorrel. And the points started to add up against her."

"Such as?" Karen asked.

"Opportunity, for one thing. She's a desirable woman, just the type who could arrange to get Uncle Charlie alone at his cottage and Humbert out to Lovers' Lane. And Sorrel's house is an easy walk from Beedle Road Extension. No problem at all to ride up there with him, kill him, and then walk home.

"Then there was the opportunity to acquire the fishing knives from Ralph's store. Since Sorrel did the inventory, she could take all the knives she wanted and doctor up the records so Ralph wouldn't know. And there was the easy way she used military jargon, like MOS and gung ho. That got me thinking about her apparent interest in nursing when she was a girl, so I added her name to the list of possibles I checked out with the Pentagon and found out about her training as a nurse. Certainly, she would know how to administer a clean killing thrust with a knife. By this time, her story about going out to California to be an actress looked completely phony. I even tested her by mentioning her SAG card—Screen Actors Guild. She didn't know what that was." I checked to see that they were all with me, then continued, "Finally, the last opportunity. The knife someone stuck in my door."

"I figured that had to be Maevis's doing," Karen protested. "Or possibly Rossiter."

"I thought of Rossiter, too," I said. "Penrose had apparently paid him to try and scare me into selling quick and beating it out of town, which explains the game of bumper cars and the attempt to foul the cottage's water supply. But then I thought of another possibility; that Sorrel had put the knife there herself, while I was asleep, as a way to warn me." I paused again. "I guess by then she had started to care for me, too."

We were all quiet for a few moments, before Karen said, "But why didn't your uncle see it coming, that night at the cottage?"

"Maybe ego." I shrugged. "But more likely, he didn't know who she was. Teddy may not have mentioned Sorrel by name when he confronted Uncle Charlie. He didn't have much of a chance to, judging by the journal entry. Anyway, Uncle Charlie probably wouldn't have matched Sorrel's name to her face even if Teddy had told him."

"Not remember a woman he fathered a child by?" Kaufman asked, incredulous.

"Remember, Sorrel had never told anyone who the father was. Charlie never knew about the pregnancy. And

215

he wasn't apt to remember a single incident out of a life of drunken one-night stands. According to his ex-wife, he'd often get loaded and end up in bed with a woman. Next day, he couldn't remember her name."

I shook my head. "Actually, it was easy for her to set up both Uncle Charlie and Michel Humbert, a pair of tipsy Lotharios. A little flirting over the counter at the diner, a date to meet somewhere later, that's all it took.

"Her guilt over Teddy's suicide provided all the incentive she needed. It ate her up until she couldn't keep it inside anymore. So she refocused it on the three people she blamed for causing the boy's misery. Charlie Dugan, who fathered the child and later rejected him; Michel Humbert, who exploited the kid's sexual confusion and drove him deeper into despair; and Maevis Kendall, the puritanical mother who could never accept Teddy, never forgive him for taking the place of the little baby girl who died in infancy. Maevis would've been Sorrel's last victim."

"Ironically," Bob Kaufman interjected, "Maevis saved her the effort. Her own guilt over killing her husband destroyed her before Sorrel had a chance to."

"Yes. I suspect the adoption was Ed Kendall's idea. Maevis couldn't handle it. She just kept sinking deeper into her religious fanaticism to somehow justify the loss of her baby. And Ed crawled into a whiskey bottle."

"And then one day," J.D. finished it for me, "Ed comes home drunk. He and Maevis argue, things get out of hand, and she kills him in a rage." The coroner's initial findings indicated that Ed Kendall died of a fractured skull.

"And I always thought my Jewish grandmother had cornered the market on guilt." Kaufman shook his head. "But those two, Maevis and Sorrel, wow!"

There wasn't much more to be said. Bob and Karen decided it was time to get back to the newspaper. Bob insisted on paying the tab, then told the waitress to bring J.D. and me one more drink on him.

I watched them leave, arm in arm, then I exhaled slowly and turned back to J. D. Staub. "They make a nice couple."

"Yeah."

The waitress brought over our drinks and set them down in front of us. Neither of us spoke for awhile. J.D. nursed his bourbon and water; I picked at the label on my beer bottle.

"You know, Sheridan," he said finally, "I guess old Dugan was really sort of a bastard."

"Yeah, I guess he was," I agreed, thinking back to all the times I'd heard my mother call him just that.

"Still, I suppose he never meant to do any harm," J.D. said. "He had his own way of living, that's all, and there wasn't much room to accommodate wives or kids."

"A selfish old bastard," I said, beginning to feel the alcohol and the sleepless night and the weight of my own emotions pushing me down. "But I can't help but feel sad about the way he ended up."

"I know what you mean." J.D. nodded. "He could be a good friend to those who didn't ask, or expect, too much from him." He lifted his glass. "What d'you think? One last toast to his memory? If we don't, nobody else will."

I smiled then and thought, Why not? This is a wake, after all. I raised my bottle and tapped it against J.D.'s glass.

"Here's to you, Charlie Dugan, wherever you may be."